Praise for the

BE WITH ME

"Three hot men and one lucky woman. I absolutely loved it! Simply wonderful writing. There's a new star on the rise and her name is Maya Banks."
   —Sunny, national bestselling author of *Lucinda, Dangerously*

"Fascinating erotic romantic suspense."
   —*Midwest Book Review*

SWEET SURRENDER

"Searingly sexy and highly believable."   —*Romantic Times*

"This story ran my heart through the wringer more than once."   —*CK²S Kwips and Kritiques*

"From page one, I was drawn into the story and literally could not stop reading until the last page."   —*The Romance Studio*

"Maya Banks's story lines are always full of situations that captivate readers, but it's the emotional pull you experience which brings the story to life."   —*Romance Junkies*

FOR HER PLEASURE

"[It] is the ultimate in pleasurable reading. Enticing, enchanting and sinfully sensual, I couldn't have asked for a better anthology."   —*Joyfully Reviewed*

"Full of emotional situations, lovable characters, and kick-butt story lines that will leave you desperate for more. I highly recommend *For Her Pleasure* for readers who like spicy romances with a suspenseful element—it's definitely a must read!"   —*Romance Junkies*

"Totally intoxicating, *For Her Pleasure* is one of those reads you won't be forgetting any time soon."
   —*The Road to Romance*

NO
PLACE TO RUN

MAYA BANKS

BERKLEY SENSATION, NEW YORK

THE BERKLEY PUBLISHING GROUP
Published by the Penguin Group
Penguin Group (USA) LLC
375 Hudson Street, New York, New York 10014

USA • Canada • UK • Ireland • Australia • New Zealand • India • South Africa • China

penguin.com

A Penguin Random House Company

NO PLACE TO RUN

A Berkley Sensation Book / published by arrangement with the author

Copyright © 2010 by Maya Banks.
Excerpt from *Hidden Away* by Maya Banks copyright © 2010 by Maya Banks.
Penguin supports copyright. Copyright fuels creativity, encourages diverse voices,
promotes free speech, and creates a vibrant culture. Thank you for buying an authorized
edition of this book and for complying with copyright laws by not reproducing, scanning,
or distributing any part of it in any form without permission. You are supporting writers
and allowing Penguin to continue to publish books for every reader.

Berkley Sensation Books are published by The Berkley Publishing Group.
BERKLEY SENSATION® is a registered trademark of Penguin Group (USA) LLC.
The "B" design is a trademark of Penguin Group (USA) LLC.

For information, address: The Berkley Publishing Group,
a division of Penguin Group (USA) LLC,
375 Hudson Street, New York, New York 10014.

ISBN: 978-0-425-23819-6

`PUBLISHING HISTORY
Berkley Sensation mass-market edition / December 2010

PRINTED IN THE UNITED STATES OF AMERICA

18   17   16   15   14   13   12   11   10   9

Cover art by Craig White.
Cover design by Rita Frangie.
Interior text design by Laura K. Corless.

A big thank-you to:
Kim Whalen, my biggest cheerleader and advocate.
Cindy Hwang, for her support of this series
and for believing I could do it
when I didn't think I could pull it off.
Valerie and Lillie, for always being willing
to drop everything at a moment's notice for me.

CHAPTER 1

HE was waiting for her as soon as she opened the door to his hotel room. Sam Kelly watched as Sophie turned, watched the wash of desire that flickered in her expressive blue eyes as she found him.

Before she could reach behind her to tug at the tie to her apron, he had her in his arms, his lips crushing hers in that first sweet taste.

"Sam."

His name came out in a breathy sigh that he felt all the way to his balls.

He reached around and took the tie from her and pulled until the work apron she wore came free.

"Any trouble tonight?"

She shook her head even as he found her lips again.

"I *hate* that you work there."

She paused in her kiss, and for a long moment they stood there, their lips barely a breath apart as she stared up at him. Her mouth turned down into an unhappy moue, and he was sorry for spoiling the moment by expressing his dissatisfaction with her job.

Who was he to say anything at all? She was working in a little dive in Bumfuck, Mexico—a place a girl like her clearly didn't belong—but maybe it was all she could do to make ends meet. It wasn't like he could offer to sweep her off her feet and carry her off into the sunset.

"Forget I said anything," he murmured. "Come here."

He tipped a finger under her chin and guided her mouth back to his. He was hungry—starving—for her. Even now his brothers and their team were doing the job he was here for because he wanted a few stolen moments with a woman he hadn't been able to resist—a woman he'd known he had to have from the moment he walked into the bar where she waitressed.

A woman who made it too easy to forget duty.

She leaned into him, warm and unsteady. He lifted her just enough that she could circle his neck with her arms, and she smiled against his mouth.

"Better," she whispered.

"I'll be better when you're naked."

He carried her toward the bed and lowered her onto the mattress until he hovered over her, trapping her underneath his body. His mouth was just over her belly, and he looked up her body, meeting her gaze.

"You're so beautiful," he murmured.

With slow, methodical movements that belied his urgency, he slid her T-shirt up, baring her slim waist.

Even as he raised it higher over her breasts, he tongued the shallow indention of her navel. She shivered beneath his lips and a fine smattering of chill bumps raced across her belly.

She arched her back almost as if she'd buck him off, but he left her shirt and gripped her hips, holding her in place.

"Mine."

She shuddered and let out a light whimper when he licked up her midline and caught his teeth on the band of her bra. He grinned and levered himself upward so that his knees were on either side of her hips, and she was effectively trapped.

Impatient to have her undressed, he grasped the hem of her T-shirt and ripped it up the middle until it lay in two pieces on either side of her. It hung from her arms, and he simply pulled until she was free.

Her nipples puckered and strained against the lacy cups of her bra. The material shielded nothing of the dark crescents. Idly he toyed with the nubs through the satin, touching and molding until they were hard points begging to be set free.

The swells plumped over the edge of the cups, and with a light flick, he pushed them free, baring her nipples so they peeked over the bra.

Her hands crept up his thighs, sliding over the rough denim of his jeans, but he reached down and grasped her wrists, pulling her away.

She started to protest, but he brought one hand to his mouth and kissed her palm before raising her arms over her head. He leaned until they were pressed to the mattress, and once again she was captured.

In a moment of inspiration, he gathered the tattered

remains of her T-shirt and tied one wrist to the head-board. She gasped, her eyes going wide when he took her other hand and secured it as well.

Her breathing speeded up and her chest heaved. She licked her lips nervously, but her eyes darkened to sapphire. His smile was slow and predatory. She was like a drug. A high he didn't want to come down from. She made him feel strong and invincible.

"Now what to do with you?"

He reached into his jeans and pulled out his pocket-knife. Her eyes widened slightly, but no fear shone in her gaze. He flipped the knife open and tucked the blade underneath the band of her bra. The material fell away, baring her breasts to his hungry gaze.

He closed the knife and tossed it aside, then turned his attention to the clasp of her jeans. He wanted to rip them from her, but he forced himself to take his time and to savor each inch of her flesh he unveiled.

He worked the jeans over her hips and then down her legs, moving so he could free her entirely. Her shapely legs drew him. He ran his finger up the slim lines and curves and then followed with his mouth, kissing and licking a path to the silky scrap of underwear that shielded her pussy.

He tucked one finger behind the lace, threading through the curls into the slick folds. She moaned and twisted restlessly when he found her clit. For a moment he played, stroking his fingertip over the sensitive nub. Then he slipped down until he rimmed her entrance, teasing her mercilessly.

With one push, he was inside. Liquid velvet closed around his finger, and he closed his eyes as he imagined his cock there, gliding through her tight, swollen heat.

"Sam!"

Her agonized cry jerked him back to awareness. Her face was flushed, her eyes glittering with need.

"Please," she begged.

He ripped the panties, no longer patient, no longer willing to prolong his seduction. He wanted her. Had to have her. Now.

His shirt came off and sailed across the room. He rolled to the side and yanked at his jeans, cursing under his breath when they snagged around his ankles.

Where the fuck was the condom? Pocket. Shit. He leaned over the bed to pick the pants back up and yanked several packets out. They spilled onto the bed as he rolled back over. He grabbed one and ripped it open as he straddled her again.

Her gaze was riveted on his groin. Her eyes flashed appreciatively, and in response he reached down, grasped his cock and stroked.

She strained against her bonds, and it only made him harder and more eager to take her.

With a shaking hand, he rolled the condom on and then reached down to spread her legs.

God, she was so soft and beautiful. Delicate and feminine. The silky blond curls were damp with desire, and he ran his thumb down the seam of her pussy before pushing her legs farther apart.

She was open to him. Open and unguarded. His to take. His to pleasure. His to taste and to touch.

He rose over her, tucking his cock against her small opening. He could never get over that first thrust, where her body fought his size and her pussy closed around him like a vise. He was sweating and shaking like a teenager, and he hadn't even gotten inside her yet.

"Are you ready for me, Sophie?"

He nudged inward just enough that the head spread her opening and he could feel her heat.

"Please, Sam. I need you."

Those softly uttered words sent him over the edge. He gripped her hips and dove deep. She gasped. All the breath left his body in a groan of intense agony.

She writhed beneath him, trapped. Her mouth opened and closed, and her arms strained against the bonds at her wrists. She surrounded his dick like warm honey. So sweet. So hot. He'd never felt anything to match the sensation of being inside her.

When she bucked upward in protest of his not moving, he withdrew, and they both moaned at the sensation of him rippling through her flesh.

"God, honey, you're so tight. You feel so damn good."

"We fit," she said on a moan. "You fit me. Perfect."

"Damn right," he growled as he swooped downward to devour her mouth.

He flexed his hips and sank deep again. He swallowed her gasp of pleasure, savored it, then returned it in his next breath as their tongues mimicked the action of their bodies.

There was no thinking. Only the slick, hot feel of her against his cock. His brain went numb as he lost himself. Deeper. Harder.

The rest slipped away. No mission. No asshole who needed killing. No frustration because KGI's efforts had met with no results.

Here it was just the two of them. And mindless, perfect pleasure.

He reached down to hook his forearms underneath her knees. He pulled hard, and the angle sent him deeper, until he was wedged so tight that his balls were crammed against her pussy.

He glanced up, meeting her gaze, making sure she was with him and that he hadn't hurt her. Only her desperate need for release stared back at him.

With a savage cry, he pulled back and then hammered into her, rocking the entire bed as he thrust over and over. Her eyes slammed shut and her cry split the air. She went tight, so tight, as every muscle in her body tensed, and then suddenly she went liquid around him, bathing him in intense heat.

He threw back his head, closed his own eyes and pounded forward one last time before his release gathered in his balls and shot up his cock. He erupted painfully, the pleasure so staggeringly intense that he lost himself for one brief moment.

His hips still flexed spasmodically as he carefully lowered himself onto her limp body. She trembled as their flesh met, and her lips brushed over his jaw as he laid his head against her shoulder.

He was still buried deep and he had no desire to move. She felt good surrounding him, holding him in her body. He moved his hips again, a shudder rolling down his spine at the nearly painful sensation over his cock.

"Did I hurt you?" he asked against her skin.

She hummed, a content purring sound that told him he'd done no such thing. Still, she spoke softly against his hair, reassuring him that he'd given her as much pleasure as he'd taken.

Though he hated to move, he knew he was crushing her. Carefully he pushed himself up and then withdrew from her body. Damn but he was still hard.

He reached up to untie her and then rolled away to discard the condom. When he moved back, she immediately curled into him all soft and limber. Her hands moved over his body almost frantically, as if being denied the ability to touch him had made her all the more desperate to do so now.

He caught one of her hands and tugged it down until her fingers circled his cock.

"See what you do to me? I shouldn't be hard again for two weeks after that, but I seem to stay that way around you."

She laughed softly and ran her hand up and down his length, exploring every inch.

"Think he'll wait long enough for me to grab a shower? Do you mind?" Her nose wrinkled in distaste. "I smell like beer."

He nuzzled her neck, licking over her pulse. "You smell wonderful, but yeah, go get a shower." He felt a twinge of guilt for having ambushed her as soon as she'd walked in. He should have let her shower and rest. She'd been on her feet the entire evening.

She reached up and kissed him before rolling away. He watched her, enjoying the gentle sway of her hips and ass as she walked naked to the bathroom.

She was one hundred percent woman. Soft and feminine, with curves in all the right places. She was everything his job wasn't, and maybe that's why she appealed so strongly to him.

He lay there for a long moment, and finally after five

minutes, he figured he'd given her enough time to wash. If she hadn't, he'd finish the job for her.

He got off the bed and went into the bathroom, where the steam from the shower had already fogged the mirror. She was standing motionless in the shower, her body blurred by the glass.

It was enough to send his blood roaring to life. God almighty but he couldn't explain her effect on him. It was crazy and left him feeling unbalanced.

He opened the door, and before she could turn around, he slipped into the shower with her, his body molding to hers. She started to turn, but he stopped her, holding her still.

He lowered his mouth to her neck, where little droplets of water beaded and rolled down her skin. Her knees buckled and she threatened to fall when his teeth sank into the slim column of her throat. He caught her and held her tight.

"Put your hands on the wall."

She put her palms on the tile and slid them up until her arms were above her head. He arched against her then reached down and hooked her right leg with his hand. He pulled up, lifting her while he held her steady with his other arm.

While the water beat down on them, he thrust into her, finding her warmth all over again. It was never enough. It would never be enough.

In the back of his mind, a warning flashed. He hadn't used a condom, but he was lost in the feel of her silky heat against his bare flesh. His mind screamed stupid, but the male roared that she was his and he'd take what was his.

She tightened around him. Her fingers curled into fists against the shower wall. She threw her head back, arching into him as he marked her neck with his mouth.

His.

It was primitive and hard core. It puzzled him even as he knew it couldn't be explained.

"Mine," he whispered.

His release when it came was quicksilver. A lightning flash that was intense and painful and had him arching to tiptoe as he strained to get deeper.

She made a small sound, and her hands slid down the walls as if she'd lost any remaining strength. She sagged and he caught her gently to him. He was filled with an odd tenderness as he reached up to turn the water off and then settled her into his arms.

He stepped from the shower and put her down long enough to wrap a towel around her. For a long time they stood there, her forehead resting on his chest as they both tried to catch up.

She snuggled sleepily into his arms, and again, guilt assailed him as he imagined how tired she must be. He kissed the top of her head.

"Let's go get some sleep. You're exhausted."

She turned her face up to his and smiled even as her eyelids drooped. Then she rose up on tiptoe to curl her arms around his neck.

"Take me to bed," she whispered.

CHAPTER 2

SAM woke with Sophie in the crook of his arm, her head resting on his shoulder. He was tempted to roll over and slide between her legs and wake them both up with a quick orgasm. But she looked tired and a little fragile, like maybe she'd had a rough night at work.

He pulled her closer and ran the tips of his fingers up and down her arm. The strands of hair closest to his mouth fluttered with his every breath, and he hooked a finger around them to pull them away from her cheek.

Her eyelids fluttered and opened, and sleepy blue eyes stared back at him.

"Good morning," he murmured

She responded by snuggling deeper into his side. Her sigh was all he heard, and her arm crept around his waist, linking them tighter together.

He chuckled lightly and kissed the top of her head. "Content?"

"Mmm hmmm."

It was easy here in this hotel room. Everything else seemed a world away and they were removed from reality. He wasn't stupid enough to embrace that, but it was nice, just for a while, to get a sense that the only thing that mattered was right here and right now.

"Feel like eating something?"

She raised her head. "What time is it?"

"Seven."

Before she could respond, a knock sounded at the door. What the hell? He frowned, then eased from underneath Sophie.

"Stay here and out of sight."

He yanked his jeans on and went to the door, opening it just a crack. The man from the front desk stood there holding a sealed envelope.

"For you, señor. It was marked as urgent."

Sam took the envelope. "Thank you." He closed the door and turned the envelope over in his hand. It didn't have a name, but then he hadn't used his real name here. It was only marked "304 Urgent." Underlined three times.

He glanced up at Sophie, who sat up in the bed, the covers drawn to her chin. Then he ripped open the seal and pulled out the single piece of paper.

At first he didn't make sense of the short message. When realization hit him in the gut, his first reaction was disbelief. Was someone fucking with him? He needed to get back to his men. This could be complete bullshit, but it was the first potential break KGI had caught in their mission to take Alex Mouton and his extensive arms network down.

For two weeks Sam and his brothers had posed as

buyers, trying to make contact with Mouton. And nothing. Either the man was a suspicious bastard or he had no interest in gaining new clients. Which told Sam that his current clientele was paying him a fuckload of money.

A chill slithered up his spine. Why the anonymous warning? Who had known what the Kelly Group was really after? They'd been careful. They'd done everything right. Blended in with the locals. Given no one any reason to believe they were anything but who they said they were. Even Sam's illicit liaisons with Sophie had gone a long way in building his cover. Because what kind of dumbass came on a covert op and then spent his time fucking a local waitress to distraction?

"Sam, is something wrong?"

Her soft voice settled over him, soothing some of the tension. He crumpled the note in his hand after committing it to memory. He shoved it into his pocket and focused again on Sophie. Sophie who sat naked in his bed. Sophie who he wouldn't ever see again.

He crossed the room and slid onto the edge of the bed beside her. She stared back at him, her eyes puzzled, and there was a hint of something else there. Fear?

He touched her cheek in an effort to reassure her. "I've got to go. Something's come up. Something important."

She bit her bottom lip. "Okay."

He inhaled, hating what he had to say next.

"I don't know when—if—I'll be back."

Her face became impassive. Her usually expressive eyes were shuttered and distant.

"I understand."

Before he could say anything else, she leaned up and wrapped her arms around his neck. The sheet fell, baring her breasts. She kissed him. Just once. With all the sweetness she'd brought into his life in just a short time.

He savored the taste and the sensation and knew he'd never have this again. Regret tightened his chest.

"Be careful," she whispered.

He touched her cheek and then kissed her again. "Always."

SOPHIE waited long enough that she was sure Sam wouldn't return to the room, and then she hurriedly dressed, making sure she left nothing behind. In the bathroom, she twisted her hair in a quick knot and thrust a pick from her bag through the knot to hold it.

The woman staring back at her in the mirror was young, amusedly fresh-faced and deceptively innocent looking. She felt none of those things but knew people only saw what they wanted to see. No one ever took her seriously or saw her as a threat.

That would end today.

Taking one last sweep of the room, she saw Sam's knife lying on the floor where he'd tossed it after cutting her bra off. She stooped down to retrieve it and then shoved it into her pocket. There would be no evidence he was here, and she might just need it later.

Taking a deep breath, she cracked open the door and peeked out of the room and down the hall. Satisfied no one was about, she hurried to the stairs, bypassing the corridor leading to the elevator.

On the first floor, there were two doors in the alcove, one leading to the lobby and one leading outside into the alley beside the hotel. She ducked outside to see the car waiting for her.

Squaring her shoulders, she strode to the dark Mercedes. The driver got out, somber-looking in a dark suit and sunglasses that completely obscured his eyes. He was nameless and faceless, just like everyone else in her father's organization. Just as she was.

He opened the door to the backseat, and she was swallowed by the armored vehicle.

The driver took her through the back edges of town, through crumbling cobblestone streets, some of which had huge gaps where sand and rock took over. The car drew no curious stares. The residents here were well used to her father's presence and had learned not to ask questions.

They left the rows of shabby houses and turned onto a winding dirt road that led into the hills surrounding the remote town. When finally they approached the stern spires that guarded her father's compound, the driver slowed and then punched a series of commands into the remote installed in the dash.

The heavy iron gate swung open to admit them, and they zoomed rapidly up the paved driveway. A thick line of trees obscured the view of the sprawling house, and in fact there was only a small hole through the dense line, where the car seemingly disappeared into a forest, only to burst through the other side to a sight that was deceptively idyllic.

To a little girl, it had been fairyland. She hadn't been that little girl in a long time.

Instead of pulling around front where the circle drive surrounded a huge fountain, the driver parked at the side of the house, under an awning that sheltered three other armored vehicles.

He opened the door, and Sophie blinked at the wash of sunshine that slapped her in the face. She stepped out and glanced up at the driver.

"Are you sure this is what you want to do?" he asked in a low voice.

She merely nodded, not trusting that she wouldn't be overheard if she responded.

"I'll be waiting."

This time she didn't react. She walked past the driver and inserted her security card into the slot beside the door leading into the house. Her father would be alerted to her presence, and he'd be waiting for her. He never came to her. She was expected to go to him and give a report just like any of his employees.

A maid met her in the hallway to her father's office. Sophie didn't meet her gaze. The maid stared straight ahead, but as Sophie approached, the maid reached under her apron and handed a small bag to her as she passed.

It was a designer handbag, something her father would expect her to have. He'd probably bought this one. She tucked it under her arm and stopped in front of the double door at the end of the corridor.

She raised her hand to knock but stopped in midair. She shook from head to toe, and sweat beaded her forehead. Each breath seemed dragged from her, heavy and sluggish. Her heart thumped wildly, until she was sure it was audible in the silence.

Swallowing back her fear, she squared her shoulders and knocked. She'd need every bit of composure she could muster. Her father could spot weakness in a second.

The doors opened automatically, and she stepped forward. Miraculously her fear subsided when she looked across the room to see her father standing against the huge picture window. It, like everything, was deceptive. What looked like a foolhardy extravagance for a man as wanted as he, was in actuality a one-way reflective plate of the highest-tech bulletproof material available. It wasn't even on the market yet.

He could see out, but no one could see in.

"Sophie, you have information?"

The casual way in which he posed the question didn't in any way fool her. Her father wasn't casual about anything. He was coldly aloof and calculating. He didn't expect obedience. He demanded it. With chillingly positive results.

She glanced around the room, searching out the position of his guards. There were two inside. At least a dozen outside. Each willing to give his life for the man who owned him. Today she was happy to accommodate them.

"I do have something that might interest you," she murmured.

He raised a speculative eyebrow as if he couldn't believe she'd proven useful. She made a show of opening her handbag as if she had something to give him.

Her fingers slid over the rubber stock of the gun, and then one finger curled over the cool metal trigger. In a lightning move, she turned and shot through the bag, downing the first guard. Before the second could react, she fired again, the heavy plunk of the bullet as it smacked his neck the only sound in the room.

The bag fell away, revealing the long barrel of the silencer. Her father stared unflinchingly at her.

"What is this, Sophie?"

She wasn't talking to the bastard. No stupid games. She had precious seconds to make her getaway before all hell broke loose on his command.

She raised the pistol, and just before she fired, she saw the surprised shock in her father's eyes. He fell heavily, blood spreading on the polished wood floors.

She yanked the knife from her pocket and rushed over to where he lay. Shoving the collar of his shirt down, she reached for the leather thong that circled his neck and slashed it free.

The thin cylindrical piece of metal lay against his skin, smeared with his blood. She grabbed it, then went to his desk and felt for the button underneath.

Across the room a panel of the floor slid open, revealing a staircase leading down into the underground network of pathways.

Without a single glance back, she hit the stairs running. She'd spent months memorizing the layout. She knew every path, every turn by heart even though she'd never been below. Relying on those long hours of studying the computerized plans, she made her way to the exit where the driver waited for her.

Ten minutes later, she rushed into the sun and breathed a sigh of relief when she saw the car there waiting. He hadn't betrayed her.

He ushered her inside, and when she was settled in the back, he glanced at her in the rearview mirror.

"It is done?"

She swallowed and nodded. "Thank you for helping me."

The slight incline of his jaw was the only acknowledgment he gave her, as he gunned the engine and roared off. She never looked back. There was nothing for her there.

As the miles passed, she let herself relax. And she dared to hope the impossible.

Freedom.

Finally, she was free.

CHAPTER 3

Five months later

SOPHIE throttled back and the boat slowed, coming to a near standstill in Kentucky Lake. Darkness shrouded her. The sky was overcast. New moon. Only one or two stars poked through the cloud cover. She was running with no lights and keeping to the middle of the lake until she was sure she was close enough to her destination to move quickly to shore.

She studied the small handheld GPS and then lifted her gaze up the shoreline to the north. According to her coordinates, her destination was another mile down the lake.

She swallowed her fear and nervousness and automatically put her hand on her belly in a soothing motion. Would Sam even be there? How would he react to seeing her again? What would he say when he knew the truth about her?

She glanced nervously over her shoulder into the darkness. The lake was a slosh of midnight ink. The only sound she could hear was the low chop against the hull of her boat.

Her nerves were shot. She knew she was taking a risk, but she was out of options. Her uncle's cronies were closing in on her. She could smell them. She could feel them in every part of her body. There'd been too many close calls in the last weeks.

A smart woman recognized when she could no longer do things on her own. She considered herself a smart woman, which was why she was here. In a damn boat on a damn lake trying to find the father of her baby so hopefully he could protect them both.

After five months of running, the idea of being in such a vulnerable place scared her witless. True, it wasn't as if she drove boldly into Dover, asked where to find Sam Kelly and then parked in front of his house. She had that much sense. Sam would be the first person her uncle expected her to run to. Which was why she'd stayed away for so long.

And then there was the fact that neither she nor Sam had been honest with the other. Both had been other people. The only real thing between them had been the intense desire. She'd fallen fast and she'd fallen hard.

For a man who'd despise her once he learned the truth.

She eased the boat forward, following the line on her GPS. With any luck, she'd dock right in Sam's backyard and hope to hell she didn't get shot for trespassing.

A noise ahead and to the left alerted her. Her head rose and she stared, her nostrils flaring as she sucked in the chilly night air.

A sudden blast of light blinded her. She threw up her arm to shield her face, but it was no use.

The roar of an engine accelerating kicked her self-preservation into gear. Without hesitation, she dove overboard. She smacked into the cold water and felt the shock to her toes.

The larger boat hit hers with a resounding crack. Debris flew into the air and pelted the water all around her. A huge chunk hit the surface in front of her and blew water over her head.

Her mouth filled with water, and she pushed it out before rolling to swim toward shore. She hadn't gotten a full breath, and already her lungs were tight with the need for air.

She surfaced and sucked in a huge breath. Pain exploded in her arm, and she inhaled another mouthful of water. Shock splintered with needle-like awareness. She touched her arm and felt warmth. Liquid warmth.

Blood.

Son of a bitch had shot her! Terror hit her like a sledgehammer. She fought to keep her panic at bay. She had to hold it together. Why the hell had he shot her?

Her hair went straight upward, and her neck popped back as a hand yanked her out of the water. She banged over the side of a boat, and she had the presence of mind to wrap her arms protectively around her middle.

Her baby. She had to protect her baby.

She landed with a crash on the deck of the boat and squinched her eyes shut against the beam of light shining into her face.

"Get up."

She cracked open one eye and stared up at the man looming over her. She glanced around and saw no one else.

"Go fuck yourself."

He kicked her in the arm and agony ricocheted through her body. Then he reached down, curled his hand in her hair and hauled her upright.

If he hadn't still been holding her, she would have gone down. Her legs refused to cooperate. Her arm was on fire and hung loosely at her side.

"Where is the key, Sophie?"

"Look, I don't even know you," she spit out. "You don't get to call me by my first name. Or at all. Do you think I'm stupid enough to carry it around with me?"

A flash of silver caught her gaze. Her eyes widened when she saw the wicked curve of a very sharp blade. The she raised her gaze higher and saw cold determination in the face of the assassin.

Forcing bravado into her voice, she said, "If you kill me, you get squat."

"A fact you're counting on I'm sure," he said in a flat tone. "My orders are to make you talk. Any way that has to happen. Trust me, you'll talk."

She swallowed and sucked in air through her nostrils. God, what was she going to do? She'd been so close to Sam. So damn close.

All these months, all this time, she'd stayed to the shadows, always one step ahead of her father's grasp. Even dead, he held her by the throat. Her uncle would carry on his legacy of selling death. There was always someone willing to take up the reins.

But without access to her father's wealth and his resources, Tomas was crippled. She planned to keep him that way.

The man hauled her close, his breath blowing hot

across her face. She felt the edge of the knife against her belly and bile rose sharp in her throat.

"You won't die. Not at first. But your baby will. Tell me what I want to know or I'll slice you open and let your child spill out of your belly."

Her stomach revolted and she gagged, the knot so big that she choked. Tears stung her eyes, and then rage blew hot like the first wave of a blast.

"You son of a bitch," she bit out.

She'd had enough. The fact that she was constantly underestimated usually worked in her favor, but this guy seemed smarter than the other assholes her father employed. Indeed he was smarter than her father, who hadn't believed she'd shoot her own flesh and blood.

This bastard wasn't going to give her any easy passes because she was cute and blond and innocent-looking. Which meant she had to rely on sheer grit and determination if she was going to keep her baby alive.

"All right, I'll tell you," she gasped out. "Put the knife away."

"I like it just where it is."

He wasn't going to make this easy.

She was careful not to glance down, not to even twitch. No advance warning when she made her move. She waited until she nearly jittered out of her skin. There. The knife eased just a bit and no longer bit as hard into her skin.

She rammed her knee into his balls and crashed her elbow down onto his wrist. The knife clattered to the deck and she kicked it hard, sending it spiraling across the boat.

He grabbed her by the neck, his fingers digging deep into her skin despite the fact he was hunched over holding his balls with his free hand.

His hand squeezed mercilessly, cutting off her air supply.

She was going to die.

Here on a boat probably not far from where Sam lived. On the lake, to make the disposal of her body easier. At the hands of an asshole who talked about murder like he would the weather.

Rage. Red-hot and searing. It splintered through her veins like volcanic fury.

Faking surrender, she let every muscle in her body go limp. Maybe it caught him off guard, or maybe he expected her to fight, because his grip eased.

Harnessing her anger, she bolted forward, throwing herself against the asshole. Forearms across his chest, she shoved, putting every ounce of her strength behind her movements.

He staggered backward, his feet stumbling to catch up with the rest of him. His hands flew up, and he tried to grab the railing.

She jumped on him, and they both went over the side.

The cold water hit her like a ton of bricks.

Down she went into the darkness. She fought off panic and struck out, swimming away from the boat. Several yards out, she broke the surface, gasping for breath.

He was out there. Probably close. But it would take him precious time to get back into the boat to look for her. Time she could use to her advantage.

This time she took a deeper breath as she dove back

under, and she forced herself to stay under until shadows grew around her consciousness. She broke the surface and kept her head down as she hungrily sucked in air.

She glanced back to see the spotlight from the boat dancing across the water.

She inhaled quickly and ducked beneath the water again. Ignoring the agonizing pain in her arm, she swam deep and hard. Eventually, her body grew numb from the cold, and the pain receded. She gave a quick murmur of thanks and pushed herself onward.

For how long she repeated the endless cycle of surfacing, taking a breath and going back below, she didn't know. It felt like hours. She wasn't cognizant of anything but the need to survive.

When her strength finally gave out and the adrenaline fled her system, she broke the surface and looked back. To her immense relief, she didn't see the boat. No lights, just murky darkness.

The lake lapped gently at her chin as she treaded water. And suddenly the pain came rushing back with the force of a car crash.

Barely conscious, she feebly struck out for shore, but it seemed a mile away. The current tugged at her legs, sucking her back and down the river channel instead of allowing her to move toward the bank.

Exhausted, she stopped fighting and turned on her back to float the best she could. She had to get out of the water. He'd be looking for her.

Her head cracked against something hard, and she let out a startled cry. She briefly fell underneath the water in panic. When she surfaced, she jerked around to see a large log bobbing in front of her.

Grateful for something to hold on to, she hauled her body up and draped herself over the trunk. The wet bark abraded her cheek, but she was too exhausted to give a damn.

She reached with her good arm and placed her hand over her belly. Her baby had to be okay. She had to be. She closed her eyes as she waited for some response from within. Just a tiny kick. Even a bump just to let Sophie know her baby was safe.

Nothing.

She ran her hand up her arm, feeling for how bad the bullet wound was. In the water, it was impossible to tell. She whispered a fervent prayer that the night's events hadn't harmed her baby.

Again she lowered her palm, feeling for movement.

She fought back the panic. It was common for a baby to be still after Mama suffered a shock. She'd read that somewhere in one of those pregnancy books.

She'd become an expert at self-treatment because she hadn't dared seek medical help. Tomas would have found her instantly. So she devoured every book she could lay her hands on. She took over–the-counter vitamins, drank her milk and exercised so she'd remain on alert. For just such an occasion as when her father's men caught up to her.

There was one star overhead. Just one, but it looked blurry and distant. It bobbed up and down, and she didn't know if it was because she shook so violently or if the lake was rough.

Her arm wrapped tighter around the log, and she pressed her cheek against the wet bark. She could ride it for a while, and maybe it would drift out of the faster current toward the calmer waters of the lake.

Her eyelids fluttered even as she fought to stay conscious. Something warm and wet ran down her arm. Blood. It smelled like blood.

Sam.

His image rose vividly to mind. Her last coherent thought was that she had to get to Sam.

CHAPTER 4

THE morning sun shone bright on the back deck of Sam Kelly's Kentucky Lake home. The wood was warm underneath his bare feet, and the rays chased the chill of the morning away. It had the makings of a truly spectacular day.

The only way it would have been more perfect is if he was on the lake, fishing pole in one hand, a beer in the other. At least he had the beer covered.

He drained the remainder from his can, then crumpled it and tossed it across the deck into the garbage can.

"Nice shot," Donovan drawled from his indelicate sprawl over one of the lounge chairs.

A brief cool breeze blew over Sam's face, reminding him that spring hadn't fully sprung yet.

He glanced over at his younger brother and motioned for him to toss him another beer.

Donovan tossed him a can and then looked in Garrett's

direction. Sam's other younger brother—not that Garrett acted like anyone's younger brother—held up his hand for one and Donovan aimed a beer in his direction also.

Garrett cracked it open and then turned his attention back to the barbeque, where he flipped the burgers.

Only the sizzle of the grill could be heard. That and the hiss of the can as Sam tabbed his open.

"Ethan and Rachel get out okay this morning?" Donovan asked, finally breaking the silence.

Sam looked in Garrett's direction since he'd know better than anyone else.

Garrett nodded. "Yeah, they left for the airport at the ass crack of dawn. Rachel was understandably nervous but very excited to be off to Hawaii for two weeks. She and Ethan both need the break."

Of all the brothers, and they all loved Rachel dearly— she was the only sister-in-law in the family—Garrett was closest to her, and the most protective. But then he had a protective streak a mile wide when it came to the people he loved.

Sam leaned back and stared over the lake. He tuned out Garrett's and Van's discussion about Rachel's recovery. They got on the subject of Christmas, and Sam tensed, withdrawing even more. Christmas was a touchy subject. Not that it hadn't been wonderful this year. Rachel's first holiday back in the Kelly fold.

Watching her smile and her eyes light up like a child's had been worth every minute.

But Christmas had been just after he'd come back from Mexico. Right after Sophie had disappeared. It was stupid to dwell on her, but inevitably his thoughts drifted to her. Her smile. Her eyes. How good they were in bed.

How she responded to his touch. How she felt when he was buried to the balls in her sweet, receptive body.

Nothing about that mission had gone according to plan. They hadn't taken Alex Mouton down. They didn't even know where the bastard had disappeared to. The only thing they had done was take down a huge arms shipment. All in all, just a stumbling block for a man with Mouton's resources.

And Sophie hadn't been there when he'd gone back.

He wasn't even supposed to have gone back. It had never been his plan. But he'd found himself making excuses about following up loose ends and had taken off, determined to find Sophie. And do what? That much he hadn't ever figured out. He just knew he had to see her again. He'd been saved making the decision of what next because she'd disappeared. No one seemed to know a damn thing about her, or if they did, they weren't talking.

It took Sam a minute to figure out that his brothers were speaking to him.

"Come on, Sam, wake up over there."

Sam looked up to see both Van and Garrett staring hard at him.

"What's with you?" Garrett asked. "You haven't been yourself since we got back from Mexico."

Sam stiffened. He hadn't realized he'd been wearing a sign advertising his issues with Mexico.

"You're not still hung up on that chick are you?" Garrett asked in a disbelieving tone.

Sam shot him a withering stare. "What the hell are you talking about?"

Garrett shook his head in disgust. He turned to Van and jerked his thumb in Sam's direction. "We're in fucking

Mexico trying to set up a buy with Alex Mouton, and lover boy takes time out to have some hot fling with a waitress in one of the local watering holes."

Donovan shrugged. "So? He still has a dick. Bound to use it sometime."

Sam choked back a laugh. God love Van. Not an uptight bone in his body.

Donovan turned his stare on Sam, and Sam began to fidget uncomfortably. He'd rather not talk about it.

As if sensing just that, Donovan turned back to Garrett. "Maybe you need to get laid, man. Maybe you wouldn't be so goddamn uptight all the time."

Garrett flipped his brother off, and Sam smiled.

It didn't do him any good to think about Sophie. They'd been good together. Damn good.

No, he had no business getting involved with her when he was involved in a highly sensitive mission. But her sweetness had provided a much-needed balm to what was otherwise a hellish assignment. An assignment that he hadn't gotten anywhere on until the very end, when an anonymous informant delivered the information Sam and his team had sought—on a silver platter.

"You hung up on this chick?" Donovan asked.

Sam glared at him. Apparently he hadn't been able to resist after all.

Donovan held up his hands in surrender. "Okay, okay, I know when to back off."

"Good," Sam muttered.

"You realize you haven't taken another mission since Mexico," Donovan said mildly. "Steele and Rio are getting restless. I didn't realize we were all on vacation."

Sam frowned. He hadn't considered that they were on vacation either, but Donovan's statement brought home to him just how picky he'd been over the last few months.

"Not that I'm complaining," Donovan continued. "I was thinking of a vacation. Somewhere south. Lots of cute college girls. Sand, sun, sex. Lots of sex."

Sam tuned him out again as he and Garrett extolled the virtues of bikini-clad college coeds. Hell, they were all too old for college girls, but then who put an age limit on fantasies?

It annoyed him that he still thought of Sophie. Then he frowned. How old was she? She was young. Not college-age young, but still young. There was a lot he hadn't found out about her. They'd always been too busy making love to do any talking.

He tuned back into the conversation when he heard Nathan and Joe mentioned.

"They're doing what?" Sam asked.

"Man, you are out of it," Donovan muttered. "Got an email from them this morning. Said they were bugging out soon and couldn't give more details. They didn't want Ma and Rachel to worry, so we're supposed to tell them they're on another training mission."

Sam snorted. "As if Mom will believe that. She has a nose for our lies. She sniffs us out every time."

"We'll let Van tell her. She always believes him," Garrett offered. "It's the rest of us who can't get away with shit."

Donovan sent them both smug looks. "Favored son status does have its perks."

"So when are you going to snap out of this funk, Sam?"

Garrett asked bluntly. "If you need a break from KGI, tell me. I can take over operations. The teams are getting restless. They need the action. So do we."

Even Donovan looked like he agreed with Garrett.

"I'm not in a goddamn funk. A lot of shit has gone down over the last year. We needed to be here with the family."

He could feel himself growing defensive, which meant they had a goddamn point, as much as he hated to admit it.

Both his brothers just stared at him, as if waiting for him to come to the conclusion on his own that he was being a dumbass.

"Yeah, okay, I get it," he mumbled. "I'll put your asses to work."

Sam sighed and rose from the patio chair to stretch his legs. He rested his palms on the railing of the deck, enjoying the sun-warmed wood against his skin.

Maybe it was time to get back on the job and work off his restlessness.

He glanced back at Garrett and studied the shadows under his eyes. Garrett didn't like time off. It gave him too much time to think about the shit that went down with his special-ops team just before he left the Marines. He hadn't been sleeping lately, not that he'd admit it to either Sam or Donovan.

Van had confided to Sam that Garrett had been tracking down any and all information on Marcus Lattimer, the man responsible for Garrett's mission going to shit and Garrett's subsequent stay in the hospital to recover from a bullet to the thigh.

Sam had been meaning to bring it up with Garrett, but he hadn't found the right time. Not that any time was ever good to try to pin Garrett down and make him talk.

"What the hell are you staring at?" Garrett asked rudely.

"You look like hell," Sam said bluntly. "You haven't been sleeping again."

"Yeah, well that's two of us. At least I'm not hung up on some chick. Quit trying to avoid the subject by making this about me."

"Find anything yet?" Sam asked mildly.

Garrett frowned and looked for a moment like he'd pretend he didn't know what Sam was talking about. He slapped a burger on the grill, banging the spatula in the process. Then he glanced over at Donovan.

"Hey, don't look at me," Donovan said, holding up his hands. "You haven't exactly been discreet about it."

"I want to take the fucker down," Garrett said.

Sam leaned back and braced his hands behind him on the railing. "Christ, Garrett. KGI can't afford to go on some damn revenge mission."

Garrett shrugged. "Who says it has to be about revenge? The world would be a better place without the piece of shit. He's dirty. He's a traitor." He stared hard at Sam. "He cost me my team. While we sit here waiting for you to snap out of your funk, we could be doing something useful. Like nailing Lattimer's sorry ass to the wall."

There wasn't a whole lot Sam could say to that. He understood Garrett's rage. He'd be doing the same in Garrett's shoes. But he sure as hell hoped his brothers would rein him in. Just like he was doing with Garrett.

"Garrett's not the problem right now," Donovan said pointedly. "You are. You need to pull your head out of your ass, and we need to go back to work, otherwise Garrett's going to go rogue on us and start some goddamn war trying to find Lattimer."

Sam blew out his breath and turned around to gaze out over the lake once more. His brothers were right. His head wasn't in it, and that was a very bad thing for KGI. They'd built their business into an extensive list of military and government contacts. They did jobs for agencies that didn't even exist.

The job to take out Mouton had come from their CIA contact, Resnick, and while KGI had thwarted one arms deal, Mouton himself had slipped through their fingers. Which meant he was still there, still viable, and he was busy rebuilding his network.

And at least for now, the U.S. government didn't seem inclined to follow up.

Sam hated unfinished business. It went against his every principle to leave a predator out there who was capable of destroying so many lives. In theory it wasn't personal. Mouton was just a job, but to Sam it had become personal the moment he failed to take the man down.

He was tempted to tell his CIA contact to fuck off and go back after Mouton, but it wasn't worth getting on Uncle Sam's bad side.

His lips twisted into a grimace. Maybe Donovan had the right idea. Maybe some sun, sex and vacation would get his mind back in the game. And off Sophie.

He had started to turn around to his brothers again when he caught sight of something that gave him pause. A large log was floating lazily down the lake. Water levels were way up in the spring as the TVA held water in so as not to burden the rain-swollen rivers and creeks that the lake fed. Recent storms and heavy rainfall had caused a debris field that had only just begun to diminish.

But it was something on the end of the log that captured Sam's attention.

"What the hell?" he muttered.

"What's up, Sam?" Garrett asked.

But Sam didn't answer him. He leaped over the edge of the deck and took off running down the dock toward the water. He heard his brothers' surprised exclamations behind him, but he didn't slow down.

When he reached the end of the dock, he dove cleanly into the water, wincing at the cold shock. He surfaced several yards away and swam hard toward the middle of the channel.

He grasped the middle of the log and maneuvered his way down. A woman's limp body was draped across the end, her wet, bedraggled hair hiding her face completely.

He hesitated a moment, afraid to reach out and touch her, to feel the rigidity of death. Then he shook off the ridiculous fear and grasped her shoulder.

To his relief, her skin was soft and pliable, albeit cold, under his fingers.

"Jesus, what the fuck?"

Sam jerked around to see Garrett approaching with swift, sure strokes.

"Help me get her to shore," Sam said as he pulled her from the log.

Her head lolled to the side, and he sheltered her face in his neck so she wouldn't accidentally inhale any water. He put fingers to her neck to check for a pulse. Weak and thready, but it was there.

"Holy fuck, she's been shot," Garrett said as he closed in on her other side.

Sam glanced down to see her blood-smeared arm. "Let's go," he said grimly as he turned on his side and began doing a sidestroke back toward shore.

Garrett kept pace, holding as much of her body out of the water as he could. As they neared the shore, Donovan waded out and reached for the woman.

Sam waved him off and curled his arms underneath her, lifting her from the water as he stood in the shallow depths. It was ridiculous, but he was gripped by the necessity to see to her himself. He didn't want anyone else touching her.

His nape prickled and the hairs stood up as he laid her on the ground. The first thing he noticed was the bruises around her slim neck. Someone had done their damndest to choke her.

The second thing he saw was the obvious bullet wound in her arm. Blood still seeped from the jagged crease.

The third thing? His gaze drifted down her body, and he froze as he met with the tiny swollen mound of her belly.

"Holy fuck," he breathed. "She's pregnant!"

"I'll call an ambulance," Garrett said.

The woman stirred at Garrett's voice, and Sam reached up to wipe the hair from her eyes.

All the breath left his body as her eyelids fluttered open and their eyes met. He took stock—took full stock of her face—and the realization hit him like a sledgehammer.

God, he couldn't wrap his mind around it. He was leaning over her, staring down at her; his mind registered who she was, but it didn't make sense to him.

"Sophie," he rasped out.

Her eyes widened in recognition just as fear slammed hard into those big blue eyes of hers.

"Sam."

It came out a hoarse whisper and dissolved into a cough. Once she started, she couldn't stop, and her entire body convulsed as she coughed water from her lungs. Her moan of pain hit him hard in the chest and jolted him out of his fog.

And then the next wave of what-the-fuck hit him so hard he nearly lost his balance.

Sophie was pregnant.

He and Sophie had been together just five months ago. She certainly didn't look beyond five months pregnant. In fact she looked *exactly* that far along.

She was hurt. Someone had shot her. Someone had tried to *kill* her.

She was *pregnant*.

"No," she said fiercely.

"No what?"

"No ambulance. Promise me."

She grabbed his arm with surprising strength. Her eyes were wild, and he doubted she had a clue where she was, who she was or the danger both she and her child were in.

"You need a hospital," he soothed. Hell, he needed a hospital. Or a stiff drink. What the hell was she doing here? Where the hell had she been for the last five months?

Pregnant. Sweet Jesus, was the baby his? His tongue felt thick and swollen in his mouth. He couldn't form the words, and he doubted she'd understand them anyway.

His hand automatically went to her arm, where the wound had started to bleed again. Her blood was warm against her cold skin, and he pressed as hard as he dared, not wanting to hurt her more.

She raised her head, and her eyes, glazed with pain, sparked with determination.

"No hospital. No police. Promise me. *Promise me*."

The desperation in her voice got to him. An uneasy sensation crawled down his spine. His gut told him this was a clusterfuck beyond all clusterfucks.

He glanced up at Garrett, who was staring at him and Sophie with a deep scowl of concentration. No doubt he wanted to know what the hell was going on. That made two of them.

"Don't call the ambulance," Sam said and turned to look up at Donovan, his hand still clamped over the bullet wound. "Get inside, find bandages, a med kit, anything you can dig up."

"Have you lost your goddamn mind?" Garrett exploded. "She's been hurt. She's been shot. And she's *pregnant*."

Sam swallowed and looked down at Sophie's eyes that were now closed.

"Garrett, please do as I asked. I know this woman."

"Who the hell is she?"

He stared both his brothers down. "She's mine."

CHAPTER 5

COLD. She was freezing. And she was having hallucinations. Sam. She'd seen Sam. But he wasn't here. She didn't know where he was. Only that there was a man who looked an awful lot like him standing over her with an expression of horror on his face. Sam wouldn't be that horrified to see her, would he? He didn't know the truth. *Yet*. No, it definitely wasn't Sam.

Then a warm blanket surrounded her, and strong arms lifted her up. She settled against a hard chest, those arms still tight around her.

Sophie opened her eyes and glanced up to see a hard jawline. Strong. Firm. With just a hint of stubble, as though he'd been too lazy to shave that morning. It was damn sexy.

Her gaze wandered upward, and then his head moved and his eyes met hers. Blue. Pale blue, like ice. Just like Sam's eyes. Was she still dreaming? If she was, she wanted to just go along with it. It was a nice dream.

"Hey," he said softly. "You're back."

Back? Where the hell had she been? Her brow crinkled in confusion. "Have I been here before?" she asked. For that matter how had she gotten here? Everything was so fuzzy. She felt funny. Not herself at all. She was having a hard time remembering the smallest of details. It frustrated her because there was something important she had to do.

He shook his head. "No."

"But you said I was back, as if I'd been here before."

He gave her a worried look and picked up his pace. "I meant that you were back. Conscious. You regained consciousness briefly when I pulled you out of the water, but then you passed out again."

"Oh."

His concern deepened and he glanced over, and it was then that Sophie saw another man striding beside them. Big. Mean-looking. He was scowling at her.

Sophie shrunk against the man carrying her and gave an involuntary shiver.

"It's all right," he murmured soothingly as he hoisted her higher in his arms. "No one's going to hurt you, I promise."

"Who is that?" she whispered.

Again he glanced sideways. "That's Garrett. He's my brother."

"He's big and mean-looking," she muttered.

He shook against her as he laughed. "He's harmless."

A snort sounded, and Sophie guessed that Garrett didn't appreciate his brother's assessment.

Then Garrett leaned over to stare at her. "The question is, who are *you*?".

She shrank back and would have crawled over her protector's shoulder and hidden behind him if she could have.

"Back off, Garrett, you're scaring her."

Garrett scowled again and gave her a look that suggested he wasn't finished. Anger surged over Sophie. Damn it, she'd had enough of overbearing, asshole males.

"Easy," the man carrying her soothed, as though he sensed her tension.

He mounted steps and then carried her past another man—just what the hell kind of mess had she landed herself in now? At least they weren't carrying guns, and so far they hadn't tried to kill her. That was a plus, wasn't it? Maybe they could tell her how to find Sam.

"Where am I?" she asked faintly as he settled her onto a bed. Not waiting on a response, she curled into a ball and reached for the covers and a pillow simultaneously. God, she was tired. She hurt from head to toe.

"Oh, no you don't," a male voice reproached. "You can't go to sleep yet."

She shoved at him with a hand and snuggled deeper into the pillow. It felt good. Her muscles started to relax into the warm covers, and then they started screaming in protest.

Her mouth and eyes flew open as pain overwhelmed her. Her arm. Fire. The numb had worn off. And then she remembered. Going overboard. Getting shot. Escaping.

Her hand climbed up her arm, feeling for the wound. It couldn't be too bad, could it?

"Easy," the Sam look-alike murmured. "I'd say some of the shock has worn off and now you're starting to feel it."

She shook violently, her fingers still gripping the area of the gunshot. A gentle hand grasped her fingers and pried them away from her wound.

"H-hurts."

"I know. You should be in the hospital."

Her head flew up. "No."

"Here's the bandages," Garrett said as he strode into the room. "Van's bringing some water and washcloths so you can clean the wound."

Sophie clutched the covers to her chest and stared cautiously at Garrett.

Garrett didn't look any more impressed with her than she did him. He regarded her with what she could only describe as deep suspicion.

A moment later, the third man crowded in behind Garrett. He at least didn't look like he'd like for her to be anywhere but here, but caution radiated from him nonetheless.

"This is my brother Donovan," fake Sam said as he jerked a thumb over his shoulders.

"How many brothers do you have?"

He grinned. "Five. Only two are here, though."

"There's three more?" she asked, trying to keep the horror from her voice.

The room spun crazily around her, and she was so cold that her teeth were going to break from chattering. There was something important she had to do, but she couldn't remember anything beyond keeping her baby safe.

She clutched her belly when she realized she still hadn't felt her baby move. Tears scalded her cheeks, and she sniffed loudly, but she couldn't manage to get air through her nose.

Through the haze and confusion she remembered the one thing she had to do above all else.

"Sam," she croaked out. "I have to get to Sam. They'll kill him."

She sank lower in the bed as the room dimmed around her.

"I'm here, Sophie."

"Sam?" No, it was that guy who looked like him. She shook her head. "No, Sam K-kelly. Have to get to, Sam. Important. They'll kill me too. My baby."

Her teeth clanked together until her jaw ached.

Why couldn't she pull herself together? Why did she feel so disjointed and murky? The room spun crazily around her, like she was stuck on some Ferris wheel from hell. Her stomach knotted and boiled. The god-awful pain was making her nauseous, and the last thing she wanted to do was puke.

Nothing made sense. She'd heard herself babble on, but she couldn't even remember about what.

Sam. That came back to her. It was her one constant.

She tried to say his name again, but found her lips stiff and uncooperative. Her lashes drifted over her eyes, and she tried to rub at them so she could see.

Darkness crowded in until the room was so dim she couldn't even make out the men. It hurt to fight the growing dark. And so she gave up.

Sam watched as she drifted into unconsciousness again. He glanced up at Garrett and Donovan to see them both staring holes through him.

"What the ever loving hell?" Garrett finally said.

Sam dragged a hand through his hair and cupped the back of his neck. "Christ, I don't know."

"Who is she?" Donovan demanded.

Before he could answer, Garrett's eyes narrowed and he stared between Sophie and Sam.

"It's the chick you were involved with in Mexico isn't it?"

Sam ignored Garrett and raised the covers higher over Sophie so she'd be warmer, but he was careful to leave her arm uncovered. The blood still seeping from the wound disturbed him. Hell, the whole thing disturbed him.

"What the hell did she mean by needing to warn you?" Donovan asked. "This stinks to high heaven, Sam. You should call Sean and an ambulance. Let him handle things."

Sam shook his head. "We're not calling the police. Not until I know what the hell went on here."

His gaze dropped to her belly. He pushed aside the covers more, and he couldn't help but slide his palm over the swell. Her skin was cold to touch, but the hard little ball of her stomach fascinated him.

"Oh hell," Garrett muttered. "Oh hell no."

"What?" Donovan demanded.

Sam knew. He swallowed and looked up at his brothers. "It could be mine. I won't know until I can talk to her, but we were together five months ago. She sure looks like she's about five months along."

"Holy shit," Donovan blew out.

"I'm with Van. This stinks like a roadkill skunk," Garrett said grimly.

Sam gestured toward Sophie. "I need to bandage her while she's unconscious. I need you to help me with her arm. If the bullet's still in there, we aren't going to have a choice but to get her to the hospital."

He glanced at the wound. Bullet or no bullet, it needed stitches. He didn't know how the hell he could keep her out of the hospital or why the hell he should.

Donovan eased onto the bed on the other side of Sophie, his expression grim.

"It looks like someone beat the hell out of her, tried to choke her, and then shot her. Not necessarily in that order."

Anger tightened Sam's jaw. "Yeah, that's what it looks like. It's a wonder she got away."

"If she got away," Garrett said sourly.

Sam shot him an irritated look. "What's that supposed to mean?"

"I find it pretty damn strange that she shows up half-drowned and beat up, with a bullet wound, and talking some shit like she has to warn you. Where the hell has she been for five months if you were so hot and heavy with her? She had to know you could protect her."

"So what are you saying?" Sam asked calmly. "You think she beat herself up, shot herself, then threw herself in the lake when she's pregnant as an elaborate scheme to get to me?"

Garrett had the grace to look a little abashed.

"Look, I know you're a suspicious bastard. I'm having my share of what-the-fuckitus at the moment myself, but until I hear what she has to say, I'm reserving judgment."

"Good call," Donovan murmured as he examined Sophie's wound. "Looks like a through-and-through. No bone. Flesh wound. It'll hurt like hell and will probably get infected after she spent so much time in the lake, but I don't think it's too serious. I'd be more worried about her pregnancy."

Donovan's statement hit Sam like a hammer. Yeah, he'd seen her belly. He'd even calmly and matter-of-factly told his brothers that the baby could be his. But not until now had he really let it sink in.

There was a baby. It might be his. He might be a father. Holy shit.

Talk about coming from left field. This wasn't something he'd contemplated in his wildest dreams. He'd left it to his brothers to settle down and have babies. He figured Ethan and Rachel would pop out a couple before he would ever consider settling down and providing grandchildren for Mom and Dad.

He winced. Holy hell. Ma would shit a brick over this.

He was thirty-six. Well past the age most men thought about having families, wasn't it? But he damn sure assumed that if and when he got around to doing it, it would be on his terms, preferably with a woman he'd married and after thoughtful consideration. Babies and his career didn't exactly mix.

"You okay, man?" Donovan asked softly.

Was he okay? He felt like someone had yanked the rug out from under him. Like someone had suddenly changed all the rules and altered the entire course of his life.

Okay, so it sounded dramatic, but hell, it was! A baby changed everything. And then there was Sophie. Why had she disappeared? No, he hadn't given her any promises. He hadn't been in a position to offer her anything at all. Not even his true identity . . .

"Fuck," he bit out.

Garrett glanced sharply at him.

"How the hell did she know where to find me? She

knew me as Sam. Just Sam. Some guy coming through the bar where she worked. Not Sam *Kelly*. I could have been from anywhere for all she knew."

"I'd say you probably indulged in some heavy pillow talk," Garrett said dryly.

Sam shook his head. "Do you think I'm stupid? Besides, talking wasn't exactly what we were doing when we were alone."

Donovan snickered but then quickly sobered. "So what the hell do we do? It's a little too coincidental that the chick you have a fling with, while undercover, just happens to show up looking like death warmed over muttering dire warnings about people trying to kill you—when in fact she wasn't supposed to know anything about you. And certainly not where you lived."

"That about covers it," Sam said as he stared down at Sophie's still form.

The sheet over her belly bumped. Just a little twitch that he almost missed. Perplexed, he leaned over and drew away the sheet. Her soaked shirt had ridden up, exposing the smooth expanse of her stomach.

He remembered touching her, running his hands over her lush body, though it had certainly changed since they'd last made love.

He put his hand to the side of her belly, only to feel the tiny little bump against his palm. In awe he stared. It was the baby.

"Guess the little critter is okay," Garrett mumbled.

Sam couldn't form a response. He was too befuddled. Was this his child he was feeling against his fingers?

"You should get her out of those wet clothes," Donovan offered. "You and Garrett both need to get into dry clothes. I'll go warm up some soup and find out if we have antibiotics in our stash of medications. She'll need that and something stronger than ibuprofen for pain. Not to mention I'm not sure what she can take being pregnant."

Sam stirred and shook himself from his trance. Then he scowled. No one but him was going to see her naked. He focused his frown on Garrett until Garrett finally got the message and walked toward the door, muttering under his breath the entire way.

"Get the soup and find what medications you can," Sam said to Donovan. "After I get her out of these clothes and into something warm, I'll assess her injuries. When she wakes up and can tell us what the hell is going on and why she doesn't want us to take her to the hospital, we'll figure out what to do next."

Donovan nodded and headed out of the room after Garrett.

Sam turned his attention back to the woman lying in his bed. His woman. His child?

He shook his head in denial She wasn't his.

He fingered a strand of wet hair, pulling it carefully away from her neck.

"Where have you been, Sophie?" he asked softly. "What secrets are you hiding and who the hell wants you dead?"

Sudden rage rolled through his body. Whoever wanted her dead had also tried to kill his child. His child.

So many questions buzzed around his head he was about to go crazy. If he didn't take care of her, she wouldn't survive to give him any answers. She still shivered, even in her unconscious state. He needed to get her out of her wet clothes and he needed to get her warm.

He shucked out of his clothing and wasted no time getting something dry on. Then he returned to Sophie.

Carefully, he peeled the soaked layers from her body, paying special care to her injuries. A variety of bruises dotted her body, and his jaw tightened as he studied the dark fingerprints at her neck.

Her nipples puckered and stood erect as chill bumps chased down her body. Her body was slim and curvy except for the mound of her belly. Sam stared unabashedly at her nude form, mesmerized by the changes her pregnancy had wrought.

She seemed too small and too thin. She'd been a little bit of a thing to begin with, but shouldn't pregnancy fill a woman out? Make her more curvy? He'd certainly heard his mom complain about gaining a cup size with each of her pregnancies and how her hips had expanded exponentially. Other than her nipples being darker, the only change in Sophie was the bump riding low on her belly.

"Is it mine, Sophie?" he whispered. "Why did you leave?"

He carefully slipped one of his flannel shirts around her and buttoned it up over the bandages Donovan had secured to her wound. He worried over the blood that had seeped through the gauze. Any blood loss couldn't be good for a pregnant woman, no matter how slight the wound was. And then there was the fact she'd obviously been in the lake for a while. Her skin was still cold to the touch and her lips had a bluish tinge that he didn't like at all.

So many questions. The smart thing would be to call Sean and get Sophie to the hospital. She was hurt and she was pregnant. But every time he looked toward the phone, he remembered the fear in her eyes and the conviction of her words.

She certainly wasn't lying about a threat. Whether it was to her, him or both of them, he couldn't afford to take chances with her life—and her child's.

He crawled onto the bed, piling more covers over her cold body. He lay on his side and pulled her carefully against him, giving her the benefit of his body heat. Then he pulled the covers tight around them, sealing in the warmth.

Gradually she stopped shivering and seemed to settle. Her lips parted against his chest, and a breathy sigh escaped. She tried to nestle closer but whimpered when her shoulder bumped against his body.

"Careful, honey," he whispered and pulled her hand down to wedge between their bodies so he could render her immobile.

"C-cold," she murmured restlessly against his skin.

"I know. You'll get warm. Just lie still so you don't hurt yourself."

"S-sam? Is that really you or am I still dreaming?"

He wasn't quite sure what to make of her confusion. Shock and cold—not to mention a bullet wound—could make a person pretty damned "off." Suspicion crept into his mind even as he wanted to discount it all as some bizarre coincidence.

Only an idiot ignored the obvious. Coincidence, my ass.

"It's me, Sophie. I'm here. You've been hurt. I need to get you to a hospital. You need to make sure your baby is okay."

It took everything he had not to interrogate her then

and there. Only the knowledge of how very fragile she was restrained him.

She shook her head against him, then moaned low in her throat.

"Don't move. It'll only hurt worse," he cautioned.

"Can't go to hospital," she said hoarsely. "He'll find me."

Sam's brow crinkled and he stared down at her face pressed so firmly against his chest.

"Who, Sophie? Who'll find you?"

"My father's—his men," she corrected.

As what-the-fuck statements went, that was a doozy. Sam stared down as her eyelids fluttered shut once more. He wanted to beat his head in frustration, and then he immediately felt guilty when he remembered that the woman in his arms had obviously had a pretty shitty day—or week for that matter.

"Sophie." He waited for a response. "Sophie," he said a little louder. "Honey, wake up. I need you to talk to me here."

She moaned and dug her face into his chest, a gesture that told him more than words that she wanted him to shut up and go away.

This was making him crazy. Van would be back any second with medicine and whatever else he'd managed to dig up. Going with that thought, Sam checked the covers to make sure she was shielded from any prying eyes. Not that Van was an asshole, but hello, a half-naked woman would draw any red-blooded man's eyes. Wouldn't matter if she was dead.

He sighed when she went limp again. Goddamn it. This was not his day, his week or even his month. Had he really been thinking just an hour ago that he missed her? It was almost as if he'd conjured her up, and while he'd had plenty of fantasies about her being in his bed again, this damn sure wasn't what he had in mind.

Donovan knocked once, then without waiting for an answer, stuck his head through the door. Seeing Sam and Sophie, he came on in, a med kit in one hand and a syringe with a capped needle in the other.

"What the hell is that?" Sam demanded when Donovan came closer to the bed.

"Antibiotics. Got it out of the field kit."

"How do you know it's safe to give it to a pregnant woman?"

"The Internet is a useful thing," Donovan said calmly. "Amazing what you can find. I don't even know why people go to doctors anymore."

"I'm supposed to trust my child's safety to some website you Googled?" Sam asked in disbelief.

"Well, yeah. You got a better idea? I still vote we call Sean and get her the hell to the hospital. And you know I'm right."

Sam sighed, then gestured for Donovan to come closer with the stuff. He also carried an assortment of bandages and ointments along with a suture kit.

"Whoa, I'm not letting you stitch her up. That's crazy."

"So is letting her arm rot off from infection."

"Damn it, Van. You're the most infuriating son of a bitch."

At that Donovan cracked a slight smile. "You and Garrett are so easy, I swear. I think you were both born with corncobs up your ass. I was trained as a medic, remember? I can do all sorts of amazing things. Fly airplanes and choppers, and I can sew limbs back on. They might rot off later, but hey that's not my problem."

"Irreverent bastard," Sam muttered. "You've spent too much time around Joe."

Donovan grinned again. "Joe always was my favorite sibling."

Sam waved impatiently at him. "Give her the shot, but I want to take a look at her arm and side again before I turn you loose with a needle and thread."

"You make it sound like I'm about to embroider a pillowcase," Donovan said dryly.

Donovan uncapped the syringe and moved to the opposite side of the bed. He looked apologetically at Sam as he moved the covers aside to bare the curve of Sophie's hip. Sam scowled, but he held his tongue while Donovan efficiently swabbed the smooth skin above her buttocks and then plunged the needle into her flesh.

She flinched and let out a startled cry. She curled her hands into Sam's shirt and trembled, but her eyes didn't reopen. Sam instinctively pulled her closer, murmuring soothing words in her ear. But he glared his displeasure at his brother as he withdrew the needle and recapped the syringe.

Donovan rolled his eyes and moved onto the bed with one knee to begin to peel back the collar of the flannel shirt she wore. When he got to the bandage on her upper arm, he carefully pulled at it. The padding came away bright red, and Donovan frowned as he wiped at the fresh blood oozing from the wound.

"She needs stitches, Sam. I know you don't like it, but if you're not going to do the right thing and take her to the hospital, I need to stitch her up. I can give her a local to numb it. It won't be as good as the stuff they give you in the ER, but if she stays under, she won't feel it."

Sam swore under his breath, closed his eyes and blew out a sound of resignation. "Okay, do it. Be quick about it. I don't want to make this worse than we have to."

Sam tucked her face into his neck, then smoothed his hand up her arm until he reached the spot Donovan was prepping. It was ridiculous that he was acting like a nervous woman over this. He'd patched up his share of bloody wounds on the battlefield. He'd seen things that would make even the most hardened soldier blanch. But the sight of Sophie, pregnant and vulnerable in his arms, while his brother was about to stick a needle through her skin, made his insides churn.

"Hold her," Donovan murmured as he prepared to place the first stitch. "If she jerks, it'll make it hurt more, and I don't want to do any more damage."

"Just do it," Sam growled.

He curled Sophie tighter into him, offering her his strength and his protection. When the needle pierced her skin, he wasn't sure who tensed more—him or Sophie.

Her face twisted and her eyes flew open in alarm. She seemed to look right through him. Her mouth opened in a soundless cry, and then when she spoke, it came out broken and hoarse.

"Please," she begged. "Don't hurt my baby."

Sam's gut twisted, and even Donovan looked up, his eyes narrowing.

"What the hell?" Donovan muttered.

"Get it over with," Sam ordered.

He turned back to Sophie and pressed his lips to hers

in an effort to stop the whimpering sounds that hit him like darts.

"Shhh, Sophie, it's Sam. I'm here. Nothing's going to hurt you. I swear. Your baby is fine. I'm fine. Do you understand?"

"Sam," she slurred out. "Have to warn Sam. No longer safe. I stayed away but now they found me. Sam has to know."

A single tear trailed down her cheek, and Sam kissed it away, savoring the contact after so many months. He didn't care what Van thought. Didn't care what he saw or that he'd tell Garrett and they'd both be on his ass. Right now this was his woman in his arms. His child. And he wanted to know who the hell had threatened her. Who she was so afraid of. And why she thought she had to protect him.

It made him furious.

"Aren't you finished yet?" Sam hissed.

"Almost," Donovan muttered.

Donovan set the needle to her flesh to do the last two stitches. Sam just prayed he'd hurry the fuck up.

Again Sophie tensed and let out a low sob. Sam wanted to moan with her.

"He'll be so angry," she said in a broken voice.

She was babbling now, flinching with each stitch, though she didn't struggle. She seemed to have resigned herself to the hell she was enduring. Sam only wished he knew what was going on inside her fevered mind.

"He'll hate me. He'll never understand. Have to tell him the truth."

Donovan tied off the last suture and cast a worried

glance in Sam's direction. Sam didn't need Donovan to tell him this was crazy. It went beyond bizarre. There was some seriously weird shit going on.

The question was, how was Sophie involved? And if she was in trouble, why the hell hadn't she come to him before now?

His hand slid down to palm her belly, and he felt the reassuring little wiggle of the baby inside her womb.

And if this was his child, what the hell did that mean for him and Sophie now?

CHAPTER 6

SOPHIE was finally warm. There wasn't a part of her body that didn't hurt, but she was warm. It took her a moment in her befuddlement to realize that the source of her warmth came from another person.

She studied the feel of the body against hers without opening her eyes. Hard. Muscled. Definitely male. And familiar.

She snuggled deeper into the wall of his chest and inhaled deeply. She knew that scent. She'd know it anywhere.

Sam.

His arm tightened around her waist, forcing her belly into his groin. It was then she felt the light flutter of her baby. Gasping, she bolted upright, nearly screaming in agony when her arm protested. But she didn't care. Her baby had moved.

She sat up in the bed, both her hands splayed over

her belly, as she willed her little one to move again. She nearly came undone when the reassuring pitter-patter tapped a rhythm against her palms.

"Oh, thank God," she whispered.

Relief staggered her and made her weak. She sagged precariously, and strong arms caught her, easing her back down on the pillow. She stared up into Sam's blue eyes, and she forgot to breathe.

She reached up to touch his cheek, needing proof that he was really here. "Sam. It's you."

She'd made it. She didn't know how. She didn't care. But she was here and safe with Sam. He'd protect her and their child. He had to.

He studied her intently. His expression was guarded, and his lips were in a firm line, neither smiling nor frowning.

"Yes, it's me, Sophie. How are you feeling? Are you in a lot of pain?"

She was too shocked to register how she felt. She was so relieved that her baby was moving, but she was flabbergasted that she was lying in Sam's bed, in his arms. How many nights had she lain alone, dreaming of being back in his arms?

Then fear rolled through her. The rush of memories, everything that had happened in the last few days, came at her, reminding her that her child's life wasn't worth a damn at the moment.

"How long have I been here?" she asked as she struggled to remove herself from Sam's grip.

Pain shot up her arm and left her gasping for breath. He let her go but assisted her in sitting up. His gaze dropped to her belly, and she swallowed nervously. He wasn't stupid. He'd put it together. He probably already had. But there was so much more he didn't know.

"A few hours," he said in a low voice. "I fished you out of the lake. You've drifted in and out of consciousness ever since. You freaked when I told my brother to call for an ambulance. You specifically didn't want a hospital or the police. Care to tell me why?"

She glanced away, but he nudged her chin back with insistent fingers.

"Oh no, Sophie. You and I have a lot to talk about. Starting with what the hell happened to you. Where the hell you disappeared to five months ago. How you knew where to find me and who I was. Why you feel the need to warn me. And most importantly. The most important issue of all. Are you pregnant with my child?"

The blood rushed from her face. He certainly hadn't pulled any punches. But then he deserved answers. He'd hate her, but he deserved to know the truth. About everything.

She swallowed nervously and stared at him with dread weighing down on her like two tons of bricks.

His eyes narrowed, and he brushed his thumb over her cheek. She should have found the gesture comforting, but it was more prompting than affectionate.

She licked her lips, then opened her mouth, but nothing came out. She stared at him in horror as hot tears rolled down her cheeks. Now that she was finally in front of him, was so close she could feel his warmth wrapping around her, she couldn't say anything at all.

His expression softened and his fingers eased around

her jaw. "Don't be afraid of me, Sophie. I won't ever hurt you. I'm in uncharted territory here, so bear with me, okay? I need to know if you're carrying my child."

As he spoke, his other hand dropped to her belly, and he cupped the rounded curve. The baby fluttered and bumped in response, and she caught her breath at the wonder of feeling her move after being still for so long.

"She's yours," Sophie said around a chest so tight she could barely breathe.

His pupils flared and his nostrils quivered. For a moment he stared at her in silence, as if digesting the declaration.

"She?" he finally said.

Sophie flushed. "I call it 'her.' I don't know for sure. Just a feeling. I don't like saying 'it.'"

"But you can tell at this stage, right? I mean, you've had a sonogram. Couldn't they tell you the sex?"

She looked down. "I haven't had a sonogram."

He nudged her chin up again, and he frowned at her. "But you've been to the doctor."

She shook her head. "Too dangerous."

His mouth screwed up into a pinched bow. He continued staring at her with those intense blue eyes.

"But she's mine."

"Yes. She's yours. No doubt about it."

"I see."

He seemed calm enough, but she could sense the turmoil beneath the deceptively calm expression.

"And you're just now getting around to telling me."

She almost laughed. She would have if she hadn't been so sure it would end up in a fit of hysteria. Tell him. As if it was the easiest thing in the world. Bitterness, sharp and quick, welled in her chest.

"Tell you?" She did laugh then. She simply couldn't hold it back. As predicted, it ended in a high, shrill sound that was anything but pleasant. "Just how was I supposed to tell you, Sam? You walked out of that hotel room after you told me I wouldn't see you again."

His eyes narrowed again, and they glittered dangerously.

"And yet you had no problem finding me. You obviously knew where I was all along, which is more than I can say I knew about you. How is that, Sophie? Just who the hell are you and what are you playing at?"

How quickly his questions turned into accusations.

She rolled, bracing herself for when her injured arm took the brunt of her weight. She struggled to get her feet over the edge of the bed and onto the floor. She stood, and the flannel shirt fell to her knees. Just as well since she was butt naked underneath.

She looked around for clothing, even as her mind rolled with just how to relate everything she needed to say.

"I'll make this quick and easy," she said in a bitter voice. "Someone wants me dead, or they will as soon as they get what they want from me. They probably want you dead too, but you've been kept alive because you're the bait. I stayed away for that reason. But they got too close, and I couldn't take a chance on staying ahead of them any longer. I'm certainly not as fast or as bright as I used to be."

She gestured down at her belly in disgust. "Not only does pregnancy make me slower, but I swear it sucks all the brain cells."

"Sophie, you need to calm down," Sam said as he put his hands out in a placating manner. "Come back and sit down. You shouldn't be up."

"Where are my clothes?" she demanded as she looked around. "I need my clothes." She knew she sounded desperate and irrational. But damn it, she needed something to wear, and she needed to get the hell out of here. Sam said she'd been here several hours. Tomas and company would know exactly where to look for her.

Her gaze lighted on a pair of sweatpants in the corner, and she bent down to pick them up. When she stood back up, pain splintered down her arm, and she bobbled like a drunken party girl wearing stilettos. Sam was there to catch her, but she yanked herself away and edged toward the bed so she could pull the pants on.

They were way too big, but she didn't care. They were warm and dry. As soon as she got them on, she stood again and reached for Sam, tugging on his arm. He looked at her in disbelief, like he'd look at a crazy woman.

"Come on, Sam. We have to go. We can't stay here. They'll come. They'll kill you. And your brothers. I didn't know you had brothers. Sorry. I didn't realize. I thought it was just you and your men."

Her pulse thudded painfully at her temples, and her chin wobbled as she chattered out the rest. She didn't make any sense whatsoever, and Sam just stood there staring at her like she'd lost her mind.

She reached again and this time took his hand between hers. She pulled until his palm rested on her belly.

"They were going to kill her, Sam. He had a knife. He said he'd slice me open and let her spill out. I can't let that happen. I need your help. Please. You have to help me."

Sam stared at her in horror, then his gaze dropped

to where his hand was splayed across her abdomen. He looked so appalled that she stopped for a moment and wrapped her arms around her stomach, trapping his hand there.

"Sweet mother of God," Sam muttered. He pulled his hand away and then yanked her into his arms.

It hurt like hell, but she didn't care. She didn't protest and she didn't try to pull away. She wanted to absorb him right into her soul. Finally she felt safe. Like maybe she wasn't so *alone*.

For just a moment she stood there, but reality crept in despite her wanting to indulge in the fantasy.

"We have to go," she whispered.

She pulled away, but he held her firm.

"Let me go," she protested. "We have to get out of here, Sam. Your brothers. They have to go too. They'll kill them."

He grasped her good arm, and with his other hand he gripped her chin and held her so that she was forced to stare back at him.

"Let's get a few things straight here, okay? One, you're not going anywhere. Period. Two, I need answers, Sophie. A lot of damn answers. Three, no one is going to hurt you or my child. Four, if you knew where I've been all this time, you damn well should have come to me the moment you knew you were in danger."

She stared at him in disbelief. Then she laughed. It was all she could do. He was so determined, and how like a man to try and simplify matters.

"You don't get it, Sam. I can't stay. I won't put my baby in danger," she said fiercely. "I barely managed to escape the bastard last night. He shot me. He would have killed my baby. I'm not giving him a second chance. I've stayed ahead of him for the last five months."

"And now he's caught up to you," Sam said calmly. "Sit down, Sophie. You and I have a hell of a lot to talk about. I want to get the personal stuff out of the way first. Because then I want my brothers here when you tell me all this other shit."

The fight left her and the pain overwhelmed her senses. She sagged onto the edge of the bed and dropped her head in defeat.

Sam knelt in front of her and carefully placed his hand on her belly.

"Why didn't you tell me?"

She glared at him again. "You didn't act like a man who wanted to know. You lied to me about everything from the moment we met."

"And yet you know everything about me. How is that, Sophie?" he asked in a dangerously low voice.

She stared stubbornly back at him.

"I came back for you," he said, surprising the hell out of her.

She furrowed her brow and frowned hard at him. "What are you talking about?"

He ran a hand through his hair and looked briefly away. "I was there undercover. I couldn't tell you things, Sophie. I couldn't share anything more of myself than I did. But when it was over, I came back, but you were gone. Disappeared. I searched, and it was as if you didn't exist."

Her cheeks warmed under his scrutiny, but she refused to feel guilty. She hadn't had a choice but to run and run hard. She'd spent the last five months hiding. All because she'd helped him. And betrayed her father in the process.

"Look at me and tell me she's mine," Sam said fiercely. "I have to know. Don't jerk me around about this."

She raised her gaze until she stared levelly at him. She let calm invade her because she had nothing to hide when it came to this. Oh, she had plenty of secrets, but in this, her conscience was clear.

"She's yours. There's been no one else, Sam. Not for a long time."

Was that relief she saw in his eyes? Regret? Joy? Maybe a mix of all three? It was hard to tell.

For just a moment, his focus shifted to her belly. He spread the material of the shirt tight over her stomach and he slid his fingers over every inch, studying the curve and the shallow indention of her belly button.

"I can't wrap my brain around it," he said hoarsely. "I'm going to be a father."

She started to thrust her fingers into his hair but held back. There was so much unresolved between them. And maybe there was nothing to resolve. She had been a fling for him—or so she'd thought—but he said he'd come back for her. Did she dare believe him? A man would say a lot to get himself off the hook when his ass was to the fire.

But then he hadn't made her any promises, and she sure as hell had kept a lot from him. So many secrets. So much betrayal. It would be a lot easier to just warn him of the impending danger to him and his family and walk away.

As if sensing her sudden desire to flee, his hand tightened on her stomach and then he rose from his knees and took her hand in his.

"We can talk more about us later," he said in a quiet voice. "Right now we need to talk about who the hell is trying to kill you and why you think me and my family are in danger. And we're not leaving my brothers out of this conversation, since they'll be the ones I'll be depending on to help save our asses."

CHAPTER 7

A myriad of emotions flickered across Sophie's face. Fear, indecision, pain and deep weariness. She should be in bed, resting, but she was as jumpy as a cricket, and she looked like she'd flee if he looked away even a second.

Sam urged her back to bed. He plumped the pillows and mounded the covers up over her body until she sat like a queen presiding over her subjects. Only she looked small and frail instead of stately.

He held up a finger as he stared down at her. "Don't move. Not even a muscle. I'll be back in a minute with my brothers."

The sudden wash of fear in her eyes made his gut clinch. Her hands went to her belly, and she rubbed in a tight circle. He wasn't sure who she was trying to reassure. Her baby or herself.

It was all he could do not to lean down and kiss her.

To tell her it would be all right, that he'd take care of her and their baby.

There was too much unsettled between them, and the uneasiness in his belly kept growing in direct proportion to the suspicion that had taken root in his mind.

When he was sure she wasn't going to bolt from the bed, he turned and strode to the door. He leaned out and didn't see Van or Garrett, but he could hear them in the kitchen. With a quick look back at Sophie and an unspoken directive for her to stay put, he hurried to get his brothers.

Donovan was stirring something in a mug while Garrett stood to the side, arms crossed over his broad chest, a typical scowl etched on his face.

They both looked up when Sam walked in, and Donovan dropped the spoon on the counter.

"I heated up some broth for her. Found some pain medication in our stash and did a cross-check for contraindications for pregnancy."

Sam nodded. "I need you both in the bedroom. Sophie's got some things to tell me that I want you to hear."

Garrett shoved off the wall and did nothing to disguise his interest.

"Like what?"

"I don't know yet. She says she's in danger—that we're in danger. Since I depend on you two to cover my ass, and vice versa, I figured it would be helpful for you to hear whatever it is she has to say."

"What if she's full of shit?" Garrett asked. "Doesn't this whole thing scream setup to you? I'd like to know how the fuck she knew where to find you. According to you she was a sweet-faced waitress with big eyes and you blew her off when we got the tip about Mouton's arms shipment moving out."

Sam's jaw clenched. "You're pissing me off right now, Garrett. You need to back the fuck off. You're not saying anything I'm not thinking, but I'm not going to go beat her down when she's hurt, scared and pregnant. She's a woman, for God's sake. Use your head."

"One of us has to," Garrett said evenly. "The right head."

"I won't tell you again. Back off."

The two brothers stood nose to nose. Garrett's eyes glittered with anger and impatience, but Sam knew he just wanted answers. Well so did he. Hopefully he'd use a little more finesse than Garrett.

Finally Garrett backed away.

Donovan cleared his throat. "So uh, are we going to be uncles?"

The casual question made Sam flinch. Then he slowly nodded. "Yeah. The baby is mine."

"Jesus," Garrett muttered.

"Hoo boy," Donovan said from pursed lips. He gathered the mound of supplies, then picked up the mug from the counter. "Not sure what you want me to say, so I'll just shut up."

"Yeah," Sam snapped. "Shutting up is good."

"You're so sure she's telling the truth," Garrett said with a hint of anger in his voice.

Sam stopped on his way back to the bedroom and turned around. He eyed Garrett evenly. "No. I'm not saying that at all. I am, however, embracing the very real possibility that the baby could be mine. She says it's mine. For now I'm going with it. I'm not going to let anything happen to *my* child."

Garrett rubbed his palm over his face and nodded. "Yeah, I understand, man. Van and I have your back. You know that."

Sam nodded. "Thanks."

He turned around and walked back into his bedroom. Sophie was listing badly to the right, her eyes half-closed. When she heard them come in, she jerked up and her eyes flew open. She winced and grabbed at her shoulder with her free hand.

"Careful," Sam murmured as he went to her. He glanced back at Donovan. "Will this pain medicine knock her out?"

"That's the plan," Donovan said. "For the first little while she needs something stronger. Then we can knock it down to ibuprofen."

Sam grimaced, then turned apologetically to Sophie. "We need to talk. I'll have Donovan give you the medicine afterward. Then you can sleep for a good long while."

She shook her head, her eyes fierce. "I can't sleep, Sam. After I tell you what you want to know, I have to go. I can't stay here. I've already been here too long. If you won't go with me, I don't have a choice but to take off on my own."

He shot his brothers a pointed look but didn't respond to her statement. He sat down on the edge of the bed and motioned for his brothers to get comfortable.

Donovan edged onto the bed on the other side of Sophie and looked at her as if seeking permission. He might as well have not even been there for all the attention she paid him. Her face was pale and strained, and it was obvious she was fighting to stay conscious.

Garrett stood at the end of the bed, arms folded over his chest, and he stared broodingly at Sophie. When she happened to glance up at him, she went even paler.

"Damn it, Garrett," Sam muttered. "Ease up for God's sake."

Garrett shifted his position with an irritated huff.

"Talk to me, Sophie. I need you to back up and tell me why you disappeared. Then I need to know how you knew who I was and where to find me and why people are trying to kill you and why you think me and my family are in danger."

She threw him an impatient look that suggested she didn't appreciate the fact that he was questioning what she'd stated as fact.

Then she looked down at her hands, and he could see the tips go white as she nervously twisted her fingers. She took a deep breath and then glanced up at him, her eyes almost challenging. Like she was gearing up for battle.

"My father was Alex Mouton."

"What the fuck?"

Sophie jumped at Garrett's explosion. Even Donovan recoiled and glared at Sophie. Sam processed the information with a sense of disbelief. He just stared at her, wondering just how badly he'd been set up and fucked over.

She stared back at him, her lips pressed into a tight line as she waited for him to digest the bomb.

It was Donovan who finally prompted Sophie to continue. Sam wasn't able to speak. He was too furious. He felt like the biggest goddamn fool on the planet.

"Okay so Mouton is your father," Donovan said in a tight voice. "Wait a minute. You said *was*."

Her eyes grew distant, and she looked at them as if measuring whether she trusted them enough to say anything.

"Just a figure of speech."

"He sent you to me, didn't he?" Sam asked before she could continue.

Her chin went up and her gaze hardened. "He did. You hit his radar the moment you came into his town. He wanted information."

Sam's nostrils flared. "Pity you failed. Or maybe you weren't good enough to get me to talk."

She winced and looked away. He felt like a bastard kicking a puppy, but goddamn it, he was pissed.

"He got nothing from me," she said. "He didn't really need it. He was on to you shortly after you stepped into his territory, but he thought it was a good idea for me to stay close to you in case you dropped any information he'd find valuable. How do you think I knew where to find you? Here, I mean. It's why you need to understand the danger that you and your family are in."

There was a whole lot more she wanted to say. Sam could tell. Her lips quivered, and he saw the flash of her teeth as she sank them into her bottom lip to squelch the flow of words. What the hell?

She'd played him from the start. Her father was an arms dealer and currently occupied the number two spot on the U.S. government's most wanted list. She claimed to be pregnant with his child. Her father wanted something from her and was using Sam's child as leverage, not to mention Sam and all his family were now in danger. And she expected him to drop everything to protect her. From what?

Donovan shot Sam a look that clearly said shut the fuck up. Was it that obvious he was ready to explode?

"We need clear heads here," Donovan said. "I get that you two have history, but right now, that's not as important as why someone's trying to kill Sophie. Why is that, Sophie?" He stared hard at her, but his expression wasn't as fierce as Garrett's or what Sam knew his own must be. "You're not telling us everything."

No, she wasn't. Sam could see the shadows in her eyes. She was holding back out of fear, but of whom? Was she afraid of him and his reaction? Or was she afraid of her father, and if so, what the hell had she done to make him turn on her after she'd prostituted herself for him.

"Look, you have to know my father was a bastard. It's not like he gave his flesh and blood a free pass. I saw my opportunity to escape, and I took it. There are people not so pleased with me because of it."

"And we figure in where?" Garrett demanded.

She threw him a disgusted look. "You encroached on Mouton territory. You fucked with the family business. You were a target as soon as you showed up looking to score a deal."

"That was five months ago," Sam pointed out. "Why now?"

Her lips twisted. "You were bait. They were waiting for me to come to you. I stayed away as long as I could. But I'm getting bigger and clumsier by the day. Soon I'll be completely defenseless. So I came here because I was sure you'd at least protect your child."

Sam looked up and closed his eyes in frustration. "So you stayed away, kept the knowledge of my child from me even though you were both in danger, and you did this all to protect me."

Rage burst in her eyes like a flare. It was a sharp mixture of anger and grief and of helpless anxiety.

"You know what? Fuck you." She looked to his brothers, including them in her fury. "Fuck you all."

She rolled to the side, shoving at Donovan as she slid to the floor. Her knees buckled, and she would have gone down in a heap if Donovan hadn't shot up to catch her.

Still, she shook him off and wrenched her arm from his grasp. A spasm of pain whitened her face, and her blue eyes went pale.

Sam moved across the room to cut off her escape route to the door. He made sure he took her uninjured arm, his other arm going around her waist to trap her against him.

She tried to shove him away, but he held tight.

"Get the shot ready," he ordered Donovan.

"No!" She struggled harder until he feared she was going to hurt herself more. "Sam, you can't keep me here. They'll find me! Are you insane? I get that you don't care about me, but for God's sake, think about your child. Your baby!"

He maneuvered her to the bed and wrestled her down until she was pinned to the mattress. Tears were trapped in her eyes, but none fell, probably held back by sheer determination not to let him see her bleed.

He grimly held her down, staring into her tormented eyes.

"Right now I don't give a damn about what you did in the past. Let's get that clear. You were a lay. A fling. You played me. Okay, fine. I can deal with that. But if that's my child—if there's any chance that you're carrying my baby, you're not going anywhere. And I goddamn well protect what's mine."

Hurt filled her eyes, and once again, he felt like he was crushing an innocent. Some innocent. Goddamn, she was Alex Mouton's daughter.

"I don't deserve to die, Sam. No matter what you think I did, I don't deserve to die."

His hands gentled on her shoulders as Donovan closed in with the syringe. Despite his anger and shock, Sam smoothed his fingers over her cheek in a gesture meant to comfort her.

"You're not going to die, Sophie."

Donovan slipped the needle into her flesh, and she jerked in surprise, her shocked gaze going to Donovan. Panic flared in her blue eyes, and she went crazy.

"No!" she shouted hoarsely. "God, please, let me go. Please!"

Her begging nearly undid Sam. Even Garrett looked discomfited by the desperation in her cries.

Sam dropped down and pulled her into his arms. He held her against him to still her struggles. When she finally figured out she couldn't win against him, she sagged in defeat, her noisy sobs echoing sharply across the room.

"Jesus," Donovan muttered as he recapped the syringe. He threw it angrily into his bag and turned away, his shoulders tense.

Sam held on to her, stroking her hair, offering her comfort even though it was the last thing he wanted to give.

There were several missing pieces of the puzzle. She hadn't told them everything. A lot didn't make sense, but now wasn't the time to try to drag it out of her. She was hysterical, in pain, and soon she'd be out when the drugs hit her system.

Most importantly, he and his brothers had to move fast. If all she said was true—if there was any possibility that she was telling the truth—they had to lock down their entire family.

He needed to contact Sean. He needed to pull in Steele and Rio and their teams. Mom and Dad and Rusty were vulnerable, as were Ethan and Rachel. They could all be targets.

He looked up to find Garrett staring fiercely back at him, and he knew Garrett was thinking the same things he was.

Sophie went completely limp against him, and he carefully pried her away from him to see that her she had finally surrendered to the painkiller Donovan had injected.

Her eyes were swollen and her skin was blotchy and red from crying. She looked delicate and frail, but underneath that deceptive façade was a devious woman who had no compunction about carrying out the orders of her father—a man who'd been responsible for more deaths than a lot of wars.

And the hell of it was she was carrying Sam's child. Which meant, like it or not, she was going to be forever tied to him through that child. No matter what she'd done in the past or what her motives were now, he had to protect her and keep both her and his son or daughter alive.

He carefully extricated himself from around her and made sure she was arranged comfortably on the pillows. He pulled the covers up over her body and then turned to face his brothers.

"Let's go," he said grimly. "We've got to move fast."

CHAPTER 8

"DO you believe her?" Garrett asked when they assembled in the living room. "Do you believe any of that shit?"

Garrett still wore a look of discomfort after the episode with Sophie just moments before, but Sam was sure his brother didn't realize how much her distress had affected him. It would just piss Garrett off.

"Whether I believe her or not, we have to treat this as a legitimate threat. Her wounds aren't faked and neither is the fact that I pulled her half-dead out of the lake."

"I agree," Donovan said.

Garrett blew out his breath but nodded.

Sam looked to Donovan first. "I want you to get in touch with Ethan. Give him a heads-up on what's going on. Make damn sure he keeps his ears and eyes open for any threat to him and Rachel. And for God's sake tell him not to come home. He could be walking into a trap."

Garrett nodded his agreement.

"Then I want you to get on the phone with Sean. Tell him to head out to Mom and Dad's until we can get over there."

He glanced over at Garrett. "We need to have a look and see if anything's out there. I'm not walking into broad daylight with Sophie when I don't know what if anything's out there waiting."

"I'll go," Garrett said. "You keep an eye on Sophie and stick by the radio. If there's anything out there, I'll find it."

While Donovan made his phone calls, Garrett escaped through the basement tunnel leading down to the lake, and Sam did a step-by-step reconnaissance of the house, checking for any possible angles a shooter could use.

The basement was solid, almost as much of a fortress as the war room on the adjacent lot, but there was only one way out of it if the house was breached, and he'd prefer to use it as a last resort.

On the main level, the problem areas were the kitchen, which had a window facing the wooded area across the road in front of the house, and Sam's bedroom, where Sophie slept. The window there was an open invitation for someone to take out anyone in the room.

He hoped to hell she was still under from the pain medication. The last thing he wanted to do was wake her up and have her wanting to split when he and his brothers hadn't fully scoped the situation.

Carefully he slid his arms underneath her warm body and lifted, inch by inch, holding his breath when she stirred and snuggled into his chest.

"Sam," she murmured in her sleepy, sweet voice. One he'd heard so many times when he woke her to make love to her again.

It was a compulsion to slide his lips over her hair. It was still damp and matted by the lake water, but she still smelled uniquely Sophie.

It pissed him off. In a situation where he needed to be in absolute and complete control of his judgment and emotions, he was decidedly . . . not.

He went back into the living room, where he'd already placed blankets and pillows on the sofa. He eased Sophie onto the cushions and arranged her arm so nothing would press on it. Before he was tempted to linger, he turned away, refusing to look at her any longer.

Donovan met him a few steps away.

"Ethan's not happy. He wanted to hop on the next plane home. But at the same time he didn't want to drag Rachel into the middle of something we don't yet understand."

"He's not stupid. He'll do what it takes to protect Rachel."

"Sean's heading to Mom and Dad's now."

Garrett's voice came in low and serious over the radio. Donovan and Sam both froze as they listened.

"Sam, I've got someone. Two o'clock. West. He's surrounded by camo netting. He's damn near invisible. He's clearly on observation duty. He's it. Rest of the perimeter is clear."

"Son of a bitch," Sam muttered. "You have a clear shot?"

"Negative. Tree's in my way."

Sam's nostrils flared. No one hunted him on his own turf. "Maintain your position. I'm going after him."

"I'm locked. He moves and I got him. Be careful, Sam. This guy looks to be a professional."

Donovan met Sam's gaze with hard eyes. "You should

stay here, Sam. Let me go after him. If Sophie wakes, she'll need you."

"She'll need you more," Sam said shortly. "You're the medic."

Donovan nodded, not arguing though Sam knew he wasn't happy with the decision.

Sam suited up, his mind focused on the fact that there was a threat out there to his family.

Stalking his prey was what Sam did best. He was patient and cunning. He'd once spent six hours closing in on a sniper and took him out without the enemy, positioned a mere fifteen yards away, ever knowing.

This was more important. This man posed a threat to everything Sam held most dear in the world. His brothers. His family. And now his child.

And Sophie.

The voice whispered in his ear, a reminder he didn't want.

When he finally got the intruder in his sights, he merely watched, gauging the man's intent. He was a soldier or a mercenary, and he too was patient.

His movements were measured. He watched the house through binoculars and occasionally he'd scout the area around the house. Looking for anyone watching him.

Sam smiled to himself. The asshole would never see Garrett unless Garrett wanted him to.

Without a sound, Sam unsheathed his knife and crept forward, pausing when the wind stopped or his target moved. He was three feet away and the man still hadn't detected his presence. Then the wind shifted, blowing from the west. The man turned up his head, nostrils expanding as he scented Sam like a wild animal.

Before he could turn, Sam was on him. The blade pressed into the neck smeared with camo paint, and Sam hissed his demand close to the man's ear.

"Who sent you?"

"Fuck you."

The intruder twisted and tried to ram his gun between him and Sam. Sam sliced, cutting the man's throat in one quick motion.

The hiss of escaping air and the slight gurgle of blood were the only sounds denting the breeze.

"Good work," Garrett said into Sam's earpiece.

Sam held up the okay sign and then signaled that he'd take care of the body. He'd have left it there to rot, but one, it was too damn close to his house and he didn't want to smell the bastard, and two, it would be a headache for Sean when the body was discovered.

Better it disappear for good.

An hour later, he returned to the house to find Garrett and Donovan both waiting.

"I've set a secure perimeter around the house," Garrett said. "No one will be able to so much as piss in the direction of this house without us knowing."

"We need to call Steele and Rio in," Sam said as he glanced toward the couch where Sophie still slept. "Mouton made the mistake of stepping onto our turf. We'll take the fight to him. This time he goes down."

Both Garrett and Donovan nodded their heads in agreement.

"Until Rio and Steele get here with their teams, we stay put. I don't want to get Sean or Mom and Dad involved in any way. We'll put big shiny targets on our asses and dare the bastards to come and get us."

"Fuckin' A," Garrett snarled.

"And Sophie?" Donovan asked.

Again Sam glanced over to her curled up body on the couch.

"She stays with me. She doesn't get out of our sight."

SOPHIE struggled in her dreams. The thing was she was aware enough to know she was only dreaming, but she couldn't shake out of the hazy world of sleep. Exhaustion held her too firmly in its grasp.

The assassin was holding her while he slowly carved a line into her belly. She felt the skin give way. Horror overcame her. She screamed, a giant, silent scream. She couldn't get her lips to work, and her mouth was as dry as sawdust.

Whimpers tore from her mouth, and she shoved invisible arms away from her. But still, she felt that blade, cutting closer to her womb.

"Sophie. Sophie!"

The gruff voice startled her to wakefulness. Panic shrieked through her spine. God, she wasn't dreaming. He was *here*. He was standing over her ready to kill her.

She came up swinging. Her fist connected with his nose, and she felt the satisfying snap as his head popped back.

"Son of a bitch!"

The snarl had her rolling over despite the scream of protest from her arm. She drew back, ready to hit him again, her other arm instinctively over her belly.

"For God's sake, it's me, Garrett. You were dreaming."

She blinked and stared up at the man looming over

her. He was holding his nose, and blood smeared his fingers.

She couldn't even bring herself to apologize. The words stuck in her throat as she remembered what an ass he'd been so far.

"What the hell's going on?" Donovan demanded as he walked up. He looked at Garrett with an expression of disbelief. Then he cocked his head in Sophie's direction and arched an eyebrow in question.

"She decked me," Garrett said.

Donovan's shoulders shook and his lips twitched. His eyes gleamed in merriment.

Garrett made a sound that came out as a grunt. "She packs a mean right."

"Look, I didn't mean to," she said in disgust. "I thought you were the asshole trying to kill my baby."

She clutched her arms tighter around herself and refused to look back up at them. The two men remained silent, and finally she heard Garrett walk away. A moment later she heard the kitchen faucet turn on.

"Where's Sam?" she asked, still not looking at Donovan.

"Making another pass. Making sure we don't have more company."

She did look then. "More? Are they here already?" She shook her head, clearing the remnants of her drugged, fogged-up feeling.

"You drugged me," she said through her teeth as she sat forward on the couch.

He stepped warily away. The memory came flooding back of her begging and pleading for them to let her go.

"Who's out there?" she demanded.

She rose unsteadily to her feet and cursed when Donovan reached out to prevent her from falling.

"Hey, you okay? Maybe you should sit back down."

"You stay away from me," she muttered as she sidestepped him.

He sighed. "You were in pain."

She bared her teeth. "When is Sam going to be back? And you never answered my question. Who's out there?"

Garrett returned from the kitchen and frowned in her direction.

"I don't know who was out there. He wasn't up for conversation," Donovan said.

"Why aren't you two out there with Sam?" she demanded. "What if something happens to him?"

Garrett shot her an incredulous look. "Nothing's going to happen to him. Sam can handle himself."

"Easy for you to say. You're in here."

"You want something to eat?" Donovan asked.

Startled, she glanced at him, trying to remember the last time she'd eaten. Powered by the suggestion, her stomach caved, and she broke out in a sweat. Her hands shook.

"Have a seat," Donovan said gently. "I'll bring you some soup, okay?"

With a resigned sigh, she sank back onto the cushion. Donovan disappeared into the kitchen, leaving her with Garrett.

"Do you always have that look on your face?" she asked.

For a moment his frown slipped and he looked startled by the question. Then he scowled but didn't reply. She shrugged and settled back on the couch, closing her eyes wearily.

Her drug-induced coma hadn't been a substitute for a good hard sleep, and now her body was nearing shutdown. The smell of chicken wafted across her nose, and she stirred but was so tired, she wasn't sure she could summon the strength to open her eyes and eat.

"Sophie."

Her eyes flew open to see Sam standing there, his gaze boring into her. Had he always been so tall and muscled? She'd spent a lot of time naked with him, but now, dressed in a black T-shirt and camo pants, he looked . . . fierce. Like a man she didn't know and wasn't sure of.

"You need to eat," he said.

It was then she saw the bowl in his hand. She swallowed nervously. They hadn't talked—hadn't said anything since she'd dropped her bomb on him. Should she tell him her father was dead? That she'd killed him? Would he even believe her?

Her stomach bottomed out again, and she covered her nervousness by shifting position on the couch. Her arm was starting to ache fiercely again, and despite her anger over the forced painkiller, it would have been nice to have the pain subside again.

She cleared her throat, hating to show weakness. She'd been forced to show strength in front of her father for so long that it was ingrained.

"Do you have something for pain?" she asked. "Like a pill. Something that won't knock me out."

The lines in Sam's forehead deepened. "Of course. Here." He handed her the bowl and slid the spoon around the inside until it rested against her finger. "I'll get you some ibuprofen."

She cupped the bowl in her palms and let the warmth

bleed into her hands. She sighed as she inhaled and closed her eyes to let the steam rise over her cheeks. It smelled like heaven.

Sam returned with a small plastic bottle and a glass of milk. He shook out a couple of the tablets and sat next to her on the couch. Then he held up the milk.

His gaze dropped to her belly. "For the baby," he said gruffly.

Carefully she put the bowl on her lap, balancing it carefully so the soup didn't spill. Touched by the gesture, she took the milk and the pills and then peered at him over the rim of the glass as she chased the medicine down.

It was hard to gauge his mood. He was frowning, but then it seemed all the Kellys loved to frown.

His eyes flickered, and again he looked down at her belly.

She drained the glass and set it aside before reaching for the bowl again. He made her uneasy, watching her as she sipped at the broth. They were all watching her like she was some bug under a microscope, some undiscovered species.

Spoonful by spoonful she concentrated on the warm liquid that coated her throat down to her empty stomach. When she was finished, Sam took the bowl, their hands touching for just an instant.

He paused and she stared down at those fingers, remembering how they felt on her body, how tender he'd been. How rough he'd been. And demanding.

She shook away those memories, determined that they not have sway in the here and now. Who was she kidding? She'd wish away the present in a heartbeat if she could just go back to those precious days she'd spent in his arms.

No, she wouldn't go back. She'd give up a lot but not her freedom. Maybe she'd made a mistake to run to Sam. She'd thought she was out of options, but maybe she should have just kept on running.

She looked into his eyes, meeting that steady gaze with steel determination.

"What do we do now?"

CHAPTER 9

SAM pulled a small digital camera from his pocket and turned the LCD toward Sophie.

"Recognize him?"

She recoiled, and her stomach heaved. She jerked her head away as her breaths hiccuped from her mouth. The man was obviously dead, a gaping cut to the throat.

"Do you?"

She glanced back and folded both arms over her belly. Then she nodded.

"He's the one who threatened to kill our baby," she said in a low voice.

"You won't have to worry about him anymore."

She lifted her gaze to meet Sam's. There was anger reflected in the blue. But there was also coldness and she shivered against the violence of it.

"Did you kill him?"

He didn't hesitate. "Yes."

Neither did she hesitate. "Good."

"He was one of your father's personal assassins," Sam said. He pushed a button on the camera and then turned it again so she could see.

Yes, she knew her father required his men to have the symbol of their loyalty branded into their arm. It was barbaric and senseless, but then he'd never had a shortage of men willing to die for him.

"You need to start talking, Sophie. There's a hell of a lot I need to know."

If he was angry, she could deal with that. Anger would be justified. But his voice was cold. He could have been interrogating a prisoner.

I'm pregnant with your child. She wanted to scream it. *Don't you remember how we made her?*

"I didn't betray you, Sam," she said fiercely.

His lips tightened. He glanced toward his brothers, who stood silently across the room, and dismissed them with a nod.

As soon as they were gone, Sam stood, as if he couldn't bear to sit that close to her. For a while he kept his back turned, and heavy silence settled over the room. Then he turned, his eyes flat.

"Then tell me, Sophie. What exactly did you do?"

She flinched and it pissed her off. She felt pinned to the couch, helpless. She couldn't stand the weight of his stare another moment.

Her hands curled over the edge of the couch, and she pushed herself up, ignoring the pain in her arm.

"Sit down, Sophie."

He didn't bark the order, but it was an order nonetheless. Her chin went up in her best go-to-hell impression.

It took courage to go to him. Courage to face him down when he could so easily turn away and crush her without thought.

It made her angry that she cared. Made her angry that it mattered. She'd done what she had to do to survive. She shouldn't have to explain herself to anyone.

"I knew you had secrets, that you weren't honest with me," she said.

"Yes, I suppose you did."

The words tripped out with a hint of sarcasm. She ignored it and went on, refusing to give him the fight he seemed to want.

"I knew and I understood. I didn't care. I wanted that time with you even though I knew when it was over that you'd walk away and that I was never supposed to know who you were or ever expect more than what you gave me."

His Adam's apple bobbed as he swallowed, and he looked away as if he was uncomfortable with the direction the conversation had turned. Would it kill him so much to admit that she'd hurt him? Did anything hurt this man? She wasn't trying to make him feel guilt. She accepted her role in deception as easily as she'd accepted his. Maybe she would have felt differently if she'd ever believed even for a moment that things were honest between them.

"I didn't betray you," she said again.

His gaze lifted, and those piercing blue eyes caught her again. This time there was a genuine question there instead of accusation and disbelief.

"Tell me."

Sweet relief sang through her mind. The weight that

hovered so unbearably on her shoulders lightened, and she forgot the pain in her arm—and in her heart.

With those two words he told her he'd listen.

"I've already explained that my father sent me to you. He wanted me to glean whatever information I could—in any manner it took."

"And you went."

She closed her eyes. She knew how bad it looked. She wouldn't apologize though, and she wouldn't allow Sam to make her feel shame for her choice.

"You were my best chance at escape. I never intended to do anything more than make my father think I was doing what he wanted. But I saw you and I wanted you more than I wanted my freedom."

The color deepened in his eyes. They went dark and his body went still.

"Why did you want your freedom?" he asked softly.

She kept her gaze even, not betraying the surge of rage that flashed through her blood.

"I hated him."

Sam's brow furrowed and he frowned. "Why?"

"You know what kind of man he was—is."

"But what did he do to *you*, Sophie?"

"Besides demanding that I whore myself for him? Is it important? I would think that's bad enough. You said it yourself. Who the hell does that? What kind of *father* asks his daughter to do that?"

It wasn't everything, but it was all Sam needed to know, and it was certainly a credible enough reason for a daughter to hate her father.

"Remember the note, Sam? The one you received that last morning?"

He nodded.

"I'm the one who sent it. I'm the one who told you about the arms shipment and when and where it was going down."

His eyes widened in shock and then narrowed just as quickly. His lips drew into a tight line, and he looked suspiciously at her.

She rubbed her chest, trying in vain to wipe away the ache. No, he didn't trust her. She didn't blame him, but it hurt nonetheless.

"Want me to tell you what was in it?"

She quoted back the contents in a low, steady voice and never broke his gaze. She wouldn't look away, wouldn't give him any reason to believe she was lying. Word for word. She knew them by heart. She should. She'd typed up the note, printed it out in the hotel lobby and paid the front desk clerk to deliver it.

Sam dragged a hand over his hair, looked away and then back at her, shaking his head as if he couldn't believe it.

"Why? I don't understand. Why not just tell me?"

She tried to laugh, but her throat closed in on her. "What would you have done, Sam? If I had unloaded that kind of story on you, would you have believed me? You would have been angry, just like you are now. You would have been suspicions of *any* information I gave you about my father."

He nodded grudgingly and sighed his acknowledgment.

"I waited long enough for you to leave and then I took my opportunity. I was helped by two employees in my father's house who were loyal to my mother and, as a result, me. I've been running ever since."

"When did you find out you were pregnant?"

She closed her eyes, remembering all too vividly the

fear and the joy. The panic that she wouldn't be able to keep herself or her child safe as her pregnancy progressed.

"It hasn't been long," she said huskily. "Maybe if I hadn't been so busy slipping from place to place, keeping one step ahead of my father's men, I would have realized that the fatigue and sickness wasn't due to stress and fear. When I noticed my pants were snug and I hadn't been eating well, I tried to remember the last time I'd had a period. Then I knew."

"That time in the shower," Sam murmured.

She smiled faintly. "Yeah."

"Why didn't you come to me immediately? If you were in trouble and you knew where to find me, why didn't you come before now?"

If only it had been that easy.

"As I said, I didn't know I was pregnant until six weeks ago—"

"Is that the only reason you came? Because you're pregnant?"

He sounded accusing, and she just stared at him. What had he expected?

"It's a big part, yeah," she said, her chin going up.

She could be as belligerent as him any day of the week. Damn it, but she was tired of having to defend herself.

"This is the first place they would have looked for me. They've probably been watching you for months, waiting for me to show up. It's the only reason you're still alive. My father had information on KGI. While he may not have had the balls to launch an all-out attack on you here, he would have done whatever was necessary to take you out. He's a patient man when it comes to vengeance."

Sam's frown deepened. "What changed then? Why now?"

The overt suspicion in his voice hit her like a poisoned dart. Yeah, she knew he had a right, but it was starting to seriously piss her off.

"What changed is that bastard caught up to me. What changed is that I'm not as fast or as agile as I used to be. Being five months pregnant with your child changes a lot, including my ability to take care of myself and protect us both from assholes that my uncle sends."

"Uncle?"

Sam latched onto her slip, his eyes sharpening.

"Uncle, father, whatever. They're partners. Either way I betrayed them both. They won't forgive that."

"We were led to believe that Tomas Mouton was a patsy of your father's and nothing more. He had no power. Alex pulled all the strings and Tomas just took up space in Mouton's organization."

"I'm sure that's true." Indeed it was. But with her father dead, Tomas would have seized his opportunity to take over the network. And his first order of business would have been to recover the key Sophie had stolen and execute her for her betrayal of the Mouton family.

She kept that information buried, unsure of how much if anything she should tell Sam about the key or the fact that she'd killed her father. There was such a thing as too much information all at once. She wanted Sam to be willing to offer her and their child his protection, not toss her out on her ass at the first opportunity.

"Sam, look at me," she begged softly.

His gaze lifted and he met her eyes. She flinched at the lack of emotion, but she swallowed her pride.

"I know what it looks like. I know you have a right

to be suspicious. You think I'm here even now on some fact-finding mission for my father, or maybe I'll take you down while you sleep because who would suspect a banged-up pregnant woman, right?"

His lips thinned. He wasn't amused by her statement at all. She wanted to reach out to him, to touch him, but she was too afraid of his rejection, and if it came now, it would crush her.

"I took a risk by spending so much time with you in that hotel. I lied to my father and said whatever I had to say not to raise his suspicions, because I wanted to be able to return to you each night. I knew you weren't offering me forever. I knew I was a fling. You don't have to beat me over the head with that. But I'm not the only one who lied here. You did too."

She sucked several steadying breaths through her nose and regained control of her emotions.

"I also knew that when I gave you the information on the arms deal that you'd leave without once looking back and that it would be up to me to escape my father's grasp. So yes, if you want to look at it like that, I used you. I used you to get away from my father, but I never gave him a damn thing about you. I didn't sell you out. He never even knew I'd leaked the information. No, I didn't sell you out, Sam. I sold my father out. For you. And for a hell of a lot of other people he would have hurt."

"And now he's after you. For what, revenge?"

She swallowed and turned her head away. Revenge? Revenge sounded personal. Tomas would make an example of her. A rite of passage in his new role of leadership. He'd want to deal effectively with her. She'd be an example to others how traitors were dispatched. The fact that she was his flesh and blood would only raise his stock among his followers. Like her father, he'd be viewed as a man not to cross. But most importantly, she held the success of that empire in her hands. And for that, he'd be willing to risk everything.

"He'll kill me and our child as soon as he gets what he wants," she said softly. "It's why I had to finally come to you and hope you would offer me your protection no matter what your feelings might be for me. I can't do it myself any longer. I almost died. Our child almost died. I'm no longer willing to take the chance of going it alone, even if it means bringing trouble to your front door."

His eyes grew hard and determined. His jaw tightened in anger, but when he reached out to grasp her arm, his touch was gentle and soothing.

"There never should have been any doubt you could come to me. I may be mad as hell. I may feel like a dumb-ass, but that's nothing next to your and our child's safety. Did you honestly think I'd turn you away once you'd explained everything?"

He sounded incredulous, and once again she was struck by how unfair it all was. She was expected to trust him, but he wasn't required to believe squat about her or her intentions.

"If I'd thought you'd turn me away, I wouldn't be here," she said evenly. "No, I didn't immediately come here. For one, I had no way of knowing how long you'd be tied up in Mexico. Two, I had no way of knowing if anything would happen to you. Three, once you no longer served the purpose of luring me into the open for my father's men to snatch, you'd be expendable. Now the clock is ticking because as of the minute I came to you, you're expendable."

"You really believe all that, don't you?"

She turned away from him, her shoulders heaving with anger.

"I'm not an idiot, Sam. You may not think what I've done has been smart or that I've had the best plan, but you know what? It's kept me alive so far. And you know what else? It's kept you alive too."

An impatient hiss escaped his lips, and then he gripped her shoulder and turned her back around to face him.

"Let's get a few things straight here, okay? Just so there's no further misunderstanding in the future. You will not make decisions in regard to your or the baby's safety at my expense or in an effort to save me. That's horse shit. My job—what I do—is protect people. From now on that's you and our baby, Sophie. I'm protecting you both, and the best way you can help me do that is to listen to everything I tell you. Don't make rash, emotional decisions. And be honest with me. Completely. From now on. Got it?"

She wanted to deck him for being a condescending jerk, but she could see he truly wasn't attempting to talk down to her. He was in total command mode, and he was talking to her like he'd talk to one of his men. No nonsense and he expected compliance. She was sorely tempted to snap him a salute and rattle off a snarky "yes sir!"

"Now come here," he said in a low voice.

The deep timbre sent a shiver down her skin. He

sounded gruff and a little unsure, but there was also a compelling plea for her to come to him.

She went and he caught her in his arms, pulling her against his chest. Warm. He was so warm that his heat soaked into her pores and invaded her stiff muscles.

He felt so good, so absolutely right, that she could do nothing more than stand in the circle of his arms and bury her face in his neck.

"I'll protect you, Sophie. We have a lot to work out, and we'll get there. But first I'm going to do everything in my power to make sure no one ever touches you or our child. If you believe nothing else, believe this."

"I do believe you," she whispered. "It's why I came."

"I just wish you'd come sooner," he said in a quiet voice.

"I'm here now."

He nodded. "And you're staying."

He turned her toward the couch and urged her down once more. After making sure she was propped in a comfortable position, he carefully arranged the blankets around her.

"You need to rest and I've got to plan our way out of here. Donovan is doing some checking on our assassin. So if you'll sit tight and let us do our thing, we'll have you out of here as soon as possible."

She tried to cover the yawn that threatened to crack her jaw, but gave up and surrendered halfway through.

He leaned in, kissed her forehead and then smoothed his hand down her face.

"Rest, Sophie, and trust me to protect you and our baby."

She stared back up at him. "I do, Sam. I do."

Nodding his satisfaction, he turned on his heel and headed out of the living room to find his brothers, and she was left alone, huddled under the blankets on the couch to ponder the mess she'd gotten the entire Kelly family in.

CHAPTER 10

"WHAT did you find out?" Sam demanded as soon as he returned to Donovan and Garrett.

Donovan looked up as Sam approached. "I ran the guy's photo and prints through the CIA database."

"And?"

"Interesting. He's one of Mouton's all right, but he was assigned to his brother's security detail."

"What's so interesting about that?" Garrett asked.

"Well, the info I gathered suggested that Tomas is a token part of Alex's network. He has no say, no power, and Alex ignores him as long as Tomas plays by the rules. Which are basically that he keeps his mouth shut and does whatever Alex tells him.

"Now, yeah this guy would have been chosen and hired and trained for that matter by Alex or his trusted head of security, but he wouldn't have had any real power or responsibility other than to stick close to Tomas, and if I know Alex, the assassin probably reported to Alex, not Tomas."

Sam frowned. "So why send this guy after Sophie? If her father's so pissed, or he wants revenge or he wants to send a message, why send this joker? He wasn't completely inept, but he wasn't hard to take down. Why not send one of his best?"

"Why send anyone at all?" Garrett demanded. "I feel like we're missing something here. Yeah, so Sophie's his daughter and she bailed. Mouton doesn't strike me as the sentimental type. Why would he give a shit about a woman? The guy's a first-class asshole. He's trafficked in women and children. I doubt he understands the first thing about familial sentiment."

"She sold him out," Sam said in a low voice.

He still wasn't sure what to make of Sophie's declaration. His gut told him she was telling the truth. Sometimes it paid to go with your gut. Other times it got you killed. Damn if he knew which was the case this time.

"Sold him out?" Donovan gave Sam a searching look that was threaded with disbelief. "Back up a second. What haven't you told us?"

Garrett leaned forward, his ever-present scowl deepening.

"She was our informant," Sam said to Garrett. "The one who tipped us off about when the arms shipment was going down."

Donavan and Garrett exchanged what-the-fuck looks. The words to defend her rushed to Sam's mouth, but he swallowed them back. He couldn't defend her. Not yet.

"She did all that because you were fucking her?" Garrett asked incredulously.

Sam turned and slammed into Garrett's chest, twisting Garrett's shirt in his hands.

"I've had enough of your mouth," Sam snarled. "You will have some goddamn respect when talking about the mother of my child, you got me?"

Garrett's eyes narrowed, then widened when Sam didn't back down. He put his hands up. "Okay, okay, my bad."

When Sam released his shirt, and Garrett took a step back, swearing the entire way.

"Will you at least try to look at this objectively?" Garrett asked. "What if it were me or Van? One of us hooks up with a chick while we're on a mission. He gets distracted. Chick shows up months later, after we failed to take down the target, and she's making all sorts of wild claims, not the least of which is she's pregnant with Van's child or my child. Then she says she sold out her flesh and blood for a guy she was with a matter of a few days. Tell me, Sam, would you be saying okay, yeah, whatever?"

Donovan remained quiet, but Garrett's thoughts were reflected in his eyes.

Sam sighed. "When did I ever give you two the impression that I'm some emotional dumbass who thinks with his dick? I get that you're suspicious. I have my own set of doubts, but so far what she's saying is checking out. And whatever you think, you'll show some respect for both me and her. If you can't live with that, then I suggest you get the fuck out, and I'll go this alone."

"Oh shut the fuck up," Garrett muttered. "You know good and goddamn well Van and I are behind you. Jesus this is one giant clusterfuck."

"You can't solve this for me," Sam said as he stared Garrett down. "I know it goes against every grain that you can't just step in with a solution. This isn't just a mission or some job, and you and I both know it. Everything has changed for me, and I'm the only person who can sort it out."

Donovan chuckled, and Sam and Garrett both glared at him.

"Garrett looks like a whipped puppy because the control freak in him can't control the situation. And Sam looks like he's swallowed a rock."

Sam held up his middle finger at the exact same time Garrett did, which only made Donovan laugh harder.

He shook his head and wiped his palm down his jaw. "If we can get back to the facts at hand. The assassin worked alone. Garrett and I have both been out. There's no one else. Not yet. We've probably bought a few days, until Mouton figures out his guy is dead and sends someone else. He hasn't impressed me with his intelligence so far, so he may or may not send enough men to get the job done. But then before he was only after a lone woman. Now he has us to contend with."

"Yeah. All of us," Garrett growled. "No one fucks with the Kellys."

Sam grinned and then let the smile fade. "We need to get to Mom and Dad's to make sure they're okay, have Steele and Rio meet us there and figure out our next move. I don't give a shit what the CIA's doing. We're going to take that bastard out this time."

Donovan nodded his agreement. "Go get Sophie. Garrett and I will have the truck ready."

SOPHIE stared out the window of the SUV as it rolled into the driveway of a quaint wood house that was at least a hundred years old. It was one of those houses you saw in television shows touting suburbia. The perfect porch, the perfect landscaping. An upstairs that probably had at least six bedrooms and a backyard that stretched over several acres.

It looked homey and welcoming like it had a soul and wasn't just a cold dwelling constructed to keep others out. No, this house invited people inside to its warmth. *Families* gathered here.

It was everything she'd ever wanted in her entire life, and it hurt her that she was going to have to walk into this place with Sam and pretend it wasn't.

The tires crunched over the gravel, and Garrett pulled the truck to a halt behind a county sheriff's police car. Sophie jerked her head around to stare at Sam accusingly.

"Sean is here for the protection of my family," Sam said shortly. "I didn't go behind your back and report you to the cops."

She relaxed a little, but the knot in her throat grew larger as she stared at the house.

This was his parents' house, and she had no concept of how to act around a normal family. But she carried their grandchild, and if nothing else, that gained her something. Didn't it?

Donovan opened the door for her, and automatically her chin went up. Sam walked around and reached in to help her out. She grabbed for the waist of the sweatpants to keep them up as Sam tucked her into his side. At least he wasn't trying to put a world of distance between them. She couldn't have faced his entire family by herself.

Garrett and Donovan hurried forward and had the door open by the time she and Sam got there. As soon as she stepped inside, she was greeted by a rush of warm air and the smell—it wasn't even one identifiable scent. It was a mixture of home-baked food, flowers, cleaner and an older musty smell that came from years of wear.

It was the best smell she'd ever encountered.

She inhaled deeply, wanting to savor every bit.

"Sam, Garrett, Donovan? Is that you?"

The feminine voice came closer, and in another moment a small woman rounded the corner as if on wheels. She collided with Garrett, bounced off and then promptly pounced on the much larger man.

"Garrett!"

She pulled him into her arms, and Sophie watched in fascination as Garrett transformed in front of her eyes. He went from surly, scowling ape to a gentle mama's boy. It was mind-boggling.

He scooped her up in his arms, though she seemed to be doing most of the hugging.

"We're fine, Ma. Quit squeezing me so hard or I won't be able to breathe."

She kissed both cheeks, patted one and then turned her attention to Donovan, who was watching with an amused smile.

"Gee, Mom, you'd think you never saw us."

She scowled at him, and Sophie could see where Garrett got it. Their mom could be quite ferocious when provoked.

She hugged Donovan fiercely, patting and squeezing in random patterns.

"I've been so worried. Sean showed up mumbling about safety and trouble and then wouldn't let your father or me out of the house. I was tempted to turn him over my knee."

Sam pushed forward shaking his head. "Sean did exactly what he was supposed to do, Ma. Don't be giving him any trouble."

Mrs. Kelly turned to Sam and her face softened. At the same time she caught sight of Sophie standing to Sam's side and her expression froze.

She looked at Donovan and then quickly back at Sam and then focused on Sophie again.

"What in the world?"

She started toward Sophie, and it was all Sophie could do not to turn around and run.

Mrs. Kelly's hands came up to brace Sophie's arms, but Sam was there to push one away from her injury.

"Careful, Ma. She's been hurt."

Sam's voice was soft and husky, almost tender. Sophie's knees began to shake because she couldn't take this. It was too much. She was scared out of her mind, and the last thing she wanted was rejection.

"Oh my word," Mrs. Kelly breathed out.

And before Sophie could expend any more time being terrified, the woman enfolded her in her embrace as carefully as she would a child. And just as suddenly she pulled away and aimed a ferocious glare up at Sam.

"Sam Kelly, what is the meaning of this? This poor girl looks like she's been in the lake."

She reached up and touched Sophie's bedraggled hair and frowned. Then she glanced downward.

"She doesn't even have shoes!"

Sam held up his hands, but his mom ignored him.

Her gaze fastened on Sophie's belly, and Sophie went completely still. She stood there in dread, chin up, her knees so locked it was a wonder she hadn't passed out yet.

"She's pregnant! Oh dear Lord. Sam what were you thinking?"

Sam's eyebrows went up, and he backed away as if unsure of what his mom was referencing.

"Mom, listen to me, okay? There are some things you need to know."

"Make it quick," she snapped.

Sam went back to Sophie's side and pulled her against him in a gesture that could hardly go unnoticed by his mother. And indeed, Mrs. Kelly's eyebrow went up, and she looked between Sam and Sophie with obvious curiosity.

"Sophie and I met five months ago while I was on a mission in Mexico. We were . . . involved. She's in trouble now and needs our help. The entire family could be in trouble, which is why we sent Sean over to stay with you and Dad. My teams will be here in a few hours—"

Whatever else he might have said was lost in his mother's gasp.

"Sam Kelly, is this my grandchild you're allowing to stand in my kitchen with its mother shivering cold and barefooted?"

Sam sighed. "Yes, ma'am."

"For God's sake, and to think I thought Joe was the son lacking in common sense."

She turned to Sophie, ignoring Sam. "Sophie, I'm Marlene Kelly and please do call me Marlene. I'll introduce you to Frank, but first my idiot son needs to take you upstairs for a hot bath and a fresh change of clothes."

Sophie smiled, or she tried, but her lips were quivering,

and she tried to control the knocking of her knees. The idea of a hot bath was so wonderful that she nearly buckled on the spot. And would have, but Marlene wrapped an arm around her waist and held her up.

"Go on, Sam, before the poor thing falls over. Garrett and Donovan can tell me all about it while you're up taking care of your responsibilities."

She pinned Sam with a stare that probably made all her sons quake in their boots.

Sam threaded his hand through Sophie's and pulled her away from his mother. She wanted that bath. Really wanted it, but she couldn't imagine how she'd manage.

"Maybe I should take a shower instead. I'm not sure I'd be able to get out of the tub once I got in."

Her face tightened, and she looked around to make sure no one had overheard her.

Sam smiled, easing the lines around his eyes.

"Don't you worry about that. I'll help you in and out."

Her eyes widened. "Oh."

He cocked one eyebrow at her. "I've seen you naked, Sophie."

She valiantly tried to control the rush of heat creeping up her neck.

He smiled again and then moved to the side of her and lifted her into his arms.

"I can walk."

"I know. But you'll put less stress on those wounds if I carry you."

With that, he headed for the stairs, striding past his family as if they weren't even there. She refused to make eye contact with any of them. She had no desire for their judgment.

When they reached the bathroom, he flipped on the light and set her carefully on the counter so that her legs dangled over the edge. Then he reached over to turn on the water in the big garden tub.

Soon steam rose and she was salivating. She *hurt* with how badly she wanted that tub full of hot water. She twitched with impatience, watching as the level slowly rose.

"I'll help you get undressed then I'll get you in the tub. I'll leave you for as long as you want to soak, and when you want to get out just call for me, okay?"

She nodded, too tongue-tied to get words past her lips. He was right. He'd seen her naked. He'd seen her wanton. He'd seen her as indelicately as a man could ever see a woman. There wasn't an inch of her body he hadn't explored, and vice versa. So why was she acting so maidenly now? She was pregnant with his child, for God's sake.

But then there hadn't been exposed lies between them. No exposed secrets. They'd just been two lovers so wrapped up in each other that the outside world hadn't been able to intrude.

"Soph?" he called softly.

She blinked and refocused on him. His fingers were in the waistband of the too large pair of sweats. He was making sure she was okay with it, and for some reason that softened her heart.

"Let's get this over with. I want to get into that tub so bad, I'd crawl in fully clothed."

He chuckled and slid the pants down until they gathered around her ankles. With a gentle tug they were gone, and he dropped them on the floor.

"I'm going to put you down and then we'll get you out of your shirt."

She gave a groan of protest when her feet hit the floor. She didn't have it in her to stand. Fatigue edged out the pain by a ratio of at least ten to one. Pain had nothing on her desire to sleep. For a year. Pregnancy was exhausting enough. Add in running cross-country, taking multiple dips in the lake and avoiding assholes with knives and guns?

"I got you. Hold still. I'll try not to move your arm too much."

She stared straight ahead as he maneuvered the shirt from her body, and suddenly she was completely nude in front of him. She hated how vulnerable and naked she felt.

Dumbass, you are *naked.*

Thankfully he didn't waste any time. As soon as she was free of her clothing, he turned to help her into the tub. She put one leg in and moaned as the hot water slid up her skin.

"Oh God."

"That good huh?"

"Oh God yes. I've never had anything so good in my life."

She gingerly sank down, holding on to his hand. Her body shrieked in protest, but she didn't care.

The water lapped to her chin, and she tilted her head back, closing her eyes. Oh sweet heaven.

Sam leaned down and gently tapped her chin until she opened her eyes again.

"Call me if you need me, okay?"

She nodded sleepily as the warmth swam intoxicatingly through her veins.

He turned to go, and she suddenly remembered what she'd wanted to ask him for.

"Sam?"

He turned, holding on to the door edge. "Yes?"

She shifted uncomfortably, seeking more of the water.

"Is there any way possible I could get some underwear? I hate to ask, but going without a bra sucks when you're pregnant. I mean my boobs are huge now and they're sensitive—"

She could see the very male shudder work over him. His eye practically twitched at the mention of underwear and bras.

"I'll get it for you. Don't worry."

She smiled, feeling warmth that had nothing to do with bathwater flash over her. "Thank you."

SAM stepped out of the bathroom and rubbed the back of his neck. Sainthood. He deserved sainthood. Not only had he stood in the bathroom with a very gorgeous, very naked woman, but he'd calmly discussed getting her things like a bra and underwear without batting an eyelash.

Give him bombs, grenades, blood, guts and gore, but bras?

Jesus.

Now, where the hell was he going to get her a bra?

"Hey, get her settled?"

Sam looked up to see Garrett and Donovan coming up the stairs. He grimaced. "Uh yeah. Sorta."

Garrett gave him a look.

"She needs a bra. Something about pregnancy and big boobs and I sort of tuned out after that."

Donovan's chest heaved in silent laughter. The bastard.

"So get her one," Garrett said.

Garrett almost pulled off that somber, stick-up-his ass look. Oh yeah, he was good, but Sam saw the flicker of amusement in his eyes.

"There are three women in this house on a constant basis. Surely we can come up with a bra," Sam muttered.

"Uh well Rusty and Rachel are smaller," Donovan said, hedging. "Not that Sophie is like big or anything, but she's bustier."

It dawned on his brothers about the same time it did on Sam. Their faces contorted, and Garrett's mouth flapped open and shut.

"Christ. That leaves Mom," Sam said.

Garrett started backing away, hands out. "Oh no. Hell no. I'm not asking Ma for one of her bras. That's just . . . wrong."

Donovan looked like he'd swallowed a bug, and then both he and Garrett stared at Sam.

"Your woman. You do it."

Sam cleared his throat. "Rock, paper, scissors?"

"Fuck that," Donovan snorted.

"You pussies."

"You go. We'll pay for your therapy later," Garrett said.

Sam turned in disgust and stalked away.

"You should probably know Ma's not very happy with you right now," Donovan called after him.

Sam turned. "What the hell does that mean?"

"Garrett and I filled her in. You know on the story. About how you knocked Sophie up, came home, then fished her out of the lake."

Sam blew out his breath and turned his face up toward

the ceiling. "Yeah, and I bet you really hated telling her all that, didn't you?"

Garrett shrugged. "You can thank us later, man."

Sam held up his middle finger and hurried down the stairs to face his mom.

CHAPTER 11

SAM hovered near the bathroom door and checked his watch. She hadn't called out, and he kept returning for fear he wouldn't hear her when she did. He couldn't decide whether to go in and check on her or wait it out.

The decision was taken from him when he heard her soft call filter through the door.

"Sam?"

He pushed in, hastily tossing the items his mom had given him on the counter. When he turned to her, he saw her drowsy eyes watching him. Her face was flushed with the steam from the bath, and her hair lay damply against her cheeks.

"You okay?"

She nodded slowly. "I tried to get out, but it hurt. I was afraid of falling."

He frowned and moved forward. "I told you I'd help you. You ready to get out now?"

Again she nodded, and he reached down, sliding his arms into the water. His hand glanced off her lush bottom and then went to the tender flesh underneath her knees. He lifted, and the water rushed over her skin like silk. He was riveted to the sight of her swollen, lush body.

He stood her up long enough to get a towel around her. She glanced shyly up at him, her blue eyes sweet. Just like they'd been the first time he ever saw her.

He'd hated seeing her work in that dive. She was too young, too innocent to be exposed to the assholes who frequented the joint. Now he felt like an idiot, because after living with her father, the guys at the bar had to have seemed like Boy Scouts.

"I can dry myself," she said after clearing her throat.

He turned to the counter and gingerly raised the bra with one finger. "I know this isn't ideal, but it was the closest thing we thought would fit you. The uhm underwear, well as long as it doesn't fall off . . . You could pull it up over your belly."

Amusement twinkled in her eyes, but she smiled as if he'd just given her diamonds.

"Thank you. This will be perfect."

She bobbled just a bit when she tried to step forward, and he picked her up and set her on the counter.

"It's all that hot water," he explained. "It'll make you light-headed, especially when you're pregnant. You probably shouldn't have stayed in so long."

She arched one golden brow at him. "How do you know so much about pregnant women?"

An uncomfortable prickle assaulted his neck. "I uhm must have read it somewhere."

He turned right and then left and realized she was still trapped in her towel and she needed to get dressed.

There was a short knock at the door, and he scowled as he turned. He opened it just a crack so whoever was outside wouldn't see in. Donovan stood there holding a pair of pants and a T-shirt. He thrust them toward Sam.

"Figured she'd do better if she wasn't running around in just Ma's bra and underwear."

There was a hint of a grin on Donovan's lips, and Sam glared a giant hole through his head.

"Thanks," he muttered.

"Any time."

He grinned again and then sauntered off.

Sam called him a few choice words and retreated into the bathroom, where Sophie was still perched on the counter, the towel gripped tight at her chin.

The towel split just at her belly, and he was afforded a tiny glimpse of the gentle mound that shielded his child. It wasn't as if he hadn't seen it a couple of times already. It was the way just a hint showed from the protective confines of the towel.

Careful so as not to spook her, he slowly dipped his hands into that little part and pushed the towel aside so that more of her belly was bared.

"Sam?"

His name came out breathless. A little hesitant. A little nervous. But there was no fear in her voice.

"Let me see her, Soph. I want to see my daughter. One moment where it's just us. No distractions. No danger. Just you and me and our child."

Her hand loosened its grip on the corner of the towel, and finally she dropped it altogether. The material fell away, baring her breasts and her belly. Even the delicate, feminine V of her legs, with the soft, silvery blond wisps of hair, was visible.

It was the most beautiful sight he'd ever seen. Here on this counter, Sophie bruised and battered, her hair wet and fatigue pulling at her eyes. Was there a more beautiful sight than a lushly pregnant woman?

He couldn't resist touching her. The tips of his fingers brushed along the tops of her thighs, around to her hips and finally up and over the tautness of her abdomen. As they gathered at her center, her belly dipped and jerked.

He drew away, stunned. "That was her!"

Sophie's face lit up like a million candles. "Yes. That's her." Her own hand came to cradle her belly, and she rocked back and forth as though she was sitting in a chair soothing her baby.

Drawn by a power he didn't understand, Sam lowered his head, inch by inch until his lips were just a breath away from that tiny little pitter-patter. He pressed his mouth in the gentlest of kisses even as he palmed both sides of Sophie's belly to hold her in place.

The tiny kick against his lips had him smiling in sheer delight.

"She's saying hello," he said hoarsely.

When he looked up at Sophie, he was taken aback by the sheer sadness in her eyes. He could swear there were tears, but she blinked and they were gone. What could possibly have upset her?

He crinkled his brow and touched a hand to her cheek. "Is everything okay, Soph?"

She smiled, though it looked shaky to him. "I'm fine. The bath did wonders. I feel like a new woman."

It was almost easy to forget that she was sitting naked in front of him—if he didn't keep getting distracted by the breasts he and his brothers had discussed in depth out in the hall.

Her nipples—one of his favorite things—were darker now instead of the delectable shade of pink they'd been. They looked browner, ruby almost. He'd give anything to taste her one more time. To run his tongue along the puckered peak and feel her come apart in his arms.

His body tightened painfully, and he nearly unmanned himself by bumping into the counter edge. Son of a bitch that hurt!

"I um got you a bra. It's right here. Donovan brought you some pants and a T-shirt. We'll get you shoes when you're dressed. Let me help you get into everything, and then we'll see what we have to work with."

She wrinkled her nose at the bra. "God, it's one of those torture devices. One of those thirty-six-hour jobs or whatever they're called."

Sam laughed. Even he'd heard enough television commercials to know there were eighteen-hour bras. But who the hell would want to stay in such a barbaric contraption for eighteen hours? Those things weren't for sissies.

"You're going to have to help me get it on. I can't put it on backward and twist it around. It'll kill my arm. I'll put the cups on and you fasten the back."

"Well hell," he grumbled. "I've had plenty of practice getting women out of bras, but I can't say I've ever helped a woman into one."

She flashed a grin. "Then you'll learn something new and useful."

She positioned the bra, looped the straps over her

shoulders, and he stared down at the dangling clasp. How hard could it be?

He fastened the clips and tried very hard not to remember where he'd gotten this or who had worn it last, because there was only so much his brain could take.

"Just hold the underwear. I'll step in," she directed.

He bent and held what looked to be grannie panties out and open while she grabbed on to his wrists for support and cautiously threaded one leg at a time into the holes. A few seconds later, she had underwear all the way over her belly and she burst into laughter.

"I look like a goober," she said, still laughing.

"The clothes will cover it." Thank God. Even as unattractive as his mom's girly things were, Sophie still managed to look sensational in them. He could tie a garbage sack around her and she'd still light up a room.

The pants weren't hard, but the shirt was more awkward. He merely stretched out the armholes until he could fit her arms through without making her do contortionist tricks.

"Want me to dry your hair?"

She blinked in surprise. "Would you? It would be so hard to do it one-handed."

He reached for the blow-dryer. "Can you stand for this long or would you prefer to sit on the toilet seat?"

She put her hand on his chest and eased her way onto the closed toilet.

He started the dryer and threaded his hand through the strands as he motioned the blower up and down. After a few minutes, he took a brush from the counter and delicately drew it through her tresses.

She closed her eyes and held her face upturned just a

bit, like she was experiencing the first rays of sun after a long winter. Wanting to continue pleasing her, he brushed the strands as he blew over them, until they shone like spun gold.

"No one has brushed my hair for me since I was a child," she murmured, her eyes still closed. "It feels wonderful."

"I've never brushed a woman's hair before," he admitted ruefully.

She opened her eyes and they smiled back at him through the mirror.

"I'm getting the idea that you were an expert at getting women out of their clothes and messing up their hair, but maybe not so much with anything that came afterward."

"Not *that* many women," he muttered.

She cocked her head, and he could see the question brewing on her lips.

Once again, a knock at the door interrupted them. Sam blew out his breath in relief, turned off the dryer and laid it aside.

"It's open," he called.

Donovan stuck his head inside. "I have Mom's med kit if you want me to look over Sophie's stitches. She's insisting on calling Doc, but I made her wait to see what you wanted."

"Yeah, okay, let me take her in the bedroom so you'll have room," Sam replied. "Tell Mom to hold her horses. Didn't you explain to her the situation we're in here? We can't be calling everyone in Stewart County to come over."

"Yeah , but you know Mom," Donovan said in amusement.

Sam touched Sophie on the shoulder as Donovan backed out of the bathroom. "Can you make it?"

She rose tentatively and then smiled. "Amazing what a hot bath and clean clothes will do for you."

Still, he took her hand and laced his fingers with hers as he led her out of the bathroom and toward his parents' bedroom.

"Just have her sit," Donovan said as he motioned toward the end of the bed. "This won't take but a minute."

Sam watched as Donovan carefully pulled Sophie's shirt down over her shoulder so he could examine the stitched wound.

Impatiently, Sam stepped forward. "Does it look all right?"

Donovan turned to his brother. "Yeah, it does. It looks really good. I'll just put on some more antibiotic ointment and fresh bandages and she'll be good to go."

Sam touched Sophie's hair, now glossy and clean. She turned her face up to him, and he wanted to touch her more.

"Are you in any pain? Van can get you some more pain medicine."

"Just ibuprofen."

"Ma's making a feast. You two should come down and eat. Then Sophie can take her medicine on a full stomach," Donovan said.

Sam saw the longing in Sophie's eyes and nodded at Donovan. "We'll be down. Have Ma set up a tray so Sophie can sit on the couch where it's comfortable."

CHAPTER 12

CLEAN and warm. And now she was staring at a tray in front of her holding more food than she could possibly eat, but damn if she wasn't going to give it her best shot.

There was a bowl of chicken and dumplings, a grilled cheese sandwich, potato salad and a plate of pot roast with mashed potatoes and gravy.

Marlene had jokingly told her that she'd cleaned out her refrigerator, and since she hadn't known what Sophie liked, she made her a little of everything.

Mouth watering, Sophie dipped into the chicken and dumplings first. She ignored the goings-on around her and dug into each of the dishes, savoring each and every bite.

When the couch dipped beside her, Sophie looked up to see a teenaged girl staring curiously at her. She didn't fit the mold of the rest of the Kelly family, and maybe that was on purpose.

She had an interesting shade of green through her chestnut hair, a nose piercing and a row of earrings in her left ear. While the girl wouldn't have stood out in most high schools, here in this seemingly conservative, strait-laced household, she stood out like orange neon glow.

Since the girl continued to stare at her, Sophie stared back, childishly refusing to back down under the teen's scrutiny.

The girl sniffed and then turned to grin in Sam's direction. "Sounds like Marlene needs to be lecturing someone else on safe sex, not me."

"Rusty, for God's sake," Frank Kelly bellowed.

Sophie jumped and looked cautiously at the burly older man. His bark seemed worse than his bite, but she couldn't be sure on such a short acquaintance.

"If you can't keep a civil tongue in your head, you can go back upstairs," Frank said. Then he turned to Sophie. "The smart-mouthed young lady sitting next to you is Rusty. Don't mind her. She likes to needle my boys."

Sophie swallowed her bite and didn't ask the obvious. It wasn't any of her business. She really didn't want to know who Rusty was anyway.

Rusty leaned over conspiratorially. "I'm the stray. Marlene sort of adopted me. Not that you could possibly think I sprang from the same gene patch as that bunch." She jerked her thumb over her shoulder in Sam, Garrett and Donovan's direction.

"Zip it, Rusty," Sean snapped. "The last thing we need is your mouth today."

Sophie looked in surprise at the young sheriff's deputy standing across the room.

Rusty curled her lip in Sean's direction. "I don't answer to you, copper. Go eat a donut or something."

Rusty turned back to Sophie and rolled her eyes. "He's another stray Marlene picked up. Though personally I think he's worn out his welcome."

"Rusty," Frank said in his gravelly voice. "That's enough, young lady."

To Sophie's surprise, Rusty shut up and straightened in her seat. Sophie could swear there was genuine respect and affection in the young girl's eyes when she looked at the Kelly patriarch.

Sophie was less sure of Frank. He watched her. He'd watched her ever since Sam had deposited her on the couch. There was nothing accusatory in his stare, but he studied her intently nonetheless and it made her uncomfortable.

She could only imagine the assumptions that were being made. She could name several, but there was no use in torturing herself. The assumptions were deserved, and she didn't have the mental energy or the desire to correct any of them.

"Are you through, hon?"

Sophie blinked and looked up to see Marlene standing in front of her, her hands outstretched to take the tray.

"Yes, thank you, Mrs. Kelly. I appreciate the food. It was wonderful."

Marlene smiled warmly. "Such a polite young woman. But please, call me Marlene. No one calls me Mrs. Kelly, well unless they're telemarketers. Most folks just call me Marlene or Mom."

She took the tray and Sophie listed to the side, no longer able to keep her head up. Sam had put several pillows behind her and to the side and she snuggled under the warm quilt. No one seemed to be paying her much attention now, so she drifted, barely listening to what was going on around her.

SAM watched as Sophie's head dipped lower and lower, until her cheek nestled against the pillow. His mother was also watching, and as soon as Sophie's eyes closed, she marched across the room, her eyes narrowed and fixed on him.

"You'll tell me what on earth is going on here," she said in a low, determined voice. "And I want all of it, not the watered-down version your brothers already gave me."

Sam expelled his breath in a long sigh. He rubbed his hand tiredly through his hair and glanced up to see his dad looking at him with the same intensity that was in his mother's gaze.

Hell.

"She's carrying my grandchild," Frank said.

Trust Dad to get straight to the point. He never was one for pussyfooting around.

"It's very likely she's carrying my child," Sam said carefully.

Marlene frowned. "Shouldn't you know?" She glanced back at Sophie, her frown deepening.

"Don't go jumping to conclusions, Ma. And don't think badly of Sophie. Not yet. There's too much I don't know. She deserves the benefit of the doubt until I find out what the hell is going on here."

If that didn't make him a flaming hypocrite, he didn't know what did. He didn't want anyone else disrespecting her or developing a bad opinion, but it didn't stop him from being suspicious and cautious with her.

He'd recognized early on that she had a lot of power where he was concerned, and that didn't sit well with him at all.

"Then tell me what you know," Marlene said fiercely.

Knowing it wasn't going to make him look good in front of his parents, he still told them the unvarnished truth about his mission to Mexico and his involvement with Sophie. He left out the part about killing the assassin, but judging by the look on his dad's face, he'd figured out that much. No need to horrify his mother more than necessary.

"Now listen to me, Ma," Sam said. "This is serious. Our entire family could be in danger. I need you and Dad to do exactly what I tell you. No arguing." He looked pointedly at his father. "I can't do my job if I'm worried that you aren't safe."

Frank put his arm around Marlene and drew her into his side. "What do you want us to do?"

Sean, who'd been standing just to the side, walked forward so he could be included in the conversation.

"My teams are due to arrive shortly. One will be assigned solely to keep you safe. All of you. No one moves without my men's say-so, and that includes Rusty."

Sean scowled. "I'll keep the little twit in line."

"Sean," Marlene admonished with a sharp frown.

Sean's expression didn't change.

"Until this is resolved, everyone will have to sit tight."

Frank cast a look over at Sophie. "What about you and Sophie? What are you going to do?"

"Sam, we have a problem."

Sam turned to see Donovan standing behind him, holding the KGI secure phone in his hand.

"What's up?"

"Resnick just buzzed me wanting to know why we were accessing their files on Mouton's assassin."

Sam's brow furrowed. "What on earth for? Not like we don't rifle through their database all the time. You didn't hack into any classified shit, did you?"

Donovan didn't even respond to the crack. "He wants to talk to you ASAP."

Apprehension seeped down his neck. The last thing they needed was Resnick poking his nose into this.

Glancing apologetically at his mom and dad and Sean, Sam walked back into the kitchen with Donovan on his heels. Garrett must have seen the exodus, because he appeared just seconds behind them.

Sam took the phone from Donovan and put it to his ear.

"Resnick."

"Sam, what the hell's going on down there? What is Mouton's assassin doing in your neck of the woods?"

"I was hoping you could tell me."

Resnick snorted. "Don't play that game with me. Mouton's daughter's gone missing. Any chance she's with you?"

Sam frowned and turned so he could look at his brothers. "Why would the CIA be interested in Mouton's daughter?"

"I'm not here to answer questions, Sam. I'm here to ask them."

Anger fizzed through Sam's blood, and he gripped the phone tighter. "Listen to me. I'm not playing games here.

That bastard is after my family. I don't give a damn about the CIA right now, you got me? This will be your only heads-up. I'm going to do what I need to do to ensure he never touches anyone close to me. The best thing you can do is stay the hell out of my way."

There was a long silence. "Sam, I need to talk to her. It's important. If she's with you, we need to question her. Mouton's missing too. He hasn't been spotted since KGI took down that arms shipment five months ago. We think . . . we think he was working with plutonium and that he had a supply. His scientists were working on a way to store it for longer periods of time in a stable environment."

"Shit. Why the hell do you think she'd know anything about it?"

"I don't. But she disappeared the same time he disappeared, and his brother has expended a lot of resources in his search for the daughter and suddenly an assassin turns up on your doorstep? He wants her back for a reason. I'm thinking maybe she either has something they want or she has information they don't want getting out."

"Good luck finding her then," Sam said.

Resnick swore long and violently. "Goddamn it, Sam. Work with me here. Don't treat me like I'm an idiot. Set up a meeting for me. You choose the location. I'll come alone. You have my word. This is too important. If Mouton has his hands on plutonium, a lot of people are going to die."

Sam rubbed his palm over his face and closed his eyes as the throb of a headache began at the base of his skull. Was Sophie still hiding shit from him? Had she been truthful about anything?

He glanced at his brothers to see both staring hard at him, questions in their eyes. Holding their gaze, he finally spoke back into the phone.

"Only you, Resnick. You break your word, you'll never get another goddamn thing from KGI. We clear? I'll call you with location and time."

Before Resnick could respond, Sam disconnected and slapped the phone onto the counter.

"What the hell was that all about?" Garrett demanded.

"Resnick wants to question Sophie."

"About what?" Donovan asked.

"Apparently Mouton has gone underground. The brother appears to be running things, which explains why his personal bodyguard came and not one of Mouton's. He disappeared the same day Sophie did her flit. The CIA has a hard-on for Sophie. They think she can give them information."

"And you're agreeing to the meet," Garrett said.

Sam nodded. "Yeah, I am. No point in pissing off Resnick. I want information too. If she's holding out on us, we need to know. I'm not taking any chances with those bastards and our family."

Both Garrett and Donovan nodded their agreement.

Sam checked his watch. "The teams will be here soon. Mom and Dad have agreed to do what we ask. We'll divide up, leave Rio and his men with them for protection, and Steele and his team will provide security for our meeting with Resnick."

"One of us should stay with Rio," Donovan said. "I'd feel better if one of us was here with Mom and Dad."

"You could both stay," Sam said. "I don't want to drag you into my mess."

Garrett shot him a quelling look. "I'm going to pretend you didn't say that. Van can stay with Mom and Dad. I'm going with you and Sophie."

"Okay then. Let's figure out where the fuck we set up the meet and greet with Resnick."

CHAPTER 13

WHEN Sophie awoke, the living room was filled with strange men, all clad in black shirts and camo pants. They looked hard, not just muscled, but hard in the sense that they'd seen and endured a lot.

These were military men. Disciplined. More than just money guided their motivation. Their loyalty couldn't be bought as her father bought those loyal to him.

Her thoughts were fanciful. She didn't know any of this for a fact. Maybe they weren't any better than her father, but she had to believe in something, and right now she chose to believe in Sam, and by default the men who worked with and for him.

Fascinated by the lone woman in the group—they called her P.J.—Sophie watched her interact from the safety of her blankets and mound of pillows. No one had noticed she was awake, and she was quite happy to observe in silence.

P.J. was small and surprisingly feminine-looking, or maybe it was because she was surrounded by much larger, terse males. She was quite pretty in an understated way. She had a tan that testified to time spent outdoors. Her hair was pulled back in a neat ponytail, simple and no nonsense, just like she appeared. Her eyes, though, were a clear shade of green, beautiful enough that Sophie found herself staring unabashedly at the fascinating woman.

She too was dressed in a black T-shirt and camo pants. A large knife was secured to her belt, and she wore a shoulder holster with a pistol tucked under her arm.

Sophie felt a rush of envy. Here was a woman who was wholly self-sufficient. She didn't need the men who surrounded her. She was obviously an equal, and she could take care of herself. These men trusted her to look out not only for herself but for the team as well.

P.J. wouldn't have run scared like Sophie had done. Nor would she have made such a pitiful attempt at escaping Tomas's assassin.

She glanced down at her hands and almost laughed. It was rather pointless to be comparing herself to a female mercenary. Though she did wonder about P.J.'s story. How awesome that she had choices, that she could do and be anything. She was in control of her own destiny.

So were about a billion other people on the planet, and now so would Sophie be. No longer would she be controlled by another human being. It was a vow she repeated often.

Her gaze drifted to where Marlene and Frank sat in the corner of the room. Marlene was on Frank's lap, and he had a firm arm around her. They were talking in low tones, and it was obvious Frank was comforting her. Every once in a while Marlene's worried gaze would seek out her sons, but there was also fierce pride reflected there. And love.

It made Sophie's chest ache. It hurt to see such love, such a sense of family in this sprawling house. Pictures and memories littered the walls and the mantel over the fireplace. Occupied every available space on the surface of end tables and over the television.

It was everything she'd ever wanted and never had.

The baby kicked, just one gentle nudge, like she was turning over to a better position in her sleep. Tears burned Sophie's lids. Already she loved her daughter so much, and she vowed with everything she had that somehow, someway, her child would grow up with the love and security that Sophie never enjoyed.

She had no experience. But she had dreams. She had imagined a thousand times how normal families lived and loved. She wanted that for her daughter.

She wanted it for herself.

"Are you all right?"

She jerked her head up to see a tall, dark-haired man—Rio?—standing over her. She froze as she studied him. He looked fierce, but there was something soft in his eyes as he stared down at her.

"You looked upset."

She cleared her throat nervously. She wasn't sure what to say, or if she should say anything at all. This might be one of Sam's men, but that didn't automatically give him a pass.

Then he smiled, and white teeth flashed. "You remind me of my little sister. Magdalena was her name."

"Was?"

It came out little more than a whisper, and when pain flashed in his dark eyes, she regretted making the distinction.

"She passed on a few years ago. She was pregnant like you. And just as beautiful. Pregnancy does that for a woman."

Sophie didn't know what to say or how to respond, so she said nothing. To her surprise, Rio held out a glass of iced tea and carefully put it into her hand.

Touched by the gesture, she gave him a genuine smile and raised the glass to her lips. "Thank you. Who are all these people?" she asked, looking beyond him to the others.

He glanced over as she did. "The man standing to Sam's right is Steele, the other team leader. I'm Rio, by the way. My team is standing to the side. All this togetherness isn't really our thing."

She followed his direction to a group of five men standing silently with no expression. They merely observed. She shivered. They looked dangerous.

"That's Cole and P.J. with Donovan. They're the two sharpshooters. They both belong to Steele. On the other side of them are Baker, Renshaw and Dolphin."

She raised her head to look at Rio. "Dolphin?"

Rio grinned. "Because he swims like one."

"Why are you being nice to me?" she asked bluntly.

His eyebrow went up and he studied her for a moment. "Why wouldn't I be?"

She shrugged. "You don't know me."

"I think maybe you're used to people not being very nice to you. Maybe it's time to alter your expectations, hmm?"

He offered a smile, then returned to where his men

stood. He leaned against the wall, propping one foot behind him, and stared at Sam and Steele with a bored expression on his face.

Every once in a while he looked back over at her and smiled. He had no idea how much that small gesture meant to her in a room filled with people she didn't know or trust. It gave her something to grasp. He may not like her or trust her—she doubted either—but he was nice to her and he didn't have to be. How silly—but unsurprising—that she was such a·weak sucker for someone showing her any sort of kindness.

She was already firmly under the spell of Marlene Kelly, and for all she knew, the woman had changed her mind about her the moment Sam gave her the story.

Talk of safe houses and leaving turned Sophie in Sam's direction. He was speaking to Steele, and Rio had closed in on the small circle of men surrounding Sam. Garrett and Donovan stood on either side of Sam, and she was struck by how fierce their expressions were.

She struggled to lean forward so she could hear, and Marlene and Sam both saw her at the same time. Sam turned in her direction, going silent as his gaze roved over her. Marlene left the shelter of her husband's arms and slid onto the couch next to Sophie.

"How are you feeling, dear?" Marlene asked as she laid a hand on Sophie's arm.

Not wanting to be rude, she yanked her gaze from Sam and turned to Marlene.

"Better. The bath and the food did wonders."

"Are you hurting? Do you want some more pain medicine?"

Sophie paused, realizing she hadn't given her shoulder any thought. She hadn't awakened with the vicious ache. Tentatively she tested her motion, raising her arm at an angle.

She winced and immediately dropped it back to her side.

Before she could respond to Marlene, Sam was next to her, his eyes flashing with disapproval.

"Don't move your arm more than necessary. You don't want to open those stitches." He glanced over at Donovan. "Van, you want to take another look before we bug out?"

Sophie blinked in confusion and then looked between Sam and his mother.

"I'm fine, Sam. He just looked at it, and I haven't so much as moved it until just a second ago. It wasn't even hurting until I did."

"Well don't move it then," he said gruffly.

"Are you leaving?" she asked. The idea of him going sent panic up her spine.

His eyes narrowed and then he blinked. "Did you think I was leaving you? You're coming with me, Sophie."

Her lips rounded to an O. "Where are we going?"

She was so relieved that her head was slightly swimmy.

"We'll have plenty of time to discuss that on the road. Sit tight here with Mom while I get all the details worked out with my men."

He touched her hand briefly as he rose, but warmth traveled her entire body. He glanced one more time at her before returning to his men.

"Is there anything I can get you?" Marlene asked.

Sophie shook her head and focused on Sam. She

wanted to hear what he had to say and find out what his plan was. She'd needed the sleep, but now she was at a disadvantage. She'd missed a lot while she dozed.

"Rio, I want you to bug out with Mom, Dad and Rusty. Donovan's staying with you. Stay low until you hear from me. Steele, you'll pull recon at Eagle One with Cole, P.J. and Dolphin. When you give me the all clear, I'll bring Sophie in. I want Baker and Renshaw on the first plane to Hawaii to watch over Ethan and Rachel. I'll send Garrett to meet Resnick and bring him in. You'll maintain the perimeter at all times. I'm not taking any chances."

"I'll take care of it," Steele said.

It was the first time she'd heard Steele say anything. He mostly stood and watched, his intense blue eyes taking in everything around him. He looked . . . cold and intimidating.

Instinctively she found Rio, and he flashed her a quick grin.

She wanted to interrupt and ask where the hell they were going, but she remained silent. She didn't want everyone's attention on her. Sam had promised to protect her and their child, and for now that was enough.

CHAPTER 14

"SAM, I think Sophie should be examined by a doctor before you leave," Marlene said in a worried voice.

Sam looked down at his mom, who had her hand on his arm. "Van checked her over, Ma. He stitched her wound and gave her antibiotics."

"But Donovan isn't going with you. He's staying with us. Garrett isn't a medic and neither are you. Besides, what does Donovan know about pregnancy?"

Sam frowned.

"This is your child, Sam," Marlene persisted. "This woman has been through hell. You need to make sure everything is all right with the baby."

Sam cupped the back of his neck and twisted his head from side to side. Fatigue and tension had a firm grip on him. "I have to see to their safety, Ma. You know that. I can't let anything happen to them. We can't walk into a clinic even using a different identity. Her father would be on to us. I'm sure he has a net several hundred miles wide around us."

"I can have Doc come here to look at her. He's delivered more than one baby. He could at least listen to the heartbeat. And give her some vitamins. She should be taking vitamins."

His frown softened as he saw the very real worry in her eyes. He leaned down and hugged her tight.

"I'll get her vitamins. I'll make sure she eats well. I'll take very good care of her. And as soon as possible, I'll get her to a doctor. You have my word. But I can't do it now. I can't take the risk and stay here any longer."

Marlene sighed and reached up to pat him on the cheek. He smiled at the gesture. It always made him feel like a boy again.

"You're my oldest, and I love you dearly but I have to say, you royally screwed up this time."

He blinked in surprise as she shook her head and pulled away. Then he laughed. There was nothing else to do. He was being taken to task like a teenager caught having sex in the backseat of his parents' car. At least then he'd worn a condom.

Blowing out a weary breath, he turned to the others.

"Is everyone ready to roll?" He glanced over at his dad. "Are you, Mom and Rusty packed?"

His dad walked toward the kitchen. "Just let me lock up the house and set the alarm."

Sam nodded, not having the heart to tell his father that locks and an alarm wouldn't stop Mouton's men if they wanted to get in.

His mom hugged everyone, including making the rounds of his men. It was amusing to watch their discomfort over being fussed over by Marlene Kelly, but it's not like they'd refuse her. She wasn't the type you refused.

Sophie watched from the sofa, and Sam could see pain that had nothing to do with her injuries deep in her eyes. He made his way over to her and reached for her hand. Her haunted gaze met his, and he squeezed her fingers, hoping to lighten some of the darkness he saw reflected on her face.

"Sit tight," he murmured. "I'm going to take some pillows and blankets out to the SUV so you'll be comfortable. Garrett's going to drive, so I'll sit in the back with you."

Now that orders had been given, everyone split up and went their way. One of the two Kelly jets would fly Baker and Renshaw to Hawaii, while the other would take Steele, Dolphin, P.J. and Cole to West Virginia, where they'd prepare Eagle One, one of the KGI safe houses, for Sam and Sophie's arrival.

Garrett slid into the driver's seat and looked over his shoulder at Sam, who was stuffing the back with the pillows for Sophie.

"So are you telling her what's going down?"

Sam paused, then met Garrett's gaze. "No."

Garrett raised a brow. "You don't think she'll see it as an ambush?"

"Probably."

"She's going to be pissed, man."

Sam stared back at his brother. "You don't seem concerned with pissing her off."

"I'm not sleeping with her either. And she's not carrying my child."

Sam punched one of the pillows, then withdrew from

the back and stood by the door, his hand gripping the top of the window.

"I don't want her to be prepared for Resnick. If she's off guard, we might learn more. She's holding back. What, I'm not sure, but she hasn't told us everything."

"We agree on that much."

Sam watched as the vehicles bearing his family to safety filed out of the driveway, and then he went back into the house. He found Sophie standing in the living room in her sock feet. She looked nervous and lost.

For a moment self-disgust held him immobile. He was feeding her to the wolves. Not that he'd allow Resnick to work her over, but he was taking Sophie into a situation with no warning. Yeah, it would work better that way, but he felt like an ass.

He had a family to protect, and he couldn't do that without all the information. Information he was positive Sophie held. If Resnick was that confident that Sophie was someone the CIA wanted to question, it stood to reason that she knew something.

"Sophie."

She looked in his direction, and he could see the strain on her face. The deep sadness in her eyes hit him deep. He stepped forward, wanting to touch her. His fingers traced down her arm until he caught her fingers in his.

"Why do you look so sad?" he asked.

Her lips trembled as she tried to smile. She looked away and stared around the room.

"Do you know how lucky you are?"

That wasn't at all what he'd expected her to say.

"Why do you say that?"

She tugged lightly with her hand, but he tightened his grip, refusing to let her move away from him.

"You have all of this." She gestured with her free hand, encompassing the room. "You have magic."

Again her blue eyes stared up at him, and he was struck by the wash of emotion there. They shone with unshed tears and his gut tightened.

"You have a family. A history. It's so obvious that there's love here. It must have been wonderful to grow up in this house."

He pulled her carefully into his arms and tucked her head underneath his chin. He didn't know what to say to her other than to agree. What kind of childhood had she endured growing up under someone like Alex Mouton? And where was her mother? She hadn't said much about her mother at all, and none of his intel had ever mentioned a woman or a daughter.

Resnick had a lot to answer for. He'd sent KGI in without important information. Like the fact that Mouton had a daughter. Sam damn sure wouldn't have gotten involved with Sophie if he'd known that little fact. Looking back, he realized it had been damn convenient.

But here, now, with her in his arms, and feeling the kick of their child, it was easy to say he wouldn't have involved himself, but he couldn't bring himself to regret it. Even if Sophie was firmly involved in her father's dealings. If nothing else, his child wouldn't live with the repercussions of her mother's or her grandfather's choices.

Surprising him, Sophie turned into his chest and hugged him fiercely. Slowly his arms came around her, and he held her there as she buried her face in his shoulder.

He wasn't at all sure what she needed from him. Oh, he could guess, but all he could offer was protection. He was determined to keep the rest of himself locked away— at least until . . . what? She proved herself worthy?

The thought sickened him even as it took root in his mind. There was no way to sugarcoat what he was doing. He hated that he didn't trust her completely, but he'd be an idiot to offer his faith blind. Too many people depended on him.

The sooner they met with Resnick, the sooner he could get on with the business of dispatching Mouton once and for all. Then maybe he and Sophie could work on the seemingly insurmountable obstacles between them.

"Come," he murmured into her hair. "Let's get your shoes. Garrett's waiting. We need to get on the road."

She didn't ask where they were going. She took his hand and let him lead her from the living room toward the front door.

Her trust humbled him and made the sick feeling in his stomach grow larger.

He was very afraid that when this was all over, he wouldn't have proven himself worthy to *her*.

CHAPTER 15

"I don't like the idea of leaving you and Sophie alone," Garrett said as he navigated traffic through Nashville, toward the airport.

Sam leaned against the door, Sophie in his arms, her lower body sprawled across the seat. She'd fallen asleep thirty miles out of Dover, and her soft, even breathing filled the back of the vehicle.

He absently ran his fingers through the strands of blond hair resting on her cheek as he stared back at Garrett's reflection in the rearview mirror.

"I don't want to give Resnick our location. He was way too damn eager to know about Sophie. Given half a chance, he'd bring in a team and take her. If you go and bring him in, I don't have to worry about that happening."

Garrett nodded. "I'll make damn sure we aren't

followed. If I have to drug and blindfold the fucker, he won't have a clue where I'm taking him."

Garrett drove into the long-term parking lot and cut the engine. Sam gently touched Sophie on the cheek.

"Sophie, wake up. We're at the airport."

Her eyelids fluttered and then popped open. She tried to rise, her movements awkward against him. He helped her to a sitting position, and she stared around, her eyes wide.

"Sam, I don't have any of my documents. My passport."

"We're not flying anywhere. Garrett is. But nobody has to know that. We're going to take a trip into the terminal and then you and I are going to slip back out and change vehicles."

She frowned. "Where is Garrett going?"

Garrett glanced at Sam and then back at Sophie. "Just a little fact-finding mission. I'll meet up with you two at Eagle One."

Sophie shook her head as if clearing the cobwebs as Sam helped her from the back of the SUV.

"What is Eagle One? Everyone keeps talking about it."

"One of our safe houses," Sam said.

He tucked her elbow into his palm and directed her toward the elevator.

"Act natural, Sophie. Smile. We don't want to draw any undue attention."

Twenty minutes later, Sam and Sophie exited through the passenger pickup and got into a cab. He directed the driver to a location just outside the downtown area and then sat back and pulled Sophie to him.

"Are you hurting?"

She shook her head against the crook of his arm. "I'm feeling much better. I'm hungry again, but I stay hungry these days."

He smiled and automatically glanced down at her belly, which was pressed to his side.

"I'll get you something to eat as soon as we're on our way again."

She didn't question him further. Didn't ask where they were going or how long it would take. She just settled against him and rested.

They got out of the cab, and Sam put Sophie into the front seat of a black Ford Expedition. Then he unlocked the back and pulled up the flooring to survey the small arsenal stashed there.

He holstered a Glock, popped the clip into one of the assault rifles, then pulled out the sat phone and a small GPS unit. He put the flooring back down and then walked back to get into the driver's seat.

Sophie's eyes widened briefly when she took in the rifle, but she didn't say a word as he laid it barrel-down between their seats.

"We're not going far today," he told her as he cranked the engine. "I've sent Steele and his team ahead to recon. We'll stay behind them until he gives me the all clear. Thought you might like hot food, a hot bath and a comfortable bed."

Her hands shook in her lap and she looked up at him, her eyes stark and hollow.

"That would be absolutely wonderful."

He reached for her hand, curling his fingers around hers as he pulled onto the highway. For a moment her hand lay limply in his, until finally she threaded her fingers tighter into his and held on.

THEY pulled into a roadside motel a few hours later. It wasn't the Ritz, but it wasn't a dive either. At the moment, Sophie didn't care as long as nothing crawled on her and it had running water and a decent bed. In fact, the bed didn't even have to be decent.

Surprisingly, she was pain-free, and she could actually move her arm in varying degrees without irritating her wound. She still ached from head to toe, but she was looser now, and if she could get another hot bath, it would go a long way in restoring her fortitude.

Sam returned with keys, and they walked to a room on the very end. The only suite the motel boasted, but it advertised a Jacuzzi tub, so she was all over that.

"I'll run you a bath, and you can soak while I order food. Do you have a preference?" Sam asked. "I'll get the bags out of the truck so you'll have clean clothes to change into."

Her brow crinkled. "Bags? We didn't bring any bags."

He smiled. "Taken care of."

Her mouth gaped open. "But how?"

"Always pays to be prepared."

She shook her head. He was feeding her a line of crap. Someone had to have packed the truck for them. Probably one of his many team members.

"Come on. I'll help you into the tub and then leave you to it," he said as he guided her toward the bathroom.

She stopped and put a hand on his arm. "I can do it. I'm okay."

He stared at her a moment, then nodded. "Okay then. I'll take care of the bags and getting food."

She didn't spend as much time in the tub as she had at Sam's mom and dad's. She could hear him outside the bathroom, and she was filled with a restless urgency to get back to him.

Other than stiffness and a little residual soreness, her wound didn't bother her as much as she had thought it would, given that she'd been shot. She tested the ridge of the stitched seam with her fingers and examined it in the mirror. It was slightly puckered, a little swollen around the sutures, but there was no angry redness to denote infection. Those antibiotic shots Donovan had given her had done the trick.

She towel-dried her hair and then realized that Sam hadn't brought in a change of clothes for her. Her baggy pants and T-shirt lay on the floor soaking up the water she'd dripped from the shower.

With a sigh, she wrapped a towel around her and cracked open the bathroom door. She didn't see Sam, so she pushed farther into the room, craning her neck to see around the doorway.

She saw Sam the same time he looked up and saw her. There was a spark in his eyes, and he quickly looked away but then lifted his gaze once more as if he couldn't resist.

"I uhm don't have any clothes," she murmured.

He moved to the bed and rummaged in one of the bags there before pulling out a pair of jeans, underwear, and a shirt. He circled around the end of the bed and stalked toward her with purposeful steps.

She almost backed away. She felt small and vulnerable,

and he was looking at her just like he'd looked at her all those nights they'd spent in another hotel.

He stopped just a foot in front of her, so close that his heat reached out and circled her like the damp towel she wore so close to her breast.

The clothes were in his hand, but he didn't move to give them to her and she didn't reach for them.

His gaze was so intense. So penetrating. She felt naked. So itchy and alive. She swallowed, but nothing she did ridded her of the knot in her throat. It ached like she ached.

The clothes dropped silently to the floor. His hands cupped her bare shoulders. His fingers caressed her skin.

Slowly and with infinite tenderness his mouth descended over hers. His breath danced across her skin, and then he captured her lips in a long, *hot* kiss. Time melted away like ice on a summer day. She was back in his arms in the hotel room where they met after she left the bar each night.

He'd always waited for her, pulling her into his arms as soon as she walked through the door. Their clothes flew and they reacted desperately to the passion that existed between them.

She'd give anything to go back to those precious nights she'd spent in his arms. But she'd always known she couldn't have forever.

Yet now, under the heat of his lips, she clung to him, wanting him so badly that the ache far surpassed the pain of her injuries.

He jerked away and took a step back, running his hand through his hair in agitation. "Goddamn it, Sophie. What you do to me."

Her lips pursed and she stared at him, hoping he'd shrivel under the force of her glare.

"I didn't make you kiss me. You wanted me every bit as much as I wanted you. Don't make excuses. Shut up and take responsibility."

He lifted one eyebrow and then his gaze smoldered. He took a step forward, and she instinctively backed away.

His hands smoothed up her shoulders, carefully skimming over her bandaged arm, until he cupped her face in his palms.

"You're absolutely right," he murmured. "I'll own up to the fact that right now I want to make love to you more than I want anything else. It's stupid. Insane, even, but there you have it. For now I'll take responsibility for the fact that I'm going to kiss you again."

She swallowed the lump in her throat just as his lips descended again. She melted into his arms, giving herself fully to his embrace.

A low moan rose from her throat, swelling painfully before it rushed into his mouth. She wanted to touch him, to hold him against her, to know that nothing bad would ever happen to her while she was in his arms.

"Tell me we can't make love, Soph," he murmured against her lips. The pet name he'd used so many times when he was on top of her, inside her, beside her or wrapped around her, sounded so sweet to her ears. She was starved for him. "There's too much unresolved between us. We shouldn't—we can't—make love."

She sighed unhappily and stared up at him as his thumbs caressed the corners of her mouth. Her face was still tenderly cupped in his hands, and she didn't want to break that connection for any reason.

"Why can't we?" she whispered. "I've missed you so much, Sam. I've stayed awake so many nights aching for you to hold me again, to kiss me and make love to me like you did before."

He closed his eyes and leaned in until his forehead rested against hers. "You're hurt. This is crazy."

She tilted back just enough that she could brush her lips over his. "I'm okay, Sam. I need you. Please say you've thought about me even just once."

"Shit, Sophie."

He sounded angry. He pulled away, his expression grim. "I've thought about you. I've thought about you a hell of a lot more than once. I wish I hadn't. But goddamn it, you disappeared. I came back for you and you were gone."

Pain—worse than the knife—sliced through her chest. Would things have been different if she had been there when he came back? Not that it had even been possible. She'd made choices—not difficult choices—but she'd made them, and now she had to live with the consequences.

"I've thought about you too," she whispered. "All the time."

She turned away and closed her eyes as helplessness fell over her. Regret knotted her throat into a tight channel. She squeezed air painfully past it until pain was all she could assimilate.

A knock sounded at the hotel door. Sam touched her shoulder then leaned down to retrieve her fallen clothes.

"Go into the bathroom and get dressed. I'll get the food."

She reached for the clothes without looking at him. Then she retreated into the bathroom and closed the door. She leaned against the old wood, hating herself for the silent tears streaking down her cheeks.

She couldn't go back. She wouldn't if she could. What was done was done, and the price she'd paid was high. Maybe too high.

Wiping at her face with the back of her arm, she dropped the towel and sorted through the bundle of stuff Sam had given her. There were panties and a bra in the correct size. This time she snapped the clips on the bra and just pulled it over her head the best she could.

A few minutes later, clean and attired in better fitting clothes, she took a deep breath and went back into the room.

The smell of food wafted through her nostrils and her mouth watered. There was an array of food spread out over the bed. A steaming pizza, two salads, a tray of cold cuts and cartons of Chinese takeout.

She stood at the side of the bed, not knowing where to start first.

"Dig in," Sam said.

He took a seat on the edge of the bed and picked up a slice of the pepperoni pizza.

"I get half that," she said in a rush, pointing to the pizza.

He chuckled and picked up a paper plate to hand to her. "Tell you what. You get what you want. I'll take cleanup duty."

She took the plate and quickly went down the row piling food onto it. When she had no more room, she hesitated, studying to find what she could put back.

Sam laughed again and handed her another plate. "It's not going anywhere, Sophie. Sit down and eat."

Feeling like a moron, she edged onto the bed and shoved aside the tray of minisandwiches.

She attacked the pizza first because it was piping hot, and while lukewarm pizza was good, it was better when the cheese was all melty.

"God, this is good," she said on a moan.

He looked curiously at her. "How long has it been since you ate decently?"

Her cheeks flamed. "A few days. I didn't dare stop to eat. I was too busy trying to stay ahead of the people chasing me. But I'd be starving anyway. I'm not one of these dainty, delicate pregnant types. I think I could eat my weight at every meal. I'll be a walrus by the time I deliver."

His gaze slipped over her body, and she found herself blushing.

"You could certainly stand to gain a few pounds. Your belly pooches out like a volleyball. There's nothing else to you."

"Boobs," she mumbled around a second slice of pizza. "Boobs are huge now. I hate it. I feel like I'm incubating aliens and they're ready to hatch."

He stared at her in astonishment for a moment before throwing his head back to laugh.

"I think the aliens are perfect."

"You would," she muttered.

She ate until she feared she was going to bust her gut. Her belly felt so tight that it was all she could do to move. She flopped back on the bed and closed her eyes, letting contentment wash over her.

Then she had to laugh because as contentment went, this wasn't exactly ideal. She was stuck on the run in a motel, with a man she lusted over with every girly hormone in her pregnant body. A man whose child she was carrying. A man who didn't trust her and seemed to fight with himself over whether he liked her or didn't like her.

Then there was the fact that her uncle's men were breathing down her neck, she'd killed her father, and she'd stolen access to his entire fortune.

When she fucked up, she went whole hog.

"What are we doing, Sam?" she asked softly. "Where are we going?"

"I told you. A KGI safe house."

She made a sound of frustration. "And what happens then? You can't tell me you don't have a plan. Where do I fit in?"

"I told you I'd protect you and our child," he said in an even tone. A tone that could have been used with anyone. A tone that told her he wasn't giving anything away.

She rolled away and got awkwardly from the bed. She went to the window because there was nowhere else to go. Her fingers curled and uncurled, denting her palm when her nails dug into her skin.

"Why won't you tell me anything?"

She hated the pleading sound of her own voice. It sounded needy and pathetic. Where was the woman who'd coldly planned her father's murder and her escape?

She dropped her head down, regretting that she'd conjured the image of her father slipping to the floor, his blood running over the polished floor.

She may have hated the bastard, but the idea that she'd so easily pulled the trigger frightened her. Was she more like him than she thought?

"Come to bed, Soph."

Sam's low voice fluttered across her neck, so soft and entreating. She shivered and clutched her arms protectively over her chest.

His hands slid over her shoulders and he pulled her back against him. Then his lips whispered just below her ear. A simple, delicate kiss that conveyed more than words the heavy regret between them.

"Come to bed," he said again.

She let him lead her away from the window. The food was gone and the covers were pulled back. He kept his gaze down, but he carefully eased her down onto the mattress before tucking her in as he would a child.

Without undressing, he walked around the foot of the bed and to the other side, where he slid in next to her. His warmth enveloped her even before he pushed up against her.

For a moment she resisted and lay stiffly as he tucked her against his body, but then, unable to resist, she relaxed and snuggled readily into his embrace.

Right now she didn't care what he thought of her. For the moment she was safe, even if it was just an illusion. Their child rolled and bumped between them, and her throat tightened at the fantasy of how it could have been if she wasn't who she was and he wasn't who he was.

They could be regular people celebrating the life of a child and their first foray into parenting. He could read pregnancy books and worry endlessly over whether she was eating properly.

He'd be there for each kick and wiggle, and they'd stay up late at night talking about names and make wishes for the future.

"Sam?"

His name spilled from her lips. She had so much to explain. She didn't even know where to start, but she could take the tension between them no longer.

"Shhh. Not now, Soph," he said in a quiet voice. "Just let it be. Sleep now. Our child needs your strength."

With a resigned sigh, she closed her eyes.

CHAPTER 16

SOPHIE woke to warm, sensual lips sliding up the side of her neck. She shivered as Sam's tongue traced the shell of her ear and lingered at the lobe long enough for him to nip it with his teeth.

The covers had been thrown aside, and his palm skimmed up her leg, pushing the oversized shirt over her hip to gather at her waist.

She sucked in her breath. Had she taken off her pants during the course of the night? She was lying there in only her panties and a shirt, and Sam's hands were fast making work of the shirt.

Or maybe he was just that good.

In past times, he would already have been over her, inside her, waking her to the feel of his cock stretching her and setting fire to her nerve endings. But this morning he was tentative. Seeking . . . permission? Her acquiescence?

Her body throbbed. A pulse thrummed in her groin, and already she was swollen and wet for him. She loved his touch. Even at his gentlest, he was strong and masterful. She'd been drawn to his strength when she had cause to fear everything else in the world.

He made her feel protected and cherished.

But now?

Her brain hurt trying to decipher where they stood. If they stood anywhere at all. She couldn't even look back at what they'd had because what they'd had wasn't real. It was built on lies and half-truths.

His hand slid over her belly and cupped their child as if bringing home the one thing they did have. They'd created a very precious life. *She* was very real.

He kissed her again, just one touch against the pulse at her neck. His body pressed into the curve of her behind. His erection was hot and turgid, pulsing against her skin. Chill bumps dotted her hip and spread rapidly down her legs.

"You said we couldn't," she said without conviction.

He moved his hand up to cup her breast, and he kneaded gently, working the nipple between his fingers.

"Are you more sensitive here now?" he whispered.

She nodded, unable to speak around the tightening of her throat.

"Then I'll be extra careful."

He touched and stroked, alternating until her nipples were stiff peaks, erect and so hard that they hurt. The simplest brush across the points sent a current of desire streaking through her abdomen.

"I'm going to take your shirt off. Just lie still. Let me do the work. I don't want you to hurt your arm."

She shivered at the raw sensuality in his voice. Low-timbred, husky, with just a bit of a rasp. It always got low and gravelly when they made love.

Oh God, they were going to make love.

He eased the shirt farther up, until it gathered around her neck. He stretched the armhole until he could slip it around her elbow. There was only a twinge as he pulled it the rest of the way up and over her arm.

"Lift your head for just a second, honey."

A moment later, she was free of the material, and she was down to her underwear.

He rose up on his elbow, and she turned her head so she could see him. He simply watched her, his gaze drifting up and down her body with lazy strokes.

"You're so unbelievably beautiful," he said hoarsely.

She swallowed. She didn't want to ruin the moment, but she had to know what had changed. Why was he willing to make love to her now?

"You said we couldn't," she repeated.

"I did," he agreed. "But right now I can't think of a single reason why we can't. I want you, Sophie. I missed you. I can't lie here without touching you. I want what's mine again. I want to give you what's yours."

Her chest fluttered, then grew tight. Her stomach flipped and she began to shake.

"Shhh, baby," he said as he stroked down the curve of her body. "Just let me love you. We'll figure this all out, Sophie. I swear it."

"You don't hate me?"

His eyes softened, and he leaned down to kiss her hip right above the band of her panties.

"I feel a lot of things for you, Sophie. But hate isn't one of them."

His thumb hooked into her underwear, and he carefully slid it down leaving her naked and vulnerable to his touch and sight.

Her hand fluttered over her belly, and she turned her face into the pillow, no longer able to bear his scrutiny.

"Do you have any idea just how beautiful you are?"

There was awe and reverence in his voice that had her looking back at him. It was there in his eyes as he simply stared down at her.

He bent and kissed her hip again and then showered a line of kisses down her leg to her ankle. He lifted her foot and kissed each toe until she twitched at the ticklish sensations.

He eased her foot down and moved behind her again. He lay down, his mouth close to her neck as he spooned against her. Her buttocks cupped his erection, and she moaned in anticipation.

He didn't move her. Didn't turn her over. He simply lifted her leg and eased it back over his until she was open and bare. His cock lay between her legs, but it was his fingers that found her heat.

"Sam . . ." she whispered as he stroked the soft folds.

He parted them and dipped one finger inside her.

"You're hot and wet and so damn tight," he said in a near groan.

Another finger slipped inside her, and she arched helplessly. She wouldn't last. Her body was painfully aware of him. She wanted him with every breath. She turned her head, and her cheek met his lips. He kissed her. The sweetness of that one kiss melted her senses and sent a trembling awakening through her heart.

How could she love someone she was so unsure of?

Sudden tears flooded her eyes. She blinked furiously, angry that she would be so weak at such a vulnerable moment.

"Make love to me," she choked out. "Please, Sam. I need you."

He paused for just a moment, and a low shudder worked its way through his body, pressing into her. She could feel his energy and his reaction to her soft plea.

His fingers left her to grasp his cock. He positioned himself at her entrance and then found her ear with his lips. One kiss. Two. And then he murmured low and sweet.

"Just relax, baby. Let me take you this way so you don't have to move. Let me take care of you."

He nudged forward, his hips pressing into her buttocks as he breached the tight clasp of her heat. She sucked in her breath, then closed her eyes when his shallow thrust sent streaks of pleasure through her pussy.

Back and forth. He rocked against her slow and measured, none of his thrusts going too deep. His hand left his cock now that he had position, and he laid it possessively over her hip. His fingers curled into her, holding her as he moved faster now but still as carefully as before.

He was driving her crazy. She flexed and pushed back, eager to meet his movements, but he gripped her hip and held her in place.

"Let me," he whispered again.

Her leg lay over his, and she tucked her foot between

his legs, enjoying the rasp of hair on her bare skin. His legs were muscled, lean and so strong. They flexed and twitched with each forward thrust.

Then his hand moved from her hip and eased underneath her leg, pushing it upward to give him room. He supported her thigh with his forearm and reached up until his fingers found her clitoris.

His thumb teased the entrance his cock rubbed back and forth over, while his fingers parted the soft flesh above and tenderly stroked the stiff, sensitive bundle of nerves at her center.

No longer able to lie still, she tightened and bucked back against him.

His thrusts got stronger, and he sank deeper, until her buttocks were flat against his abdomen.

"Are you ready, honey? Go with me. Come with me now."

"Just one more second," she breathed.

She closed her eyes and rocked against him. His fingers grew more assertive, and he moved his thumb up to roll over her clit in a demand for her to respond.

"Yes. Oh my God, yes. Just like that, Sam. Don't stop please. Don't stop."

She was pleading. Her voice was hoarse and needy, and each demand came out in a short burst of air.

He drew back and then pumped deep just as his thumb rolled in a tight circle.

She cried out and tensed. Her fingers curled into balls, into fists so tight that her hands shook with the strain. Cascades of color flashed, little and big spots that floated through her vision even when she closed her eyes.

Sam was thrusting hard and fast now as he sought his own release. His hoarse shouts mixed with her agonized sounds. It sounded as though she was in the worst sort of pain, but the pleasure, ah the pleasure, was so intense, so beautiful that she didn't want it to end.

She reached down to still his hand when the sensation became too intense to bear. He eased his thumb away but continued a gentle rocking motion that sent his cock gliding through tissues slick with his release.

Finally he stopped, lodged deep within her. She didn't move for fear of displacing him, and she lay there simply enjoying the feeling of being so intimately connected to this man.

He kissed her back, rubbed his thumb in circles around the ball of her shoulder and then kissed her again, his erratic breaths sending goose bumps over her skin.

"I need you."

His voice was quiet and regretful, as if he had no liking for the admission and hated voicing it even more. She wondered why he'd been honest; maybe he too was tired of all the deceit between them.

"I can't explain it. Not sure I want to, but damn it, I need you, Sophie. It's not just physical. It can't be. I've had physical before."

He moved slightly, and for a moment she feared he was pulling out of her, but he stayed locked tight, their bodies joined as he shifted closer to her.

He slid his hand over her waist and splayed his fingers over her belly. His grip was possessive and tender and told her more than words that he was claiming what was his.

He continued to pet and stroke her belly, his touch light and soothing. He rested his mouth on her shoulder, and neither spoke. She floated on a cloud between sleep and awake, existing in a state of delicious lethargy. Finally she dozed, and only came awake when she felt him finally pull away in a warm rush of fluid.

"Be right back," he said.

He returned with a warm towel and gently cleaned between her legs. Then he settled next to her in bed once more and pulled her in close to him.

"Don't we have to leave?" she mumbled.

"No, not yet. My team will notify me when it's safe."

She stirred and frowned. "Are we safe here, just us?"

She felt him smile against her neck.

"Yes, Soph, we're safe. I wouldn't risk you or our baby. I'll know if anyone steps within ten feet of our door."

"How?" she asked drowsily.

He chuckled. "Security. I did a lot while you were taking your bath. Sleep now and don't worry about anything."

She sighed as some of the postcoital euphoria faded. It was hard not to worry when she faced so much uncertainty. She still hadn't told him everything, and when he knew, he might not want anything to do with her.

He hated her father, and if the apple didn't fall very far from the tree, she couldn't imagine Sam being overjoyed with spending time with her, loving her or allowing his child to be raised by a monster.

Fear churned in her stomach until she was sucking deep breaths through her nose to quiet the nausea. He couldn't, he wouldn't take her child from her.

She closed her eyes. She was being an idiot. Nothing

of the sort was going to happen. She just had to be careful, pick the right time and make sure her uncle never got close.

And the last she couldn't do without Sam.

CHAPTER 17

SAM woke to a warm, sweet body sprawled across him and a tiny pitter-patter thumping him in the side. It took him a moment to process that it was his child kicking him.

He smiled and slid his hand down Sophie's spine, down to cup her plump little rear as he lay there soaking up the utter domesticity of the scene.

His woman, limp and sated, draped across him in a possessive manner that gave him a ridiculous sense of satisfaction, and his child, waking him up with a tiny foot to his gut.

If the little imp was anything like her mama, he was in for a hell of a ride.

As he continued to caress her behind, she stirred and murmured something against his neck before burrowing deeper into his arms.

"What was that?" he asked against her ear.

"Shower," she muttered. "I need one. But God, I don't want to get up."

"Then don't."

He tightened his hold on her, content to stay just like this. He raised his hand from her hip to check his watch and then lazily trailed his fingers down to the cleft of her ass.

Chill bumps raced across her back, and he soothed them away with his palm. For a long moment, she lay there, the only sound her soft breathing against his neck.

Yeah, he liked it. He'd liked it five months ago and he liked it now.

Finally she shoved herself up, and her blond hair spilled over his chin. To his surprise, she leaned down and kissed him.

It wasn't a tentative brush but a hot, open-mouthed kiss that sent a surge of electricity through his body.

She drew away, and her pupils dilated until there was only a thin ring of blue around the black. She laid her palm over his jaw and let her thumb glide across his lips.

"Why'd you tie me up before?"

He blinked. "Huh?"

"That time in the hotel. You tied me up."

His chest shook as laughter escaped. "I don't know. It seemed like the thing to do at the time. Maybe I'm a kinky bastard. Did you like it?"

She seemed to think about it as she cocked her head to the side.

"Maybe."

He leaned up and kissed her quickly on the mouth.

"Then maybe I'll do it again sometime."

Her eyes widened and went even darker. He smiled. Oh yeah, she'd liked it. The thing was, he didn't really know why he'd done it. At the time he'd wanted her completely at his mercy, and the idea of her tied to his bed had been a huge turn-on. Not that he needed much encouragement around her.

"Okay, I'm really going to take a shower now," she said.

She tried to push away, but he caught her against him and then rolled with her until he was over her, staring down into wide swirls of blue.

His cock ached like a son of a bitch, and when she squirmed, the tip brushed through swollen, damp folds. He groaned and pushed, forcing his way through tight, liquid heat. She gasped and surged upward.

"Oh fuck," he whispered. "This is going to be quick."

He thrust and felt his skin peel away, leaving him raw and exposed. He tried to be gentle. He needed to be gentle, now of all times, when she was still sleepy and unprepared, but her channel hugged him, had a stranglehold on his cock.

Her nails scoured his back and then dug in. He thrust and rocked, and she opened her legs wider to take him.

When she whispered his name in sweet, husky acceptance, he lost it. He came apart while she held him. Her hands, like little feathers, whispered up and down his back.

He swallowed and tried to regain his composure, but he felt shattered by this one, quick encounter. He shook almost uncontrollably and went suddenly weak.

He lowered himself to her, and she enveloped him in her embrace. He buried his face against her neck and inhaled her feminine scent.

"Sorry, baby. Sorry."

She turned her head until her lips met the skin behind his ear. She kissed, just once, and whispered softly, "Don't be sorry for wanting me, Sam."

He pushed himself up. "Never that. I'm just sorry I was such an inconsiderate asshole."

She smiled. "Come take a shower with me."

"No soak in the tub today?"

She shook her head. "No just a quick shower and then you can feed me again. When will we have to leave?"

He checked his watch, wondering the same thing.

"You go ahead to the shower. I'll call and check in, make sure everything's going according to plan."

He carefully pulled himself away and then reached a hand to help her out of bed. He watched her walk into the bathroom, mesmerized by the gentle sway of her ass.

She was one beautiful pregnant woman. He'd always thought that pregnant women were beautiful. He loved to look at them, at the swollen lushness of their bodies, the spark in their eyes, and imagine the softness of their skin. But nothing had prepared him for the reality of a woman pregnant with *his* child.

He shook himself back to awareness. The devil of it was he knew he was on a clear collision course with something he wasn't prepared to deal with, but at the moment he didn't care.

He only knew that somehow, someway, he had to sort all of this out. Not only was he not letting go of his child, but he wasn't letting go of Sophie either. That was as far as he'd thought, and he wouldn't allow himself to go any further.

SOPHIE walked out of the bathroom in bare feet, her hair still damp from the shower. She rubbed it with a towel as she glanced around for her shoes.

"Looking for these?" Sam asked as he tossed her tennis shoes onto the bed. "We need to get moving. We have a few hours on the road before we get to the safe house."

She dropped the towel and reached for a pair of socks that Sam had placed by the shoes.

"I'll get the rest of the stuff out of the bathroom and then we'll head out. I've already got everything else."

She nodded and slipped on her shoes, quickly tying the laces. She was brimming with curiosity over this safe house. How long did Sam plan for them to stay? Did he intend to leave her there while he went after her uncle?

He hadn't told her anything, but she wasn't an idiot. In his shoes, she'd do the same thing. She wouldn't be sad to see the rest of her father's network taken down. Tomas was crippled because he didn't have the key that Sophie had stolen. His resources would be stretched, and he'd just become more and more desperate.

"I'm ready," she said as she stood to her full height again.

Sam ushered her out of the hotel, his gaze scanning the night around them. His body was tense and alert as he put her into the SUV. He even buckled her in before walking around to the driver's side. She smiled and shook her head. The man was conscientious. She'd give him that much. He didn't do anything half-ass.

He was intensely loyal to the people he loved. His family. His friends. If he gave even half that loyalty to their child, she'd grow up the luckiest of little girls. But Sophie knew Sam would give his all. There would be no one more important to him than his child.

Her chest ached with sadness. What would it be like to have that kind of love and loyalty? She only hoped she could give what she'd never been given. She hoped she knew how.

It didn't really matter whether nature prevailed over nurture or vice versa. She was fucked both ways.

"It'll be light soon," he said. "Maybe an hour. We'll roll in midmorning. Just in time for breakfast. I know you said you were hungry, but do you think you can wait a few hours?"

"I was teasing you," she said with a grin. "I ate so much before that I don't think I'll be hungry for a week."

He glanced over at her belly. "Uh-huh. I've heard that it's never wise to believe a pregnant woman when she says she'll never be hungry again."

She laughed and enjoyed the sensation of feeling so light. It was absurd and incongruous given how they'd come to be here and how tenuous her grip on the situation was. It had been too long since she'd felt safe enough to enjoy a stolen moment where she didn't have to worry that taking joy in something meant its death or removal.

She looked away, embarrassed by the fact that she could so easily forget what was at stake here. She cleared her throat as if that somehow would make the feeling go away.

The sky turned lavender, and only one star hung stubbornly in it, bright like a diamond against velvet. Her gaze was fixed on the star, and she was unable to look away. Stars had always fascinated her. She'd spent countless hours wishing on them as a child.

She'd learned young that wishing was an exercise in futility, and that the only useful trait was self-reliance. She'd spent years trying to make the wistful little girl inside disappear. At first she'd been bent on protecting her, and then she'd tried to ruthlessly drive her from existence.

The woman who'd shot her father and felt no remorse was a long way from the child who'd only ever wished for love and a family—a real family.

"What are you thinking about over there? You're about to chew your bottom lip off."

She immediately relaxed her mouth and managed a faint smile. "Nothing important. Tell me about KGI. How did you get it started and why do you do what you do? It seems an odd career choice."

He cast a sideways look at her and shrugged. "It pays well."

She arched an eyebrow. "That's it? It pays well?"

"I suppose you could say it's in the blood. My entire family is military. Never a time we weren't. My father, his father, his father's father. Uncles, cousins—you name it, we served."

"But you're not still enlisted right? I mean KGI is private."

There was only a brief flicker in his eyes, and if she hadn't been watching she would have missed his hands tightening just a bit on the steering wheel.

"Your father didn't tell you about us? You said he knew what we were."

Her lips thinned. "My father only told me what he thought I needed to know in order to get close to you. He didn't give me your life story or anything."

He glanced back to the road. "No, I'm not enlisted. I was an army man. Garrett and Donovan both joined the Marines. There's also Ethan, Nathan and Joe who you haven't met. Ethan was a Navy SEAL."

"Was? So none of you are still in the military then?"

"Nathan and Joe are still active duty. Army."

"And does Ethan work with you?"

Sam grimaced. "Some. Probably more in the future. He and his wife have had a rough time. His focus is her right now."

"Oh. I mean that's good."

"Yeah, they need the time. They'll be fine though. Rachel's tough. She's a fighter."

Sophie looked at him curiously. A warm glint had entered his eyes when he spoke of his sister-in-law, and it made Sophie curious to know the story lurking behind those enigmatic words.

"So you formed KGI when you left the military? That seems like such a daunting undertaking. I can't even imagine."

Sam smiled. "Not so much. I had a lot of good contacts. I saved an upper-level CIA operative's ass during an incident at one of the U.S. embassies. He told me if he could ever return the favor to call him. So I did. Call him. It's through him that a lot of our jobs are done, but we take jobs in the private sector as well."

"Like?"

She couldn't imagine normal, everyday people needing a military operation. Her father yes, but then he was as far from normal as one could get.

"Most of our hostage recovery missions are contracted through governments and not always our own. We've been hired by smaller countries without the military might of a more developed nation.

"In the private sector we've taken jobs to recover kidnap victims and we've also done fugitive recovery."

Her eyes widened. "You mean like prison escapees?"

He smiled. "No, not quite. More like criminals who haven't been apprehended yet or are on the run before they've been tried for their crimes. The job is a lot of things, but predictable and boring it's not."

"It sounds very dangerous," she murmured.

"It can be, but we're good at what we do. We hire and train the best."

She grinned cheekily. "You sound like a commercial now."

He reached over and chucked her on the chin. "No one likes a smart-ass."

She caught his hand and kissed the tip of one finger. His eyes went molten, and for a moment he swerved as he took his attention from the road.

"You're a menace," he muttered.

Her eyes widened innocently. "What?"

He shook his head and chuckled but faced the road and returned both hands to the wheel.

CHAPTER 18

"I'M in position," P.J. said into her receiver.

Out of habit, she took a wide, slow sweep from left to right with her scope and took in any potential problem areas.

"There's a weak area to the west of the house. Three large trees connected by a mass of honeysuckle so thick you can't see through it. Someone could hide in there and never be seen."

"Should I break out the chain saw?" Cole drawled.

P.J. rolled her eyes. "You probably couldn't handle that much power."

"I'll show you power," he muttered.

"Children," Dolphin reprimanded.

P.J. grinned and mentally counted to three. Yep, Steele broke in with his dry, no-sense-of-humor voice.

"Cut it, you two. We have a job to do here. I'll take a look at your problem spot, P.J.," Steele said. "You and Cole stay in position. Sam will be rolling in soon."

P.J. pulled her field glasses up and watched, curious as to whether she'd actually be able to see Steele in the area. She knew she wouldn't, but it was a game she never tired of. The man couldn't always be that good, could he?

After several long minutes, Cole chuckled in her ear. "You won't find him, P.J."

She frowned. "How the hell do you know what I'm doing? I know damn well you can't see me."

"I could mess with you and say I can, but you're predictable. I knew you'd be looking."

Prompted by his needling to take him down a peg or two, she raised her rifle and did a meticulous sweep of the area where he'd taken position. She'd find his ass and nail it to the wall. Then he wouldn't be so smug.

It took several sweeps and intense concentration, her eyes nearly crossing as she looked for any pattern that didn't fit. She would have missed it if she'd so much as blinked, but there it was. A shoelace. Just the end between two leaves.

"Gotcha," she whispered.

"Who you shooting now?" Cole asked in amusement.

"You. Just found you."

Dolphin's laughter broke in.

"Bullshit," Cole said in a terse voice.

But there was a pause, and then the shoelace disappeared, and the foliage surrounding it shifted slightly as if blown by a breeze.

She laughed. "Nice move, but I'd have already nailed you. You gotta watch those huge feet of yours, Cole."

"Son of a bitch," Cole muttered.

"Is it true what they say about men with big feet?"

"Come down here and I'll let you find out."

She snorted. "You dream big."

"As amusing as I find you two, I want radio silence and I want it now," Steele ordered.

P.J. complied with the order and went silent. But she was still smiling as she went about her surveillance.

THE safe house was a large cabin ensconced in a wall of trees and buried in the foothills of the Appalachians. The area surrounding it was wide open and gently sloping. She could see its appeal from a protection standpoint. No way anyone could sneak up on you here.

Still, Sophie nervously surveyed the terrain and wondered if it would be safe. If her uncle would find her here, and if he did, would Sam and his team be enough to protect her?

Sam touched her hand, and she turned to look at him. His fingers curled around hers and he squeezed reassuringly.

"You'll be fine here, Soph."

She smiled and hoped it looked genuine. "How long do we have to stay here? Will you be going with the others when they go after my unc . . . my father?"

He looked startled by her question. "You're so sure that's what I'm doing."

She shrugged. "It's what I would do. He's a threat to your family."

"He's a threat to you and our child."

"Yes."

"I don't intend to let him remain a threat."

She raised a trembling hand to her forehead.

"Are you okay? Is your head hurting? What about your arm?"

"I'm fine."

He frowned but didn't press. The SUV rolled to a stop, and Sam cut the engine before looking up to where Steele strode across the yard to meet them.

"Stay put until I come around for you," Sam said as he opened the door and stuck a leg out.

She nodded, and he stepped out of the truck and shut the door, leaving her in silence.

He and Steele conversed, and Steele made several gestures at the surrounding area. Fear knotted her belly. Not fear for her safety. She felt at ease for the first time since she'd fled her father's estate. This was a different fear.

She had to tell Sam everything. Soon.

Sam walked around the front of the truck and opened her door. He reached in to help her down and then hurried her toward the cabin.

She shivered as the cool, damp air brushed over her skin. The sun still hadn't burned off the fog, and the ground was shrouded in light mist. She inhaled deep and pulled the moisture into her dry throat.

The wooden steps creaked under their feet as they climbed up to the porch. Sam opened the door and a rush of warmer air hit her in the face.

The inside was sparsely decorated, with only a couch and one well-worn armchair in the living room. A large stone fireplace dominated the back wall, but the hearth was empty and no fire blazed.

It wasn't fancy, nor was it furnished beyond the bare necessities, but it *felt* safe. She had no idea if that was any real intuition or just a product of her wishful thinking. But for once it was nice to depend on someone other than herself for her well-being. She was tired—beyond tired—of running, of always fearing the current day would be her last.

Sam ran his hand up her back and over her shoulder before giving her a light squeeze.

"You okay?"

She turned and smiled at him and marveled at how nice it felt to really smile. To feel like smiling even amid such adversity.

"I'm okay. Better than okay. I was just thinking how nice it was to feel safe and to feel like I could depend on someone other than myself."

Puzzled by the sudden discomfort that crossed Sam's face, she cocked her head to the side.

"Did I say something wrong?"

He recovered quickly and shook his head. "No, of course not. I'm glad you feel safe. I want you to feel safe."

She glanced around at the empty cabin and lifted her hands. "So what do we do? Play cards? Monopoly?"

Though it was a joke, a tingle of excitement jolted through her at the idea of doing something so simple as play childhood games, games that Sam had probably played a million times growing up. She'd never done such mundane things. Never had those moments of playful, mindless fun.

He chuckled. "I need to get back with Steele and make sure the perimeter is secure, see what if any concerns he has. I'm afraid I didn't pack cards or Monopoly, but we can always play truth or dare."

He waggled his eyebrows suggestively and grinned. It transformed his face from serious hard-ass to light and playful. Her heart fluttered. He really was extraordinarily good-looking.

"I've never played truth or dare, but it sounds interesting."

His eyes widened in mock horror. "Never? Your education has been sorely neglected. What about spin the bottle?"

She solemnly shook her head.

"I can give you the abbreviated version of both games. You end up in a closet kissing me with my hand up your shirt."

She held a hand over her mouth to stifle the giggle. "If that's supposed to warn me off, I'm afraid it didn't do the job."

His blue eyes went molten, and he swaggered closer to her. He chucked her chin upward with his knuckle and then fused his lips to hers in a long, hot kiss.

She leaned in closer, her knees going weak. She loved his taste. Loved the slight bristle of beard stubble over her chin. She loved how he smelled—couldn't put a name on it—but it was a heady mixture of blatant masculinity and comfort. If she could bottle it, she'd make a fortune.

He drew away long enough to touch her swollen lips with the tip of his finger.

"Hold that thought," he murmured. "I'll be back and we can take up where we left off. I'll even trade the closet for the bedroom."

She parted her lips and nibbled at his finger, then sucked it inward. He stiffened and his pupils dilated. Let him imagine her mouth around his cock. It would give him something to think about.

With a saucy grin, she let his finger fall away, and she started in the direction of the bedroom.

"I'll be waiting," she called back. "In the closet."

His bark of laughter followed her as she stepped into the small bedroom.

She hadn't seen anyone when they'd driven up, but there had been another vehicle parked on the side of the cabin. She knew they were here—somewhere—but she was happy to hold on to the illusion of privacy for her and Sam.

Sam could do his thing, check in with his team. She knew he'd see to their safety. She trusted him, which was an odd—and new—sensation for her. Trust wasn't a word she'd even contemplated before. But she decided she liked it. She liked it very much.

SAM entered the bedroom to find it empty. The sound of running water reached his ears, and he followed the trail of clothing on the floor from the bed to the bathroom. He smiled when he stepped into the bathroom and saw Sophie's silhouette behind the glass door of the shower.

He ducked back out and positioned his radio and the sat phone on the small dresser for easy access, and then he went back into the bathroom. When he heard the water turn off, he swiped a towel from the rack and waited for Sophie to open the shower door.

A fist slammed into his gut when the door swung open and he saw her standing there, her water-slicked body glowing in the light. She looked up and her wide, startled eyes met his gaze.

God but she was beautiful. Droplets slid down her neck, over the swell of her breasts and then to the swollen mound of her belly. He couldn't get enough of simply watching her.

Mechanically he moved forward and held the towel open for her to step into. Shivering, she melted into his arms, and he wrapped the towel around her and then rubbed briskly to dry her.

The towel fell to the floor, and his hands glided over her warm, soft skin.

"I just want to touch you," he said. "I can't get enough of how you feel."

She moaned and arched into his hands like a cat wanting to be rubbed. The tips of her breasts brushed over his shirt, and he suddenly wanted to be as naked as she was.

He positioned his hands underneath her breasts and then turned his palms up to cup the swells. The motion plumped them up and her nipples puckered and grew hard. He had to taste them, wanted them in his mouth. He wanted to suck them and let her sweet taste explode on his tongue.

Impatiently he hoisted her into his arms, swiveled around and started to set her down on the counter next to the sink.

"Shit," he murmured.

He put her down, grabbed the towel and quickly spread it over the cool tile. Then he lifted her again and eased her down on the towel.

"Perfect."

He lowered his head to one pink-tipped breast. He blew over it gently, watching it in fascination as it puckered again. She shivered in reaction and leaned back to give him better access.

He swiped his tongue over the crest. Velvety. He loved the way it felt in his mouth, loved the way she tensed and danced under his touch. She was so honest in her response and didn't shy away. She gave everything to him.

He leaned farther in to suck the tempting little bud into his mouth and winced when his groin pressed into the edge of the counter. Jesus, but he was hard, and he was dying to get inside her.

"Spread your legs," he whispered. "Let me see you."

Tentatively she pulled her knees up and then parted her thighs. Blond curls guarded soft, pink flesh. He ran his thumb down the seam and then pressed inward, finding her damp center.

"I have to taste you."

He heard her quick intake of breath even as he lowered himself to his knees in front of her.

"Put your feet on my shoulders," he said. "And relax."

The balls of her feet dug into his shoulders. Using two fingers, he parted the delicate folds of her pussy. His mouth hovered precariously close, and he inhaled her scent just as he kissed the opening. Keeping his mouth pressed tight to her, he pushed his tongue inward, savoring the hot, silky essence.

She moaned and shuddered, and for a moment her feet left his shoulders. Her fingers shoved forcefully over his scalp and then she guided him back when he drew away.

"Please. Oh Sam, touch me."

He licked gently, wanting to bring her as much pleasure as he was taking. He kissed his way up to her clit and then tongued it before sucking carefully to bring it farther into his mouth.

She began to shake. Her excitement spurred his. His cock swelled and strained against his jeans, and he knew if he didn't get inside her soon, he was going to come regardless.

He stood abruptly and fumbled with his zipper. He was as clumsy and unpolished as a teenager with his first girl, but nothing mattered except finding her sweet heat.

He moaned his relief when his cock came free and jutted forward. His hand closed around it while the other shoved his jeans down over his hips.

He fitted himself to her opening, then rubbed the tip of his cock up and down and finally inside. The opening flared around the head, and he closed his eyes, gritted his teeth and hoped to hell he could maintain a tight leash on his control.

He pumped his hips forward and thrust to the hilt in one hard push. She gasped. He gasped. He locked his jaw and stood still, absorbing the sensation of so much tight, wet flesh surrounding his dick.

Her hands curled around his shoulders and her fingers dug deep. He opened his eyes and searched her gaze for any sign that he'd hurt her, that he'd gone too fast.

He felt callous. A first-rate ass. But he was lost in the feel of her and helpless to do anything but drive. He withdrew and thrust. He strained up on the balls of his feet in an effort to get deeper.

"Tell me if I hurt you," he gritted out.

Even as he said it, he hoped to hell he wasn't, because he wasn't sure he had the strength to stop.

Her fingers cut into his skin and her breaths left her lips in soft little bursts.

"No. Don't stop."

Her breasts shook with each thrust, and his hands left

the edge of the counter to cup the supple mounds. His thumbs brushed the tips in rapid strokes to mimic the motion of his hips.

Fire centered in his groin, balled in a painful knot and then exploded outward into his gut and to his balls. His release lurked, menacing in its power, and he stopped, wanting to prolong the moment.

He rested against her, his sac pressed against her ass, his dick completely encased in her heat. She twitched and pulsed around him and she twisted restlessly, telling him without words that she needed more.

"Hold on to me, baby. I can't wait any longer. You feel so good."

He withdrew, and the ache intensified as she rippled across his length. He pushed forward again, taking care even as his mind screamed at him to take her as hard and as rough as he could.

He reined in that urge and sank deep, then stood motionless before repeating the act all over again. His release drew his balls up, so tight it hurt, and when he plunged deep again, it shot up his cock. He spilled hot and liquid even as his hips jerked spasmodically against her.

He dropped his hand down her body, let it slide over the tight ball of her stomach and then dipped between them through the soft curls until he found the tiny nub of flesh between her folds.

She gasped, arched up, and he pressed in, rotating in a tight circle until he felt her flutter around his cock. He thrust one last time and she cried out. Her hands fell from his shoulders and she gripped the edge of the counter, her knuckles going white.

He rolled his thumb over her clit and she went liquid

around him. He continued to slide back and forth, until finally he slipped from the welcoming grasp of her body. He stood, trying to squeeze air into his tortured lungs. His knees shook and he'd never felt so limber, so completely satisfied, in his life.

He leaned forward, gathered her in his arms and rested his forehead against hers as they both struggled for breath.

Her soft blue gaze found his, and she smiled, a gesture he felt to his toes.

"Well, it was almost a closet."

He laughed and kissed her and wondered not for the first time how he could ever stand to let her go.

CHAPTER 19

"THIS blows," Rusty complained as she stared at the television set in boredom.

Marlene Kelly gave her one of those enduring motherly looks that suggested she didn't appreciate Rusty's assessment.

Frank made a grunt from his seat in the recliner and rubbed a hand over his chest. "You'll make this a lot easier if you keep a decent attitude, young lady."

Rusty nearly groaned. She hated the young lady bit. Frank pulled it out only when he was calling her down about something, and it made her feel about two inches tall. Amazing how he could do that without ever raising his voice.

She and the "parents" had been herded into some podunk little house several miles away from Dover, all in the name of safety, and here they sat twiddling their thumbs like morons while Sam and company were off saving the world, or at least the chick Sam had been dumb enough to knock up.

Donovan was out playing superhero with Rio and company. Maybe they'd do something cool like plant explosives to keep the bad dudes away.

"If it weren't for missing school, this would double blow," she muttered. "At least the eye candy isn't bad."

Frank rolled his eyes and looked over at Marlene. "You see, *this* is why we didn't have girls. They're all hormonally deranged."

Rusty grinned. "I just call it like I see it."

Frank rubbed absently at his chest and grimaced. He shifted in his seat but never moved his palm.

"Frank, is something wrong?" Marlene asked in a worried tone.

"Nah, just a case of indigestion. I wonder if they have any antacids around here. Place seems stocked well enough."

Rusty snorted, but she got up from the couch and headed toward the kitchen. Well stocked? Well stocked would be having something to do in this godforsaken place. They didn't even have cable TV, so they were stuck watching two of the major networks, and she hated sitcoms.

She rummaged around in the cabinets but didn't find anything that resembled antacid. She did find some ibuprofen, so she shook out a few of the pills and poured a glass of milk from the fridge.

She returned to the living room and handed Frank the glass of milk.

"No antacid, but isn't milk supposed to help? I got you some pain stuff. Maybe that'll work."

Frank smiled and took the medicine from her

outstretched palm. "Thank you, Rusty. I'm sure this will do the trick."

She shrugged and headed back to the couch to sit next to Marlene.

Family sitcoms were the worst. Watching dysfunctional people trying to be funny while appearing all happy happy was worse than watching paint dry. She knew all about dysfunction, and it didn't go hand in hand with happy or funny.

She sighed and tuned out the laughs of the studio audience and wondered how long it took to save the world. A few days? Weeks? She'd ask Marlene how long, but it would only earn her another one of those motherly looks that made her cringe.

She turned when she heard Frank move. He sat forward in his chair, holding his arm. He looked pale and strained and he huffed for breath.

Alarmed, she glanced at Marlene, to see her staring at Frank as well.

"Frank," Marlene said sharply. "What's wrong?"

"It's nothing, Marlene. I just need to get up and move around. Feels like a damn elephant is sitting on my chest."

He struggled to his feet and for a moment stood stock-still before he swayed. With a groan, he pitched forward and hit the floor with a thud.

Panic hit Rusty like a ton of bricks. She surged to her feet and screamed for Rio and Donovan at the top of her lungs.

Marlene threw herself onto the floor beside Frank at the same time Rusty scrambled over the coffee table to kneel beside him.

"Is he breathing?" Rusty asked fearfully. "Oh my God, is he dead?"

Before Marlene could respond, Rusty leaned her ear down to his chest, feeling for any movement. She reached a hand up to his neck. You were supposed to feel for a pulse, right?

He wasn't moving. God, he wasn't breathing. She didn't think his chest was moving at all. She couldn't feel a pulse, but her hands were shaking so bad that she doubted she could have felt one anyway.

Rio and Donovan burst into the room, one of the other men tailing them. They all had their guns up, but when they saw Frank on the floor and the two women surrounding him, they tossed the guns aside and rushed over.

Donovan shoved Rusty out of the way and immediately checked for breathing and a pulse. Rio bent next to him and tore open Frank's shirt at the chest.

"He's n-not breathing," Rusty said.

Rio's gaze found hers for just a moment, and she saw steady reassurance there. Then he doubled his hands and positioned them over Frank's heart. Face drawn and pale, Donovan tilted Frank's neck back, then leaned down and began mouth-to-mouth.

Marlene was on her knees, her face so white that it scared Rusty. She looked like she was in shock, and worse, there was such fear in her eyes that it hit Rusty in the gut like a punch.

"Marlene. Marlene!" Rio added the last more forcefully.

Marlene snapped to awareness and looked at Rio.

"Call 911. We have to get him to a hospital."

Rusty started to shake. There wasn't a part of her body that wasn't trembling violently. Oh God, not Frank. No, no, no. Tears welled in her eyes and she wrapped both arms around herself in an effort to gain control.

Rio's expression was grim as he and Donovan continued CPR. Donovan wouldn't look in her or Marlene's direction. His steadfast focus was on forcing air in and out of his father's lungs. Marlene raced to the phone, and Rusty could dimly hear her relaying the situation to the dispatcher.

Only seconds later, Marlene returned and stood anxiously over the men. "They said an ambulance would be here in ten minutes."

Donovan didn't acknowledge her. He kept on with the breaths.

The wait was the worst Rusty had ever endured in her life. It was like a bad video that was stuck in a replay loop. It didn't seem real. It couldn't be real. This wasn't happening. She couldn't lose Frank. He believed in her. No one else believed in her.

When the paramedics finally arrived, they had to force Donovan away. It was a blur. There was a tube and needles. Lines and a machine. When they paused in CPR to check for a rhythm and the thin, red, flat line streamed across the monitor, Rusty lost it.

"No!"

She threw herself forward and shoved the paramedic out of the way. She hugged Frank to her, sobbing, her heart breaking.

"No," she cried hysterically. "You can't leave me. Please don't leave me. You can't die."

Rio plucked her off, and she kicked and fought him

until he wrapped both arms around her and held her immobile. The medics quickly wheeled Frank out of the room to the waiting ambulance, and when Marlene would have followed Donovan, Rio's man gently reined her in.

"Listen to me, Rusty," Rio said in a low voice next to her ear. "He's not gone. Not yet. They can save him. You have to believe that. You can't give up on him. He'll know."

Tears ran down her cheeks. She'd never felt so lost in her life. Not when her stupid mother ran out on her. Not when her asshole stepfather made her life miserable. Not when she'd tried to turn tricks just to find a way out of her life.

"Rio, why can't I go with him?" Marlene asked in a stricken voice. "Where are they taking him? I need to be with him. I need to be with Donovan."

Rio gently set Rusty down on the couch and took the seat beside her. He cupped her cheek even as tears splashed over the back of his hand. He glanced over at Marlene.

"My job is to keep you safe. All of you. I'll take you to the hospital. But we'll do this right. You go with me. You don't go *anywhere* without me. Understood?"

Marlene nodded numbly, her eyes glazed with fear and grief. Then she crossed the room and sat down next to Rusty, pulling her into her arms.

Rusty hugged her fiercely and buried her face against her breast. All moms needed to smell like Marlene. Warm and comforting. Rusty's only experience with mothers' smells was one of alcohol and stale cigarette smoke.

"Shhh," Marlene said as she rocked Rusty back and forth. "He's a fighter, Rusty. All the Kellys are. It'll take more than a heart attack to put Frank down. He's survived worse."

Rusty choked back another sob and clung desperately to those words. She knew Marlene was putting up a brave front for her, and she appreciated it—loved Marlene for doing it—but she felt Marlene's betraying tremble and the fear that was laced into those words of comfort.

Rio put a hand on Rusty's back and then slid it up to squeeze her shoulder. "If you two will come with me, we'll get you to the hospital."

CHAPTER 20

SOPHIE woke to an empty bed and the sun streaming through a crack in the blinds. She turned from the glare, reached for Sam's pillow and hugged it to her, inhaling his scent.

She was deliciously tired and sore from their love-making, and for the first time she didn't dread telling Sam everything. She'd confide in him about the key and trust him to do the right thing with the information. He was a good man, and she didn't think for a minute he'd betray her trust.

Smiling, she got out of bed and pulled on one of the pairs of elastic-waisted jeans she'd found waiting for her. She'd been ridiculously touched that there had been actual maternity clothes in her size along with all the accoutrements, including a bra that fit and underwear.

With a satisfied sigh, she went in search of Sam. She didn't want to put off the inevitable any longer. She'd tell him, get it over with, and then hopefully she could put the past behind her.

The murmur of voices from the living room grew louder as she ventured down the hall. When she rounded the corner, she was surprised to see someone standing with Sam and Garrett. She knew Garrett was supposed to arrive today, but Sam hadn't said what he'd been doing.

All three men turned when they heard her, and now, subject to their scrutiny, she wished she'd just stayed in bed.

"If I'm interrupting, I can just go back . . ."

She started to turn, but Sam strode over, his expression indecipherable. He took her hand, but tension radiated from him, and she glanced nervously over at the new guy again.

"Sophie, I want you to meet Adam Resnick. He's here to speak to you."

She blinked in surprise, and her gaze rapidly went from man to man. Garrett as usual stood there looking like you could break a rock on his face. The Resnick guy looked . . . eager, for lack of a better word. Sam looked . . . worried.

"To me?"

Her heart pounded harder. She broke out in a sweat, and she swallowed in vain at the knot in her throat. How would this man—whoever he was—know anything about her? Why would he want to talk to her?

Resnick stepped forward. "Sophie. Can I call you Sophie?"

She nodded stiffly and waited, her dread increasing with each second.

"I'm with . . . Well let's just say I represent the interests of the United States government, and I'd like to talk to you about your father."

She sucked in her breath, and her shocked gaze went to Sam. He'd sold her out. He'd actually sold her out! Sam frowned and reached out for her, but she flinched away, putting half the room between them.

For a long moment she stood, fists clenched, facing away from the occupants of the room. When she turned, she refused to look at Sam. She directed her gaze at Resnick and asked in a cold voice, "What do you want to know?"

Resnick moved toward her, and she took a quick step back. Her chin went up, and she forced calm she didn't feel.

"Where is he now?"

"I don't know," she said truthfully.

"Okay, where is he likely to be? If you'd give us information on his holdings we can match it to what we know of him. Maybe we're missing something."

"I don't know."

Resnick made a sound of frustration. "What *can* you tell us, Sophie? If you cooperate fully, we'll make allowances for you."

A chill went down her spine.

"Resnick," Sam growled.

Sophie ignored Sam and stared straight at Resnick. "Allowances? What sort of allowances should I expect? What is it you're threatening me with?"

Resnick held up his hands. "I'm not threatening you. I'm merely pointing out that we can do more to help you if you cooperate with us."

"Oh nice," she said bitterly. "What you're saying is I'm

on my own unless I play nice with the FBI or CIA or whoever the hell you are. You know what? I'm fine with that.
I never should have relied on anyone but myself anyway."

"Sophie," Sam cut in, his voice hard enough to direct
her gaze toward him. "He doesn't speak for me."

"You're wrong, Sam." She pressed her hands to the
sides of her legs to keep them from shaking. She stared
at him unflinchingly as she delivered her judgment. "The
moment you brought him here, he spoke for you."

"Sophie, damn it."

She looked away again, anger vibrating in her throat.
She wasn't getting into this with him in front of others—
or anytime.

"I'm asking you to help me," Resnick said. "He's hurt
a lot of people. As his daughter you know this. We think
he's trying to put together technology to build a nuclear
weapon and auctioning it to the highest bidder. He has to
be stopped."

"He never—that is he doesn't—confide in me. I'm not
privy to the details of his business dealings," she said
stiffly.

"Okay, yes, I understand that," he said in a placating
tone. "But there are things you can tell us about him,
small details that you might not think will help."

"Tomas is who you should be looking for."

Resnick blinked in surprise and then looked at the
others, as if gauging their reaction to her statement.

"Why is that? We were led to believe that Tomas had
no power whatsoever."

She stared coolly at him, her hands still tight against
her sides. "You asked, I told you. He wants me dead, but
maybe you don't care about that."

Resnick stared intently at her. "Is he dead, Sophie? Did Tomas kill Alex in an attempt to seize power? Is that why he's after you now, because you're Alex's heir? Or do you have something he wants?"

The blood left Sophie's face. She willed herself to keep it together. Her stomach revolted, and now her skin felt hot and clammy.

"If you'll excuse me, I need to go to the bathroom."

She bolted, ignoring Sam's worried question as to whether she was okay. Okay? How could she be okay when she'd been played for the biggest fool ever?

God, when was she going to stop being so damn trusting?

Hearing footsteps behind her, she slammed the bathroom door behind her and locked it. Last thing she needed was Sam hovering over her.

"Sophie," he called through the door. "Damn it, Sophie, open the door so I can see if you're all right."

She leaned over the sink and breathed deeply, sucking air through her nostrils as she fought the urge to puke. She sensed Sam's presence for several more seconds before she finally heard him retreat and walk back down the hall.

She splashed water on her face and stared at her reflection in the mirror until she was sure she didn't look like she was about to fall apart. She looked down at her hands and raised them in front of her and waited for the shaking to stop. When she was satisfied she could hold it together for however long this "questioning" lasted, she opened the door and quietly walked back into the hall.

When she reached the end, Resnick's words stopped her cold in her tracks.

"I have to take her in. You know that, Sam. She's too valuable to let go. She knows something. Even you can see that."

Fear nearly knocked her to her knees. A dull roar started in her ears as her blood pounded furiously. Hell if she'd escape her uncle only to fall prey to some government lackey who was eager to put a notch in his belt by taking down the Mouton family.

She didn't escape one prison only to enter another. Her child would have a better life than she had, and she'd do anything to ensure that. She already had.

She turned, her mind working frantically for an escape route. There were windows in the bedrooms, but she certainly hadn't inspected them to see if they opened. Now seemed a good enough time.

"YOU are out of your goddamn mind," Sam snarled. "Sophie stays with me and that's nonnegotiable."

Resnick blew out his breath and dragged a hand through his hair. "Look, Sam, I don't have a choice in this. This is a matter of national security. Surely you can see that. I have to do whatever it takes to stop Mouton, even if that means taking his daughter into custody. Hell, I'm not going to hurt her. I'd make sure she was taken care of. She'd have the best medical care for her and the baby."

Sam grabbed Resnick by the collar and slammed him against the wall. "My child. Mine. That's *my* baby and Sophie's my woman. I don't give a fuck about what your superiors are saying. She stays under my protection."

Garrett stuck an arm between Sam and Resnick and

pried Sam away. "Cool it, Sam. You two need to chill the fuck out. This isn't helping."

Sam jerked away and cupped a hand over the back of his neck as he paced across the room.

"Christ, Sam, you have to know my hands are tied here," Resnick said.

Garrett held his hands up. "I think Mouton is dead, and I think Sophie knows it."

Sam and Resnick both glanced sharply at Garrett.

"We have that as one of the possible scenarios," Resnick said. "But what makes *you* say that?"

"Sophie's been holding back from the start. She's been as jumpy as a cricket, but she's slipped up a few times and referred to her father in the past tense. She's said nothing of him being after her, but she's mentioned the uncle. What if you're right about Tomas making a power play? He kills Alex, maybe even tries to kill Sophie in the takeover. She escapes, Tomas catches up to her, puts a bullet hole in her, and she comes to Sam for help and protection."

"It's plausible," Resnick said. "It's something I've considered, but the only thing that makes no sense to me is why there is such an emphasis on Sophie. Women have never meant anything in Alex's empire. They're used and discarded or kept under tight wraps, as I suspect Sophie has been. If she escaped, while Tomas might be annoyed, I can't imagine him risking so much to pursue her on U.S. soil."

"Unless she has something he wants," Sam said grimly.

Garrett nodded. "Exactly."

Sam started to head toward the bathroom, but he stopped. Impatience simmered in his veins, but he had to handle this just right. He'd hurt Sophie by keeping this from her. She wasn't going to be very cooperative now because he'd lost her trust.

For the hundredth time he questioned his decision to allow Resnick to meet with Sophie. He hadn't wanted to anger a man who handed them so many of their missions, but in agreeing, he'd placed business ahead of his child, and that made him a huge dumbass.

He'd hoped that Sophie wouldn't know anything, Resnick would be satisfied, and then he'd leave and Sophie would be free of any "interest to national security." That wasn't going to happen now, and he was going to have to contend with a woman who felt betrayed.

P.J. scanned the area in two-minute intervals, her eyes peeled for anything that wasn't supposed to be. It was a damn boring job, but she never allowed boredom to interfere. A single lapse could cost lives, and she'd had to learn patience the hard way when she'd worked in SWAT.

Some lessons you learned by the book. Others you learned from cold hard experience. The latter may not be the best way to learn, but it damn well stuck.

She swept the perimeter again, and when she got to the house, she stopped, not believing what she was seeing.

"Well hello," she murmured.

Sophie was climbing out the window. Impressive for a pregnant lady. P.J. had always imagined pregnancy making a woman awkward as hell and about as graceful as a moose, but Sophie made quick work of the window and ran like a rabbit for the woods.

Shit.

"Steele, we've got a problem. Subject is escaping into the woods. Heading north. Fast."

"Say again?"

Yeah, she didn't believe it either.

She repeated the information and heard Steele's soft curse.

"Dolphin, you're with me. Cole, you and P.J. stay on lookout, and P.J., relay that to Sam. Tell him Dolphin and I are on it."

"You two always have all the fun while I get stuck in the trees," she complained. Not that she really wanted to mess with a pregnant woman. There was too much similarity between them and pit bulls for her liking.

She'd take on a man anytime, thank you very much.

She tapped the button to switch from the privacy of her communication with her team and then fired a message Sam's way.

CHAPTER 21

"SHE *what*?" Sam demanded.

He yanked the receiver from his ear and stalked down the hallway to the bathroom. Son of a bitch. Son of a bitch! The bathroom was empty. So was the bedroom. Only the cracked window told him the story as P.J. relayed it.

"Goddamn."

"What's going on?" Garrett demanded from the doorway.

Resnick stood to the side of Garrett, his brow drawn in concern.

"She's gone. She went out the window. P.J. saw her running into the woods. Steele and Dolphin are in pursuit."

Resnick swore, and it set Sam off. He closed the distance between them and slammed Resnick against the wall in the hallway.

"You stay away from her. You leave here and you forget you ever knew she existed, you got me?"

"I can't do that, Sam. You know that."

"Do it for me."

Resnick blew out his breath and sagged. "Goddamn it, Sam. What a time to call in a favor."

Sam let go of his shirt. "We have to get moving. Sophie is out there. She probably thinks I'm set to turn her in."

The peal of Sam's cell phone stopped him as he strode down the hall. Seeing Rio's number on the LCD, he jerked it to his ear.

"Sam here."

"Sam, we need to talk. I have a situation."

Shit. Fear slithered down his spine and his grip tightened on the phone.

"Can it wait? Sophie took off. Dolphin and Steele have gone after her. Garrett and I need to go as well."

"No, it can't wait."

Sam glanced up at Garrett.

"I'll go after her," Garrett said.

"I can help," Resnick offered.

Garrett shook his head. "You show your face, she'll run hard in the other direction. You stay here with Sam until we can get you the hell out of here."

"I feel so valued," Resnick said dryly.

Garrett ignored him and hurried out the door.

Sam turned away and put the phone back to his ear. "Talk to me, Rio. Make it fast."

"It's bad, Sam. Your father had a heart attack."

Sam stumbled and had to catch himself on the kitchen cabinets. "What?"

"He's in ICU. They're monitoring him closely."

There was a pause.

"What else? Just say it," Sam demanded.

God, don't let him die. Don't let his dad die.

"Your mom's gone missing."

"What? What the hell? What do you mean she's gone missing? She'd never be anywhere but at Dad's side."

"I know. Goddamn it I know, Sam. I'm sorry. I've let you down. I still don't know how the hell it happened. I wouldn't even let her ride in the ambulance with him to the hospital. I told her that she and Rusty weren't to go anywhere without me. Period. I took them myself. My men are here in the family room. I requested something private. We have tight security around the intensive care unit. I have someone at all possible entries. Your mom was allowed in to see him a couple of hours ago. She came out and Donovan went in. She seemed to be okay. She spoke to Rusty for a few minutes and then excused herself to go to the restroom. I sent a man with her. He stood outside the door. When they didn't return, I found him dead inside one of the stalls and your mom was nowhere to be found. I'm going over hospital surveillance now, and I have the rest of my team turning the hospital inside out."

"Jesus. Son of a bitch!"

He'd never felt more out of control in his life. Everything was crumbling around him and he felt helpless to stop it.

"I want this son of a bitch," Rio seethed. "The bastard preys on helpless women. First Sophie and now Marlene. He killed one of my men."

"I don't know what he wants, but I expect we'll find out shortly," Sam said. "I just hope to hell he'll want to negotiate."

His gut knotted and he wanted to puke. His hand

shook around the phone, and he mashed it against his ear
to keep from dropping it.

"Make sure Rusty and my father are safe. Do whatever you have to do. I want you to keep me posted on his
condition. And for God's sake sit on Donovan and make
sure he doesn't do anything stupid. I'll be there as soon
as I can."

"I'll guard them with my life," Rio said softly. "I'm
sorry I let you down, Sam."

Sam closed his eyes and slowly pulled the phone away
from his ear.

"Is everything okay, Sam?"

He turned to see Resnick standing a few feet away, his
hands shoved into his pockets.

"He has her," he said hoarsely. "That bastard has my
mother. My father is in the hospital with a heart attack,
and that son of a bitch took her when she went to the
bathroom."

Resnick ran a hand back and forth over his head.
"Christ, Sam, I'm sorry."

Sam's fist curled into a tight fist and he rammed it into
the cabinet. The wood splintered and pain shot through
his hand.

"I have to go find Sophie. Then I have to go to my dad.
Then I'm going after this son of a bitch."

He stared Resnick down, letting the full force of his
fury bleed into his expression.

"You stay the hell out of my way. Make damn sure no
one makes a move on Mouton. Last thing I want is for
you guys to finally decide to make a move and have my
mother caught in the cross fire."

Resnick pulled a crumpled pack of cigarettes out of

his breast pocket and hastily shoved one into his mouth. He lit it and sucked in a deep breath. Then he exhaled, blowing a steady stream of smoke from his lungs.

"I can only buy you so much time, Sam. We can't allow whoever it is in charge—whether it's Alex or Tomas—to sell a fucking nuclear weapon to some shit-hole third world country with a terrorist agenda."

"I'll bring him down. Or I'll die trying."

Resnick nodded and sucked on his cigarette again. He paced around the living room in agitation, taking jerky drags and spewing the smoke in noisy exhalations.

Sam checked his sidearm, then reached for the rifle lying on the counter. He shoved his earpiece in and positioned the mic in front of his mouth.

"Report in. Any sign of Sophie yet? I'm coming out."

"Negative," Steele responded. "We're looking."

Sam swore and shoved out of the door.

SOPHIE huddled between two of the three large stone outcroppings and forced herself to slow her breathing. Her pulse thudded like a hammer, until all she could hear was her heartbeat and each breath, in and out.

She'd climbed over the tall stone face and slipped behind it in an effort to find a hiding place. Unless someone climbed up the same way she had, no one would find her here. She was protected on all sides and had enough room to stretch out in the craggy moss. It was damp and chilly, but she'd be safe here.

All she had to do was be patient. Sam would search for her. They'd fan out, cover the territory surrounding the cabin, and they'd gradually move outward until she was behind the search radius. If she could outlast them and they didn't find her, she could double back and escape undetected.

Her plan was brilliant, and she wasn't out running like a headless chicken, but it was only brilliant if it worked.

She stifled the hysterical laughter that threatened to bubble up. She'd had plenty of experience running. Hiding like some fugitive. But she hadn't imagined having to flee the man she'd trusted to protect her.

She drew her legs farther into her, molding them against her belly. She dropped her head to her knees as anger worked over her skin, hot and itchy.

If she hadn't gone to Sam, she wouldn't have felt hope. She wouldn't have touched the sun for one brief, shining moment, only to have that warmth and joy extinguished.

She'd been a fool, and now she not only had to keep ahead of her uncle, but she had to keep from being taken into custody and having God knows what done with her by whatever agency Resnick represented. If he represented one at all.

Goddamn them. Damn them all. Especially Sam.

Whoever Resnick was, the U.S. government wanted her father enough that they'd do whatever it took to achieve their goal. She was expendable. Her child was expendable. They might suspect her father was dead, but they didn't know it. Not yet. And while they could do nothing with the knowledge that she'd killed him, they could certainly use the information that he was dead to their advantage.

She leaned against the cool rock face and closed her eyes wearily. Just last night she'd lain in Sam's arms and summoned the courage to confess that she'd killed a man in cold blood. She already had so much working against her in Sam's eyes. What would he think about the mother of his child being a killer?

Then she'd woken up feeling certain that everything would be okay. Sam would understand. He wouldn't judge her. She would confess everything to him, he'd take the necessary steps to take her uncle out, and then she could live in safety—finally—with her child. Sam's child. They could be a family.

Only Sam had never had any intention of them being anything.

For hours she sat there, until her muscles screamed in protest. Her bladder ached and she grew twitchier with each passing minute. Still, she wouldn't move. Not yet. She'd wait until nightfall if it killed her.

She dozed lightly, her sleep interrupted every time she heard the slightest sound. Her neck was sore and her back was killing her. She had to shift her position.

Inch by inch, she adjusted, until she stretched her legs across the small area shielded by the rocks. A sigh of relief whispered past her lips as she curled on her side.

She looked upward to the sky, watching thin, wispy clouds roll by and the blue grow pale as the sun began to set. It wouldn't be much longer now. Her patience would be rewarded.

She slept again, and when she woke this time, she was surprised by the darkness surrounding her. She'd slept longer than she'd thought she would, and now she was disoriented as to time. It was well past dusk and already stars had popped above her. Maybe Sam had given up, or broadened the search radius such that he would be miles away by now.

She rolled to her knees, braced her palms on the ground and slowly pushed herself upward. Her knees creaked, her back popped, and her wound protested the strain she was putting on it.

For several seconds she stood and stretched, working the kinks out of her stiff body. She was cold and hungry, but she shrugged off both discomforts. Neither was new to her.

As carefully as possible, she climbed over the shortest rock facing, testing her footholds to make sure she didn't fall or make unnecessary noise.

On her way over, she slipped and landed with a thump that knocked the breath from her. She wrapped her arms around her belly and lay there, mentally examining herself for any injury.

After catching her breath, she picked herself up and stared around, trying to gain her bearings. It was dark as a well bottom and there was no moonlight to guide her. Good for not being seen. Not so good for being able to see.

She crept through the trees and the underbrush a lot slower and stealthier than she'd done hours before. She'd had all day to come up with a plan, but the only thing that stood out was that she had to find transportation. She couldn't make it on foot if she hoped to put any distance between her and her immediate threat.

When she was but a short distance from the cabin, she paused and rubbed at the stitch in her side. She could barely make out where the trees fell away, and she inched forward, trying to make out whether the lights were on in the cabin and if the trucks were still parked out front. She didn't know how stubborn Sam would be or how long he would persist in searching for her or if he'd searched at all.

"Going somewhere?"

She whirled around and slapped a hand over her mouth

to stanch the reflexive scream. The light from a flashlight blinded her, and she threw up her other arm to block it.

Poised for flight, she shot to the right, but Garrett's hand snapped around her wrist, and he hauled her up short.

"Let me go," she said desperately.

"You're going to hurt yourself. Stop struggling," he said in a calm voice.

Tears knotted her throat. "Damn you."

The light went down, and then he turned it upward so the immediate area was illuminated. She expected his face to be his usual thundercloud, but he wasn't frowning.

"Let me go," she pleaded. "You don't even like me. You haven't liked me from the beginning. Let me go and I'll never bother you or Sam again. But at least give me a chance to protect my baby."

Something that looked like regret and unease flashed across his face. His features softened and his grip lessened on her arm. For a moment hope sparked in her chest. He was going to let her go. But when she tried to pull away, his grip tightened again.

"Listen to me, Sophie. Sam is frantic with worry. Whatever you heard or think you heard, he isn't about to sell you out."

"He already did," she said bitterly. "I shouldn't have expected anything else. He doesn't owe me anything. I was just some chick he picked up in a bar. Knocking me up wasn't part of the deal."

"If you knew Sam, you wouldn't be spouting that horse shit," Garrett said. "I get that you're hurt. I get that you feel betrayed. But give him a chance to explain. We *will* protect you, but we can't do that if you take off on us."

" 'We'?" she questioned. "Are you including yourself in that promise?"

"I am," he said evenly.

"Why?" she blurted. "You've made no secret of the fact you despise me. You don't trust me. You don't want me anywhere near your brother."

"You're carrying my niece or nephew. You're important to Sam." There was resignation in his voice, as if acknowledging that left a bad taste in his mouth. "That makes you important to me."

She stared back at him and he met her gaze. There was no anger, none of the disapproval she'd grown so used to in his eyes. She swayed in his grip, suddenly so fatigued that she would have fallen if he hadn't reached his other hand out to steady her.

"Let me take you back, Sophie. You're tired, you're hurt and you have no business running like you've been running with you carrying a baby."

"I can't."

Her voice turned pleading, and she stared imploringly at him, hoping she could sway him.

"I can't go with that Resnick guy. Don't you understand? I'm expendable to him. I'm nothing in comparison to what they gain by taking down my family's network. They won't care about me or my baby. I want her to have better than I had. Please, just let me take care of my baby."

Garrett's entire face softened, but he didn't let go of her arms.

"I swear to you, Sophie, Sam will never allow Resnick to take you anywhere. That was never his intention. Not only that, *I* won't allow it. You have my word."

"You aren't really offering me a choice," she said dully.

He sighed. "No, I'm not. I'd like you to come back willingly, but if you don't, I'll be forced to bring you back by whatever means necessary."

Her chin dropped and she closed her eyes.

"All right," she accepted quietly.

CHAPTER 22

WHEN Garrett pushed into the cabin, Sophie saw that she and Garrett were the only two occupants. He closed the door behind them and shot her a look that suggested she not think of running again.

He gestured toward the table. "Have a seat. I'll get you something to eat and drink."

She sank wearily into a chair and folded her arms over the tabletop so she could rest her head. When Garrett set a glass of milk in front of her, she drank greedily and then returned her head to its perch. She closed her eyes and rested while Garrett rummaged around in the refrigerator. She was hungry, but she was too tired to eat.

A moment later, the door burst open, startling her from her lethargy. She bolted upright to see Sam stalk in, his eyes blazing. She barely had time to register her alarm before he was in front of her.

He yanked her to her feet, cupped one hand around her nape and then dragged her to him. He kissed her long and hard, his mouth molded so tight to hers that neither of them could draw a breath.

She inserted her hands between them and shoved as hard as she could. He didn't budge. Instead he deepened his kiss, as if convincing her of his ownership.

His tongue flashed over hers. Warm, wet, tasting. His fingers rubbed firmly over the column of her neck and then up into her hair, tangling with the strands.

Finally he drew away, but he kept a hold on her nape as he stared down at her through half-lidded eyes.

"Don't ever scare me like that again," he said in a low voice.

She tried to pull away again, but he cupped his other hand to her cheek and smoothed his thumb over her swollen lips.

"I know I hurt you, Sophie. I'm sorry. Sorrier than I can say. I don't have time to explain everything to you now. I hope you'll understand that."

With that, he turned and strode toward Garrett. She listened in horror as he told his brother that Frank had had a heart attack and that their mother had been abducted from the hospital.

She swayed and had to brace herself against the table. She didn't chance looking at either man. She couldn't bear to see the rage in Garrett's eyes. Rage that would be directed at her.

Nausea boiled in her stomach like acid, and she gulped breaths through her mouth. Her chest heaved, and she closed her eyes before finally sinking back into the chair.

All she wanted to do was bury her face in her arms and weep.

"Sophie, we need to go."

She raised her head to see Sam standing by the table, his expression grim. Beyond him, Garrett was already striding from the cabin.

"Where?" she croaked out.

"Back home. To my father. I need to see him and then we have to find my mom."

She shakily rose, nodding her agreement. Of course they had to go. She went out ahead of Sam and nearly ran into Garrett at the bottom of the steps. He grasped her arm to steady her before Sam took over and ushered her to the truck.

The ride was silent and tense. The two men didn't speak. Garrett stared moodily out the window while Sam's gaze remained fixed on the road.

She alternated feeling guilty for bringing her uncle to their doorstep and feeling angry for feeling guilty. Her uncle going after Sam and his family was inevitable. Once Sophie had been caught, her uncle would have taken steps to eradicate the Kellys.

But now she needed to give Sam all the necessary ammunition to take the fight to her uncle and hopefully rescue his mother in the process. She prayed that Marlene would be kept alive. If her father were still in charge, Marlene would have already been killed and left for Sam and his family to find as a message. Her uncle wasn't as ruthless as her father, though. Not that he didn't try to be. He was just weaker. He wanted to be seen as someone who was strong and as capable of running a criminal empire as her father, but not many men were. Alex Mouton had had no conscience when he was living, and Sophie could only hope he was consigned to hell in death.

She pressed her lips together and inhaled deeply through her nose. Then she straightened in her seat and pushed away from the window so she could readily see both men from her position in the back.

"My father is dead."

Sam's head came up to look at her in the rearview mirror at the same time Garrett whipped around to stare at her.

"You're sure of this?" Sam demanded. "This is important, Sophie. We have to know for sure. We can't afford to assume anything."

"Did you see his body?" Garrett cut in.

"I saw," she said softly. "I'm the one who killed him."

Sam braked suddenly and pulled onto the shoulder. He shoved the truck into park but left the engine turning. Then he rotated around so he too could stare back at her.

"You want to run that by me again?"

"I killed him. I shot him to be exact."

"Holy fuck," Garrett muttered.

Sam closed his eyes and pinched the bridge of his nose in a gesture of frustration.

"You shot him."

"Yes."

"Christ, is that why your uncle is after you? Revenge?" Garrett asked.

"I have something he wants."

She chased the tremble from her voice, refusing to wimp out now that she'd boldly made her confession.

Sam immediately became more alert. His eyes sharpened, then narrowed.

"What do you have, Sophie?"

"They key to my father's vault."

Garrett frowned harder. "And? That has significance why?"

"The vault houses my father's wealth. Not only his wealth, but all the details of his business transactions, his contacts, prototypes of the weapons he has developed over the years. Your Mr. Resnick was concerned about the idea of him developing nuclear technology. If he has, the details are there with everything else."

"And he just keeps this shit locked in a vault?" Garrett asked incredulously.

She almost smiled. "It's not just any vault. It's an underground, state-of-the-art, completely secure, climate-controlled vault. And when I say vault, don't imagine some bank vault–type thing, something you could maybe fit a car into. This is a vast compound. It's a huge chamber with only one way in and one way out. And once you enter, you can't exit the way you came in. It's all one way."

"And you have the key to this. He just left this lying around for anyone to get," Sam said.

Ignoring the sarcasm, she nodded once again. "I cut it from his neck with the knife you left in the hotel room. After I shot him. It was my insurance policy. It was my way of making sure I stayed alive. I knew they'd come after me for killing my father. They'd hunt me down and they'd dispatch me like they would any other enemy.

But I wouldn't die quickly. Because I'm blood and I betrayed my blood, they'd make my death long and painful. Because I turned on my father, I'd be made to suffer until I begged for death. That key prevents them from killing me. If they find me, they have to take me alive or risk never retrieving the only way into Alex's vast underground network of wealth and business. Tomas can only temporarily take over as leader of the Mouton family 'business.' Soon he'll run out of resources, money and support. Without a way into my father's vault, Tomas will be nothing."

"Christ," Sam swore. "He keeps that shit in a vault? It's insane."

She raised an eyebrow. "How so? He deals in gold. Gems. Untraceable wealth. He doesn't trust banks. He never leaves records of his transactions. Everyone else? He keeps meticulous accounts of everyone he's ever had dealings with. In his books he has the names of countless world leaders, many from the West who would die were their crimes to come to light. Many would kill for this key. I never plan to give it up."

Garrett blew out his breath and looked over at Sam. "Hoo boy, this just got a hell of a lot more complicated."

"Can you drive for a while, Garrett? We can't afford to get held up. We've got to get to Dad."

In response Garrett got out and walked around to the driver's door. He waited for Sam to slide out before he settled into the driver's seat. Instead of going around to where Garrett had been sitting as Sophie had expected, Sam opened the door next to her and slid in beside her.

Garrett pulled back onto the road, and Sophie sat

staring at Sam, dreading his scrutiny. Dreading the inevitable questions. And the change in the way he'd look at her from now on.

She slowly bowed her head and stared down at her fingers curled so tightly together in her lap.

"What did he do to you, Sophie?"

Her head came up in surprise. That wasn't what she'd expected him to say or ask.

"What do you mean?"

"Why did you shoot him?"

"Because he needed killing."

"I believe you killed him," Sam said softly. "But I don't believe for a moment that you killed him to rid humanity of a first-rate bastard."

"Then you don't know me very well," she taunted. "I killed him for just that reason. He's a bastard. He's a cold, calculating sociopath. Life means nothing to him. Everyone's but his. I took from him the one thing he valued. His own life. It was the only thing he was passionate about."

She hadn't realized that Sam's hand had slid up her arm until he rested his palm against the curve of her neck, waiting until she hushed her tirade. Suddenly he was caressing her skin, soothing some of the horrible tension emanating from her.

"And I took the key because it meant no one could take over his legacy."

"That was a pretty damn stupid . . . brave . . . thing to do," Garrett said grudgingly. "More stupid, mind you, but still amazingly brave."

"Where is the key now?" Sam asked.

He kept his voice as even as the light caresses he feathered over her skin. But she didn't want to talk about the key. She wanted to know why he'd set her up with Resnick. If his father hadn't had a heart attack and his mother hadn't been abducted, would Sophie even now be on her way to some dark hole the U.S. government would put her in, where she'd never be seen or heard from again?

It was obvious Sam was going to need her now. Now that circumstances had changed so drastically and it was likely he was going to need to trade Sophie for the one thing that mattered the most to him.

She tried not to think about how much that hurt. It seemed everywhere she ended up, she was expendable.

"Why Resnick?" she asked hoarsely. "Why did you lie?"

"I didn't lie."

"You withheld information. Same thing."

His mouth curled into a snarl. "Let's not get into withholding information, Sophie. You've been holding out on me from the start."

She bared her teeth and pushed forward into his space. "Exactly what was I supposed to do, Sam? Show up on your doorstep, say hey I'm pregnant, and oh by the way, you're the father, and since I know how much you hate your potential father-in-law, I shot him down in cold blood and then ran like hell?

"I'm thinking you wouldn't have been very receptive. I think you would have packed me off to Resnick even faster than you ended up doing. I think you would have backed off me so quick that you would have broken a leg doing so."

She sighed and fought the exhaustion that beat at her so relentlessly.

"Just tell me why, Sam. Don't answer my questions with accusations. I'm sure we have plenty to accuse each other of."

"Goddamn," Sam bit out. "Sophie, I had to agree to let Resnick question you. He wields a lot of power. I couldn't say no. It was obvious you were holding something back. Something that scared the bejesus out of you, and Resnick was convinced you could give him information that would help him. Now I see why he thought that."

He paused and slid both hands under her neck and delved into the thickness of her hair with his fingers.

"But honey, listen to me. Never. Never was there even a remote chance that I'd let him take you away from me. He was there to ask you a few questions. I was there to pacify him by cooperating. I didn't lie to you when I said I'd protect you."

His voice lowered until it was barely above a whisper and no one but the two of them could hear.

"I didn't lie to you when I said I needed you."

He leaned in until his forehead pressed to hers. Then he kissed the tip of her nose.

"You and I both know we have a lot to work out. But we can't do it if we aren't together, Sophie. We can't do it if I can't be with you to make sure you're safe and that our child is protected from your bastard uncle. I need you to trust me and I know that's asking a lot."

She raised her gaze until she stared up at him. "I need you to trust *me*, Sam. You want and expect a lot from me, but you aren't willing to give me anything in return."

He brushed his hand over her cheek and smoothed away her hair. If he'd answered right away, she wouldn't have believed him. She would have thought he was saying whatever it took in that moment to persuade her. But he stayed silent for a long moment, and then finally, he tilted her head so that their gazes were locked.

"I do trust you, Sophie. My gut tells me that I believe you, but my head is screaming I'm a fool. I'm sorry if that hurts you, but I'm being one hundred percent honest with you."

"Just tell me you believe I never betrayed you," she whispered. "That you know I didn't whore myself for my father."

His gaze softened and he kissed her, just a light smooch to the lips, and then he raised his mouth to press a kiss to her forehead.

"I believe you, Sophie."

She wrapped her arm around him and burrowed into his chest. He held her tightly against him while she absorbed his warmth and strength.

"I'm scared, Sam."

He rubbed her back and dropped a kiss on the top of her head. "I know, honey. I am too."

"He's going to demand the key. He'll want me back. I have to go. If it had been my father, he would have already killed your mother, but Tomas will try to trade. He's desperate. He just wants the key . . . and me."

Sam tensed beneath her. His arms tightened painfully around her. "This is where I need you to trust me, Soph. I'm not handing you and my child back over to that bastard, but neither will I leave my mother. I'll find a way. I swear it."

She pulled away and braced herself against his chest so she could look into his eyes. All she saw was unwavering determination. She wasn't as convinced as he was, but she knew he believed absolutely in what he was saying.

She put a hand on his face and smoothed her fingers over the lines carved deep into his brow. "I know you will."

And she prayed with everything she had that he would.

CHAPTER 23

THE convoy of SUVs rolled into the narrow alley at the side of the rural hospital. Rio strode from the building, his mouth set into a grim line. He came immediately to greet Garrett and Sam as they stepped from the truck.

"How is he?" Sam demanded.

"Stable. He was awake for a while. A little disoriented. Asked where your mom was. Donovan is with him. I don't know if he's told him about your mother yet."

"Stable?" Garrett parroted. "He's still in ICU, though, right?"

"He'll remain in ICU until the cardiologist releases him. They want to monitor him closely, but they've listed his condition as stable. I'm sure the doctor can tell you more than me."

Sam reached into the truck for Sophie's hand and pulled her out beside him. Rio, Garrett and Sam formed a protective circle around her while Steele and the others brought up the rear. When they reached the inside of the hospital, Sam paused briefly to issue a directive to Rio.

"Give Steele and his team the report. Coordinate your efforts. I want my family safe. We can't allow another breach in security."

Rio nodded, and Sam could see the wash of guilt in his eyes.

He put his hand on his team leader's shoulder. "I don't blame you, Rio."

Rio didn't react or respond. Sam knew he wouldn't. He dropped his hand away and curled his arm around Sophie once more.

"I want Sophie to see a doctor while we're here," he said to Garrett as they hurried toward the elevator. "After we see Dad."

They shoved into an elevator, and Sam pulled Sophie even closer. She trembled against him, and her eyes looked so sorrowful. The same guilt he'd seen in Rio's gaze he saw in Sophie's.

He squeezed her hand. It was all he could offer right now. Words weren't good enough, and until he could see his dad, his tongue would be so knotted he couldn't speak anyway.

When the elevator doors opened and he saw the sign overheard pointing the way to the intensive care unit, fear squeezed his chest so tight he felt light-headed.

Rio had said he was stable. That was good, right? But he'd had a heart attack. A serious one. Did it mean he could have another? Was his heart damaged?

He didn't want to imagine a world without his dad in

it. Growing up, his dad had been his rock. He'd been the rock of six rambunctious, rowdy boys, and he'd infused his core values into all of them.

Be a good man, have honor and integrity, protect those weaker than you, and never suffer injustice.

Those values had formed the cornerstone of KGI.

He hadn't realized he'd stopped outside the entrance to the family room until Sophie's small hand circled his and squeezed.

The ache in his chest intensified until he felt bogged down with emotion. Sorrow. Fear. Anger.

Oh God, he couldn't lose his father. Not Dad. And his mom. Oh God. It took everything in him to stand there, steady, and not break as he stared at the closed door to the room.

Garrett turned to him, and he saw that his brother fared no better than he did. They were both supposedly so tough. The older brothers. Leaders. Sam felt like a fraud.

Then Sophie reached out and touched Garrett lightly on the arm. It was a simple gesture that softened some of the raw grief in Garrett's eyes. Garrett reached for her hand and gave it a quick squeeze.

"Thanks," he murmured.

Sam nodded toward the door. "Let's go in. I want to see him as soon as I know how Rusty and Sean are doing."

When they entered, Sam saw Rusty seated in the far corner, her face splotchy and her arms hugged around her drawn-up knees. Sean was standing across the room, hands shoved into his pockets, and two of Rio's men stood guard just inside the door.

When Rusty saw them, she shot to her feet. Fists

clenched at her sides, she stormed over to where Sam stood.

"You promised you'd keep them safe! You left them!" she accused, her voice ravaged by tears.

She turned her furious stare to Sophie and then back again at Sam. "This is all her fault, isn't it? She's the reason you took off and why you left them unprotected. They could die. They could all die."

Sam moved from Sophie so she was behind him, and he reached for Rusty. She tried to pull away, but he hauled her against his chest and wrapped his arms around her.

She struggled but he held on, and finally she went limp against him and broke into heartrending sobs. She wept against his neck, and her entire body shook uncontrollably.

"Shhh," Sam said as he stroked her hair. "Dad's going to make it, Rusty. You know how ornery he is. Can you imagine a heart attack ever taking him out? It would require a tank, and even then my money would be on him."

"What about Marlene?" she sobbed. "They believed in me. They're the only people who ever gave a damn about me."

Sam swallowed back his own tears and hugged her fiercely. It was the first time he'd ever reached out to Rusty in the almost year she'd been with his family. He and his brothers tolerated her much like a splinter. Annoying but there. They'd indulged Marlene's motherly fits over her just like they indulged her mothering everyone else in the world. But they hadn't ever accepted her. Only Marlene and Frank Kelly had done that.

"We'll get her back, Rusty. I swear it. We'll get her back."

He led her over to the sofa against the wall and eased

her down. She covered her face with her hands as though she were ashamed that he'd seen her cry.

"Rusty, look at me," he said gently.

Slowly her chin lifted and her haunted eyes found his.

"I know you're angry. I am too. But Dad needs you to be strong for him, especially now that Mom is missing. I swear to you I'll bring her home."

"You swore you'd keep us safe," she said bitterly.

Sam sighed. "Rusty, you're old enough to know that shit happens. Playing the blame game gets you nowhere. If it makes you feel better to blame me, then by all means do so. It won't change a damn thing, though. If I have to move hell to find my mother, then that's what I'll do."

Tears crowded her eyes again and her face crumpled. "I'm sorry. I'm sorry. I'm just so scared. If I lose them . . ."

She broke away and buried her face in her hands.

Sam pulled her against his chest again. "You will always have a home," he said quietly. "No matter what."

She jerked her head up and stared at him, tears sloshing over the rims of her eyes. "Do you mean that?"

"I wouldn't say it if I didn't."

She smiled, really smiled, and it occurred to Sam that it was the first sign of true joy he'd ever witnessed from her. She was always so reserved and on guard. Way tougher than a girl her age should ever have to be.

"Thank you," she whispered.

"I need you to promise me something now."

She cocked her head. "What?"

"You don't go anywhere, even to the bathroom, without an armed escort. No exceptions. I can't focus on getting Mom back if I have two people to rescue. Okay?"

Her face fell at the mention of Marlene, but she bit her lip and nodded. "I promise."

He rose, leaving her on the couch. Before walking away, he reached down and squeezed her hand. "I'll be back. I need to see Dad."

Sophie was standing where he'd left her. She was pale, her face drawn, and she looked like she'd have preferred to fade into the wall.

Garrett was absent, probably gone back to see their father already. Rio stepped into the waiting room, and Sam went to meet him. He reached for Sophie and pulled her into his side when he stopped in front of Rio.

"Watch over them for me," he said in a low voice. "I'm going back to see Dad and then we have to put our heads together."

"Steele and I are working on it," Rio said. "Sean coordinated with the local and state police and they set up roadblocks within an hour of her abduction. If I had to guess, I'd say they left by air. There were reports of two helicopters in the area and we're trying to run down information on both."

Sam reached up to touch Sophie's cheek. "Stay here with Rio. Don't go anywhere without him, okay?"

Sophie looked uneasy as she glanced over at Rio, but she nodded.

Sam glanced at Rio one more time and Rio nodded. Then Sam walked out of the room and to the door that led to the glass-enclosed rooms in the intensive care unit.

It took a moment for a nurse to answer his summons, and when he told her he was there to see Frank Kelly, she informed him there were already two visitors with him.

Sam ran a hand through his hair in frustration. "I just

got here. I have to see him. My brothers are with him. I'd like to be there with them. Please."

Her face softened and she glanced back toward the nurses' station. "Come with me."

He followed her to the far end of the unit, to the last cubicle on the right. She paused at the door and motioned him in.

"I can't let you stay long. If the charge nurse comes back, she'll insist on the two-visitor limit."

"Thank you," Sam said.

He nudged the already ajar door and stared at his father lying motionless on the bed, wires and tubes and machines everywhere.

Garrett was sitting on one side of their dad with a chair drawn up to the very edge of the bed, while Donovan was slumped in a chair on the other side. When Donovan looked up and saw Sam, he immediately got up and walked over.

After a moment's hesitation, Sam enfolded Donovan in a bear hug.

"How is he?" Sam whispered.

Donovan drew away and murmured low, "He's woken up a few times. First time he asked for Ma. At first I don't think he had any idea what had happened."

"And now?"

"He knows," Donovan said grimly.

Sam closed his eyes. Then he nudged by Donovan and went to his father's bedside. Garrett looked up, his eyes bleak.

Sam eased into Donovan's chair and leaned forward until he grasped his father's hand. It shocked him how weak and human Frank Kelly looked lying so pale in the bed.

"Dad," he said softly. "It's Sam. Garrett and I are here. Can you hear us?"

To his surprise, his dad's eyelids twitched and fluttered open. For a moment he stared at Sam as if not recognizing him. Then his lips parted.

"Sam."

It barely came out as a whisper. More as a raspy sigh than an actual word but it was the sweetest sound Sam had ever heard. Tears burned his eyes when his dad carefully turned his hand in Sam's until he could curl his fingers around Sam's palm.

Slowly Frank turned his head until he locked onto Garrett.

"Garrett? Is that you?"

Garrett leaned forward and grasped his father's other hand. "I'm here, Dad."

"Where's Van?"

"He's here too," Sam said. "Standing right here behind me."

"Get your mother back. Don't worry about me. I'll be fine. You go get your mother. Bring her home to me." Pain spasmed across Frank's face and a tear rolled down his wrinkled cheek. "I've never been without her. Not in forty years."

"We'll find her," Sam vowed. "You just concentrate on getting well so when she gets home you're not stuck here in the hospital."

Frank nodded. "Ethan and Rachel. Are they safe?"

"Yes, they're fine. I need . . . I need to tell Ethan about Mom."

Frank shook his head. "No. You leave them as far away from this as you can. He has no business bringing

Rachel home and into danger. You boys will find Marlene. I have every faith in you."

"I love you, Dad," Sam said as the knot grew bigger in his throat. "Take care of yourself please."

"Love you too, son. Be careful."

Frank seemed to sag deeper into the bed. His face was gray, and he looked exhausted by the few minutes of talking. Alarmed, Sam called for the nurse. She came in immediately and did an assessment.

"He's overtired. You really should leave him to rest now."

Reluctantly Sam rose and filed out of the room with his brothers. They gathered in the family waiting room, where Steele, P.J., Cole and Dolphin had joined Rio and his men. Rusty still sat on the sofa, her hands curled tightly in her lap, and Sophie had retreated to the far corner and stood with her arms wrapped around her waist, as if protecting herself and her baby from the world.

Despite his need to talk to his men, Sam left the knot of people and walked to where Sophie stood. He had a very real need to touch her, to feel her against him. He ran his hands up her arms and then carefully pulled her into his embrace.

"Is he okay?" she asked anxiously. "I mean I know he's not okay, but will he be?"

He kissed her lightly on the lips. "I think so. He looks bad, and he's worried about Mom, but I think that worry is what will keep him fighting."

Her face fell. "I'm sorry, Sam. This is all my fault. I should have stayed away longer. I shouldn't have come at all. I knew . . ." She sucked in a wavering breath. "I knew what would happen, that my uncle would come after you, but—"

He put a finger over her lips. "You most certainly should have come to me. I don't even want to imagine you out there still running, hurting, maybe even dead by now. We'll work this out, Soph. I don't want you blaming yourself. Put the blame where it belongs. On your father and your uncle."

She buried her face in his chest and clung fiercely to him. All his reservations melted away, and all he could see or feel was her. Where she belonged. With him. Him standing between her and the world.

A phone rang and Sam turned sharply to find the source. The community phone on the wall, the one for the family to use, rang loudly, interrupting the quiet in the small room.

Donovan picked it up and muttered a hello. His entire body tensed and his expression became dark and forbidding. His hand curled so tightly around the receiver that Sam could see his knuckles whiten.

Sam stepped away from Sophie just as Donovan extended the phone in his direction.

"It's Mouton. He wants to speak to you."

CHAPTER 24

SAM heard Sophie's gasp behind him. A dull roar began in his ears, and he crossed the room to snatch the phone from Donovan's hand without any realization that he'd done so.

"Sam Kelly," he barked.

Tomas Mouton was short and to the point. "I have something you want. You have something I want. If you want your mother back alive, you'll hand my niece over to me, and you better make damn sure she has what she stole from me."

Sam's lips curled into a snarl. "From you? Don't you mean what she stole from her father? Some would argue it's hers now. Are you taking over, Tomas? I didn't think you had the balls to run Alex's organization."

A low hiss was all he heard in response, and then he heard a startled cry. Feminine. His mother.

"Sam? Sam is that you?"

His heart fell. His hands and knees shook so bad he had to sit down on the couch.

"Mom, are you all right? Has he hurt you?"

Her voice was tight with anger. "No. I'm fine, son. He wants me to tell you to do what he says or he'll go after every member of our family." She broke off and there was a muffled sound as the phone was taken from her again.

Sam lifted his gaze and sought out Sophie, who stood as still as a statue across the room. Everyone else had turned to look at her as well, and she only grew paler.

Then, as if gathering herself, she straightened. Her eyes went flat and no hint of emotion was reflected in the cool blue. She strode to where he sat and extended her hand for the phone.

"Let me speak to him," she demanded in a low voice.

"Yes, Sam," Tomas demanded. "Let me speak with my beloved niece."

Slowly, Sam handed the receiver over to Sophie and watched her expression grow even colder as she put it to her ear.

He rose to stand beside her, but she turned away, and when he touched her shoulder, she flinched and shrugged him off.

"Tomas, this is Sophie. Listen to what I have to say and listen well. I have what you want. I'll bring you the key."

Sam lunged for the phone, but Sophie wrenched it from his grasp and backed away as far as the cord would allow. She angrily held up a finger to stop him and glared fiercely, a clear order for him not to interfere.

He stood there seething, his rage growing with each moment.

"If you harm Mrs. Kelly, if you so much as scratch her, I'll disappear with that key and I'll destroy it. You'll never find it. You'll never have access to my father's wealth or his dealings."

She paused for a moment and seemed to listen to something Tomas said. Sam tried to lean closer, but again she twisted away.

"Don't fuck with me, Tomas," she said softly. "I have nothing to lose. I'll come to you, but you get nothing until she's freed. Do we have a deal?"

She turned back to Sam and slid the phone down to her neck before finally handing it back to him. Sam jerked it away and put it to his ear, only to hear a dial tone.

He exploded. "Sophie, what the fuck?"

He was furious at her for agreeing to trade herself for his mother and furious because he knew nothing of the deal. No location, nothing. He hated the helpless feeling that gripped him, and he hated being dependent on Sophie for information.

"I did what needed to be done," she said calmly. "If it had been my father, your mother would already be dead."

The room erupted in various exclamations and curses. Garrett and Donovan pushed up next to Sophie, and both of them looked as furious as Sam felt.

"What the hell was that all about?" Donovan demanded.

Hurt flickered in Sophie's eyes for a brief second before she steeled herself once again and any emotion was lost as she stared first at Sam and then the others.

"Tomas isn't as disciplined as my father was. My father would have killed Marlene to send a message. He didn't negotiate. He didn't bargain. He demanded, and if his demands weren't met, he acted. Tomas is weaker.

It's why your mother is alive. All he wants, all he craves, is wealth and power, and with my father gone, he sees it all at his fingertips. Only I am standing in his way. His sights are on me. No one else matters. Not your mother, not you, not anyone else."

She said it so matter-of-factly that it could have been the weather they were discussing. Sam stared at her incredulously. Did she honestly believe he was going to throw her under the bus?

He stared at his brothers, who were still glaring at Sophie, but now he wasn't sure whether they were pissed because she'd so readily agreed to the trade or whether they were pissed because she'd taken control out of their hands.

"That was a goddamn stupid thing to do," Garrett all but roared at her.

She did flinch this time and took a step back. Garrett ignored it and stepped forward until he stared down at her from his full height.

"Do you honestly think any of us would just hand you and our niece or nephew over to that bastard? Are you out of your mind?"

Now she looked panicked, and her gaze jerked to Sam in a plea for help, only he didn't feel particularly helpful at the moment. He was too goddamn pissed.

Even Donovan, who from the beginning had treated her much more gently than Garrett, advanced on her with a deep scowl on his face.

"You may not realize it yet, but you're part of this family," Donovan all but snarled. "We'll find a way to take down that bastard and rescue our mother, but it won't be because we handed you over like a bunch of fucking pansies."

Sophie's eyes widened and tears shimmered there, turning the blue to liquid. Sam wasn't ready to rescue her yet. She needed to hear this, needed to understand what he himself hadn't been able to say yet. Maybe he hadn't realized it himself.

Steele stepped forward, and soon the remaining members of KGI formed a circle around her. She was trapped. Nowhere to run. No place she could deny her value.

"KGI doesn't hide behind a woman. Even one as courageous as yourself," Steele said in his quiet, stern voice.

Rio glanced at Steele in amusement before adding his own statement to the mix.

"And I rarely agree with anything Steele has to say, but in this I do. You may have never had anyone you could count on in the past, but you do now. And we're not going to let you do something foolish like walk into a certain death."

All the color leeched out of Sophie's cheeks. She looked stunned. She glanced frantically from face to face and then finally came back to Sam. She looked at him, her eyes pleading. For what? Confirmation? Understanding?

His heart turned over in his chest. Did she really not think she had any value except as a bargaining tool? His breath caught and held. Of course, she wouldn't. He hadn't given her any reason to believe differently. Things had gone so crazily fast in the days since he'd pulled her from the lake that he hadn't really given her presence in his life any thought beyond the immediacy of the here and now. He didn't even know if she wanted a place in his life. He hadn't offered her one. Hadn't made her believe in her value.

"Sophie, what did Tomas say?" Sam asked gently.

"What else did he say? About the exchange. Where are we supposed to make it?"

Some of the light left her eyes, but damn it, he couldn't tell her everything he wanted to tell her in front of all his men, and their first priority had to be the information.

Her voice was scratchy, and she wiped at her cheek with the back of her sleeve as she spoke.

"He's here. In the U.S."

"Where?" Garrett bit out.

"My father owned a large estate in West Texas. It's isolated and I'm sure the local law enforcement is on his payroll. He moved into places and took over. That's how he operated. Tomas took your mother there. He wants to make the exchange. We have forty-eight hours."

She looked up at Sam. "He wants you and me to go alone."

"Fuck that," Donovan muttered.

Sam turned to Donovan. "Do we have intel on a holding in Texas?"

"There were two to my knowledge," Donovan said.

Sam glanced back at Sophie. "Where, Sophie? Where are we going?"

"Rock Springs. Not far from Del Rio and the border."

Sam faced his men. "Okay, I want all the intel we can gather on this place. Sat imagery, the local climate, topo maps, the works. I want to know who takes a piss and when, and I want it yesterday. The clock is ticking. Garrett, you and Donovan need to get with Sean and see what kind of local cooperation we can have to keep this hospital locked down and provide protection for Rusty and Dad."

He sighed as the weight of their mission settled over

his shoulders. The mother of his child—and his child—
for the life of his mother? It didn't even bear thinking
about. If he had anything to do with it, it would never
come to that.

"Garrett," he said as his brother started to leave with
the others.

Garrett stopped and glanced back at Sam.

"Get on the horn with Resnick."

Sophie stiffened and turned away.

"Yeah, and?" Garrett said.

"Tell him to stay the fuck out of our way."

CHAPTER 25

SOPHIE was shaking so bad she was going to fall if she didn't sit down. Her senses were shattered, and she needed to get away from the overwhelming presence of so many people. There was no friendly welcome from Rusty, who sat isolated in the corner of the room, and Sam would never let her get a foot outside the door without him.

She'd never been more scared or more overwhelmed in her life.

Sam pressed in and put a hand on her shoulder. She jumped and skittered sideways, the light touch hard on her already frayed nerves.

"Sophie," he said softly. "I'm going to take you down the hall so a doctor can examine you."

Her baby. Yes, she wanted to make sure everything was okay with her baby.

Numbly she allowed Sam to lead her from the room.

He kept her tight to his side, and they only traveled three doors down to what looked to be a private doctor's lounge.

It was empty when they went inside, and he directed her to sit on one of the leather couches that lined the wall. Then he sat beside her and took her hands in his.

She stared down, watching as his fingers grazed lightly, soothingly over her palms.

"The doctor will be here in a moment. I wanted a chance to talk with you privately."

She raised her head in alarm.

He held her gaze, and she was surprised by the tenderness in his eyes. No anger. No judgment.

Never before had she felt quite so overwhelmed. The events of the last few minutes had somehow unhinged her. She felt so desperately adrift, and she was more afraid now than she'd been when she'd run so many months ago, and kept running.

Before, she'd had nothing to lose, and now? She stood to lose so much and maybe nothing at all.

Angered by the tears that slithered down her cheeks—had she done nothing but cry for the last hour?—she scrubbed at the wetness with the back of her hand and looked away so Sam wouldn't be witness to her awful, gut-wrenching weakness.

But he turned her back. Ever so gently, he touched her chin and brought her back around. He swiped at one damp trail with his thumb, and his gaze softened all the more as he stared into her eyes.

"I lied, you know," she said brokenly.

He looked startled by her admission. "About what?"

She pulled away from him and stood, unable to just sit

there when every muscle in her body fidgeted uncontrollably. She paced three steps and then stopped, her back to Sam. Her heart raced, and even as she wiped at the tears, she felt the uncontrollable urge to weep more.

"I gave you a bullshit line about why I killed my father, and maybe some of it was true. But I killed him for my mother. And now because of that, you could lose yours."

She turned then so she could at least look him in the eye.

"I'm so sorry, Sam. I never meant for this to happen. I never dreamed . . ."

"What did he do to you, honey?" Sam asked. "What about your mother? You never mentioned her."

"You're so lucky," she said with all the envy in her heart. "Even with all that has happened, you're so fortunate. You have such a wonderful family."

He rose to stand in front of her. He seemed indecisive as to whether he should touch her or not, and finally he just stood there and watched her.

"And you didn't have a family."

She slowly shook her head. "My mother was the closest thing to family, but even she was too cowed by my father to ever do anything to gain his disapproval. He didn't marry her. He didn't want me to have his last name. He thought it would be inconvenient were his enemies to ever try to use me to weaken him. *Inconvenient.* What they didn't know was that he wouldn't have cared. He would have never given or sacrificed anything for me or anyone else. But he didn't want to be inconvenienced. God."

"Ah Sophie," Sam said quietly.

"He killed her. And do you know why? He wasn't

angry with her. She had nothing to do with it. She was unfortunate enough to be in the room when a man my father was cutting a deal with questioned whether or not he had the stomach to do what it took to get the job done. Want to know what my father did then?"

Sam closed his eyes. "Jesus, Sophie, you don't have to tell me this."

"Yes, yes, I do, so maybe you'll understand, because even I don't understand. I don't understand any of it. We were eating dinner. He had this asshole over to discuss business. When the man questioned him, he simply pulled out a gun and shot my mother in the head. *At the dinner table.* And then calmly went back to eating. His only comment? 'Do you doubt me now?' "

"Holy shit, how old were you?"

She was quiet for a moment because all she could think of was the image of her mother, slumped forward in her chair, the sound of her fork clattering to the table. And the blood. So much blood. It had run onto the pristine white tablecloth. Sophie hadn't screamed. She hadn't reacted. She'd known even as young as she was that if she'd made any sound, it was likely her father would have killed her too. Just to make a point.

"I was ten," she finally said. "He went back to eating and then complained because his steak was too well done. I remember being afraid for the cook, but his mood was strangely relaxed, and aside from pushing his plate aside and wiping his mouth, he did nothing more than stare at the man across the table. Then he asked him if he'd like an after dinner drink. They retired to my father's study while I sat there staring at my mother. I sat there until the maid came to lead me away, and my father's men then disposed of my mother's body just like they disposed of everything else in my father's life that displeased him."

She lifted her gaze once more to Sam's. "You wanted to know why I killed him. I killed him with the same disdain that he once killed my mother, and I killed him so I would finally be free."

"Jesus, baby, I don't even have words. I don't know how you survived as long as you did." He pulled her into his arms and cradled her protectively against his chest. He stroked her hair with one hand and held her tightly with the other. "I'm sorry. I'm so sorry."

She closed her eyes and inhaled his comforting scent. Hot tears continued to leak down her cheeks, absorbed by his shirt. She'd never cried for her mother. She'd been too afraid. Even in the darkness of her room at night, she'd been too afraid her father would hear. He abhorred weakness, and she'd spent years removing any hint of it from her demeanor.

A knock sounded at the door, and she quickly stepped away from Sam, wiping at her face in an effort to hide her distress. He gave her a moment, then leaned in to kiss her on the forehead.

"That's the doctor. Have a seat and get comfortable. I want him to give you a thorough checkup before we leave here."

She sagged onto the couch and only half-listened as Sam went to the door and spoke in low tones to the doctor. A moment later, an older man walked in, pushing a portable piece of medical equipment, with Sam close on his heels. It didn't escape her notice that Sam's hand was on his gun, and he watched the doctor closely when he stopped in front of Sophie.

"Sophie, I'm Dr. Richards. I'd like to check you over, listen to the baby's heartbeat, and if you consent, I'd like to do a sonogram as well. Just to make sure everything's as it should be."

He smiled as he spoke, and Sophie relaxed a little.

"I get to see the baby?"

Hope and excitement welled in her chest, and ridiculously, she felt like crying all over again.

"Yes, we can even see if you're having a little boy or a little girl if you want."

Her gaze flew to Sam. He looked a little gobsmacked.

"I do," she breathed. "Do you?" she asked Sam.

Sam circled around the doctor and slid onto the couch beside her. "I do. I'd love to know."

The doctor began with a cursory exam of Sophie. He listened to her heart, took her blood pressure, asked her general questions about her health history. He asked to see her arm, poked and prodded at the stitches and seemed surprised that the sutures looked so clean and that there was no sign of infection. Then he asked her to recline on the couch, smiling as he did so.

"I'm afraid it's not the best of exam tables, but Mr. Kelly felt strongly about me performing the exam here and not in one of our rooms."

"No, it's okay," she said hastily as she looked right and left to determine the best way to lie down.

Sam answered her dilemma by simply rotating and easing her down until her head was in his lap. He smoothed a hand over her forehead as the doctor slipped the waistband of her jeans below the swell of her belly.

There was a muffled sound from the machine as the doctor placed the wand over her belly and moved back and forth. Then he settled on a spot and a rhythmic *whop whop whop* echoed over the room.

Sophie yanked her head to the side to see a pulsing blob on the screen.

"That's the heart," the doctor said. "A good, strong heartbeat. Right where we want it."

She was mesmerized by the sight. This was her baby! She stared in awe as the image moved. Occasionally the doctor stopped and typed on the small keyboard attached to the sonogram machine.

He pointed out arms and legs, the head and even a tiny mouth. And then a hand, seemingly held out as if to wave, the little fingers splayed.

Sophie's heart contracted. She was hit by a wave of love so fierce that it paralyzed her. Her child. A tiny life nestled in her womb. She couldn't even wrap her head around the idea.

"Okay, here we go. Let's see here. We have a shy one."

Dr. Richards probed harder on her stomach and then turned the wand.

"Aha, there she is. Take a look, Sophie. You have a daughter."

Despite her vow not to shed another tear, the screen went completely blurry. A daughter.

"I was right," she whispered. "A girl!"

"You called it right," Sam said softly above her.

The catch in his voice had her tearing her gaze from the screen to look up at him. He was staring at the monitor with such awe in his eyes that she felt her chest squeeze a little harder.

Then he glanced down and their eyes caught and held. He touched her cheek, and the emotion in his gaze nearly undid her.

"She's beautiful, Soph. Just like her mama."

She looked back at the monitor and smiled. The small burst of joy was so welcome, so wonderful that she wanted to hold on to it forever.

Dr. Richards pulled the wand away from her belly and carefully pulled her pants back up over her waist.

"I'd leave those stitches in your arm for another few days. Keep the area clean and a bandage over it. It's healing quite nicely though. Everything else looks good. I'd say you have a healthy little girl there."

"Thank you. Thank you so much. It was so nice to see her for the first time."

The doctor smiled and backed away from the couch. "I'll leave you two now. I have patients to get back to."

He wheeled the sonogram machine away, and a second later, she heard the door close behind him. She tried to push to a sitting position, but it was awkward. Sam helped her up, and she leaned against the couch, suddenly exhausted, but euphoric at the same time.

"A daughter."

Reverently she palmed her belly and rubbed softly over the swell. Sam put his hand over hers and squeezed.

"I just want her safe," Sophie said.

Sam cupped her chin and pulled until she faced him. His expression was hard now, devoid of his earlier tenderness. There was determination there.

"She will be, Sophie. We'll find a way. I need you to believe that."

"I want to," she said honestly.

"Help me then. I need information. I know you're tired. But I need you to tell me and my men everything you can about your uncle, about your father's holding in Rock Springs. Every detail you can think of. They're gathering intel now and we need to move quickly, but you can help us a lot if you tell us what you know."

"Of course I will."

"Where is the key? I asked you in the truck, but you never answered."

She covered her face in a tired gesture, knocking his hand from her chin in the process. She rubbed at her eyes and sighed.

"The night I took the boat, when I was coming to you, I hid the key in a box and buried it in the planter that was at the bait shop where I got the boat. It's there. The Ice Box. That's the name of the store."

"I know of it. It's a few miles down the lake from Paris Landing. I'll send one of Rio's men for it."

She shook her head. "No, I should go."

He frowned. "You're not going anywhere you're unprotected."

There was determination in her eyes as she stared back at him. "That key is all the insurance I have, Sam. All the insurance our child has. I won't take a chance with it."

"I know I don't have a right to ask, and you have every reason to be unsure and scared, but trust me, Sophie. Trust me. Trust that I won't do anything that puts any of you at risk. I'll send him for the key and he'll return it to us—to you."

She swallowed hard, and he could see the conflict so readily apparent on her face. His hand closed over hers, and he felt her tremble in his grasp. Finally she nodded.

"Okay, send him."

He lifted her hand and kissed her fingertips. "Come on then. Let's go find the others."

CHAPTER 26

AFTER issuing instructions to Rio to send a man to retrieve the key, Sam went back in to see his father. This time he didn't disturb him. He simply stood by his bedside and watched the up-and-down lines on the heart monitor and took reassurance in the rhythmic sounds of each breath.

Now more than ever he needed to take steps to ensure the safety of his family. It would take months to see to fruition the detailed plans for a veritable fortress on the land he'd purchased, but no longer would he put it off.

His family would be safe and under his watchful eye—all of them.

He reached down to touch his father's hand. It was cold—too cold—to the touch. His mother should be here, sitting by his bedside, not scared out of her mind in some shithole in West Texas.

He hadn't prayed in a long time, but he prayed now. He recalled every trip to church with his parents, and knew his mother found comfort in scripture and the steady words from the pulpit. He hoped she reached back for that now and that she didn't lose hope.

"I'll bring her home, Dad," he whispered. "Somehow I'll make all this right."

He turned and walked out of the cubicle and came face-to-face with the nurse who'd shown him in earlier.

She gestured toward a man on one of the phones at the nurses' station a few feet away. "The doctor is here if you'd like to talk to him about your father."

"Thank you, I would."

"Wait here and I'll get him," she said.

A few seconds later, the doctor hung up the phone and the nurse spoke to him and pointed in Sam's direction. The doctor walked over and extended his hand.

"I'm Dr. Caldwell. I'm in charge of your father's care."

Sam shook his hand. "Sam Kelly. How is he, Doctor?"

"He's doing well, considering. He had a major blockage that we went in and stented. There was another artery with about sixty-five percent blockage that we ballooned. He'll have to be on medication, and he'll need to make some drastic changes to diet and lifestyle, but he should do well with proper treatment."

Relief nearly crushed Sam on the spot. "When do you think he'll go home? I mean is he even near that point? How long will you keep him?"

The doctor smiled. "I'd like to keep him for a couple of days and monitor his recovery, make sure there aren't any problems. I'll run some tests to see how much, if any, of the heart was damaged, but he'll be able to go home in a couple of days."

"Thank you," Sam said.

The doctor put his hand on Sam's shoulder. "No problem. That's my job. If you'll excuse me, I have other patients to see."

Sam nodded and the doctor walked away. Sam glanced back toward his father's room before walking out of the unit himself.

When he rejoined the others in the family room, he briefed Donovan and Garrett on what the doctor had said and then he turned to the matter at hand.

"Sean give me the details on what you've worked out for security here at the hospital," Sam said quietly. "I need every man I can get when we go to Rock Springs, but I also won't leave Dad and Rusty unprotected."

Sean looked haggard, like he hadn't slept in a week, and grief was raw like a storm in his eyes. Frank and Marlene were like parents to him, and he was another son in an already large family.

He was young, but he was a damn good cop, and Sam trusted him to keep his loved ones safe from harm.

"The state police were screaming, but your pal Resnick called and they calmed down," Sean said.

Sam's brow furrowed in surprise, and he turned to Garrett. "Did you know anything about this?"

Garrett shrugged. "All I told him was to keep Uncle Sam off our asses and out of West Texas. Figured that's all he needed to know."

Resnick had come through in spades. He was a good man when the chips were down. Sam knew he'd put him in an untenable position. His ass would be on the line with his superiors. But he'd gone out on a limb for Sam. Debt paid.

"Okay, what else?" he directed at Sean.

"We have three troopers assigned to the hospital. I also have two locals and two of my guys from the county. We've alerted hospital security, and they've called in backup so they've doubled their field. I'll stay with Frank and Rusty myself."

Sam inhaled and looked over at his brothers and broached the topic that had been troubling him since their conversation with their dad.

"I know Dad doesn't want Ethan involved, but I have to call him. I *need* Baker and Renshaw, and Ethan will be pissed if we don't tell him what's gone down. I wouldn't blame him. I'd want to know if I was out of town and all this shit had happened, and heads would roll if I was left out of the loop."

Garrett grimaced. "I agree, but what about Rachel? If we call Ethan, he's going to race home, and he's going to want to go in with us."

"We need him," Sam said.

"Rachel could stay with Rusty and Dad," Donovan offered. "Ethan's going to be in a hell of a position. He won't want to leave Rachel, but he's not going to stay behind while we go after Mom."

"I'll guard them with my life," Sean said in a tight, grim voice.

Sam put his hand on Sean's shoulder. "I know you will, Sean. I just worry about dragging Ethan into this fight when Rachel is still fragile."

"I don't like it, but you're right, we do need him," Garrett said.

Sam looked at Donovan for confirmation, then heaved out a huge breath. "Okay, I'll call Ethan and bring him in. The Kelly jet could have him home by morning, and we'll take out as soon as we have things in hand here."

He looked back over at Sean. "I want Sophie to stay here with you and the other women."

He caught a blur of movement from the corner of his eye. Sophie had sat quietly through the entire conversation, but now she leaped to her feet.

"Are you insane?" she demanded. "I'm not staying here."

Sam caught her hand and brought her next to him. "This isn't up for negotiation, Sophie. I want you safe. I'm not bringing you into the middle of a war with your uncle."

Her pale face crinkled with anger and outrage. "You're signing your mother's death warrant. Whatever your plan is, you cannot go in there without me. The moment he realizes I'm not holding up my end of the bargain, he'll kill your mother. Oh, he won't do it himself. He doesn't have the balls. But he'll have her killed. Are you willing to risk that?"

"I won't trade her for you."

She pulled her hand from his and faced him, her mouth set in a fierce line. "I made the deal with him. The key in exchange for your mother. We have to at least give him the semblance of that. What if your plan goes wrong? Are you prepared for the worst? Are you willing to pin everything on your ability to go in and flawlessly execute a rescue?"

"Sophie . . ."

"Don't ask me to *trust you*, Sam. This has nothing to do with trust and everything to do with me not being willing to be responsible for your mother's death. How about you trust me? Trust me to know my uncle and know what'll happen when he realizes he's not going to get what he wants."

Sam closed his eyes. Goddamn but he didn't want to involve Sophie in any of this. How could he?

"How close do you think you'll be able to get without me? Are you willing to take that chance, Sam? You want me to trust you. Well, I do. I trust you to keep me safe when I go with you. I trust you to come up with a plan that has your men going in for your mother while I face my uncle. You know I'm right. You may not want to take me, but you know you have to. You *know* it."

Her impassioned plea impressed the men gathered around Sam. They shifted restlessly, and he could see they battled the same dilemma he did. None of them wanted her in harm's way. They didn't want her anywhere near her uncle. But they also all knew she had a very valid point.

And it pissed him the fuck off.

"Christ."

"I don't like it," Donovan said. "We can't risk Sophie and her baby on the off chance we don't get the job done."

"I don't like it either," Garrett muttered. "But do we have a choice? Do we really want to take that risk? We can protect her, Sam. You know we can goddamn protect her. You don't want her to go. I don't want her to go. But do you really want to face Dad and tell him we didn't do all we could to bring Mom back to him?"

"That's a low blow," Sam said fiercely.

Sophie's small hand slid over his arm and she tugged, turning his attention back to her.

"Don't I get a say in this?" she asked softly. "I brought this to your door, Sam. I brought it to your mother and father's door. They didn't get a choice. Let me do this. Let me save your mother like I couldn't save mine. Do you think I could live with myself if I stayed here and she dies?"

Her courage astounded him. It humbled him. He felt wholly unworthy of her selflessness. And as much as he wanted to deny her, as much as he wanted to tie her down if necessary to keep her safe, he knew in his gut she was right. She was right and it made him so furious, so afraid for her that he wanted to break something.

He stared into her eyes and then closed his. His hands found hers and he hung on. God forgive him, but what was he supposed to do? How did you make a choice between keeping your woman safe or possibly causing the death of your mother?

Sophie moved against him. He opened his eyes just as she leaned up on tiptoe. She kissed him. A soft, gentle kiss that held a wealth of meaning. And support. It was the first time she'd made any overt gesture in front of the others.

"I have faith in you," she whispered.

Her fingers squeezed his, and she rocked back on her feet. There was more trust in her gaze than he deserved. He just prayed he didn't betray it.

Feeling empty, he turned to the others, but he kept a tight hold on one of Sophie's hands.

"We rework the plan," Sam said bleakly. "I'll go in with Sophie. I want P.J. and Cole on sniper duty. As soon as the bastard shows himself to us, I want him taken out. Everyone else will surround and go in. This has to be precisely timed. There's no room for mistakes."

"We won't fail," Steele said. "We never have. We won't start now."

Sam pulled Sophie closer to him, needing in that moment to feel her warmth, to remind him of what was at stake. He slid his hand down her body to her belly, feeling for the reassuring kick of his daughter.

His daughter.

"This is your niece," he said to his brothers. "Sophie's having a girl."

He needed them to know. Needed to make it personal, to make this as real to them as it was to him. Then they'd know what was at risk.

Donovan's face split into a wide grin. He moved forward, swept Sophie into his arms and spun her around. Even Garrett smiled, and when Donovan set her down, Garrett reached for her hand.

She hesitated only for a split second before she went willingly into Garrett's embrace. He hugged her close.

She seemed shocked by their gestures, and when Garrett let her go, she teetered a little, her eyes glazed.

"If she's half as fierce as her mother, she'll be a force of nature," Garrett said in a gruff voice.

A wry smile curved her lips. "If you keep this up, I'll get the idea you actually like me."

"I regret that I ever gave you the idea I disliked you," Garrett said, his eyes serious. "And maybe I did. I was wrong."

She stared at Garrett in stunned disbelief. Sam smiled. Garrett admitting he was wrong was a sight to behold.

Sam held out his hand for Sophie to return to him. She came willingly, and he pulled her to his side.

"This has to go right," he told the men surrounding him. "I can't lose her."

CHAPTER 27

WHILE Sam and his men entered the final planning stages, Sophie slept and Sam watched over her. He wasn't entirely focused on the conversation and the intense strategy session because his gaze kept drifting to the small woman who held such a big part of him in her hands.

He hated that he couldn't keep her here, safely tucked away from anything that could hurt her. He despised it. Before, KGI would have planned a ruthless extraction, gone in with precision, rescued the hostage, been in and out in an hour. Wiped their hands, moved on to the next job.

That had all gone to hell because this was his mother, and if Sophie was to be believed—and he did believe her—her uncle was a wild card. No one really knew how he'd react, because he'd never been tested. He'd never assumed any leadership in Alex Mouton's organization.

That made him unpredictable, and they couldn't afford to risk his mom's life by assuming anything.

Goddamn but he hated this.

"P.J. and Cole will be on sniper duty," Steele said in a low voice next to Sam.

Sam turned to his team leader and knew he'd been caught napping. He'd been staring down at Sophie, who was curled on the small couch in the family room, her face tense and drawn even in sleep.

It was all he could do not to run his fingers over her lips to ease the worry stress, but he didn't want to disturb her. The next hours would be tense and she needed her rest.

"You and Sophie can make nice and meet Tomas for the trade, if the bastard will even show himself. The rest of us will stage around the house and go in. If Marlene is inside, we'll get her out. If she's with Tomas, P.J. or Cole will take Tomas out at the first opportunity."

"He knows I won't be coming in with Sophie alone. He can't be that stupid. He'll be expecting something. We have to give him something else entirely," Sam said. "I won't risk her. I want Garrett and Donovan with me. Protection for Sophie. If I front enough men with me and Sophie, the rest of you might come as a surprise."

"And Ethan?"

Sam blew out his breath. He needed Ethan, but he didn't want to involve him either. Hell of a note.

"Ethan comes with me. You and Rio will take your teams and take down everyone in your path. It needs to be clean and quiet. The longer it takes for Tomas to figure out you're there, the better."

The door to the room burst open and Ethan strode in, his hand curled tight around his wife's hand. Baker and Renshaw flanked the couple and were armed to the teeth.

Sam went to meet his brother just as Donovan and Garrett broke away from the others as well.

"How is he?" Ethan asked hoarsely.

"He's resting. He'll be okay. I spoke to the doctor earlier."

Sam's gaze dropped to Rachel and he extended a hand. "Rachel, honey, how are you?"

To his surprise she walked into his arms and hugged him fiercely. He responded by enveloping her in a hug. She'd gotten better about expressing affection with him and the other family members, but this spontaneous outburst caught him off guard.

"I'm sorry," she murmured. "You must be so worried."

He dropped a kiss on the top of her head and relinquished her to Garrett, who stood impatiently to the side. Garrett and Rachel had always had a special bond, and next to Ethan, Rachel was the most open with Garrett.

"Tell me what the hell's going on, Sam," Ethan demanded. "The report I got was sketchy at best, and I still don't understand what's happening here."

Sam caught Garrett's eyes and nodded for him to take Rachel away. Garrett responded by wrapping an arm around her slender form and guiding her past Sophie and over to where Rusty sat.

As succinctly as possible, Sam gave Ethan the story from the top. The parts about him and Sophie were abbreviated, but his warning was crystal clear. His brother wasn't to place blame on Sophie's shoulders.

Ethan stared dumbly at the couch where Sophie lay sleeping. Then he dragged a hand over his short-cropped hair and shook his head in disbelief.

"I'm going with you," he said firmly.

His stare was challenging, as if he expected Sam to shoot him down. But Sam nodded.

"I need you on this, Ethan. I've made arrangements for Rachel and Rusty to be cared for. Sean's going to stay with them, and we have a veritable army around the hospital so they and Dad will be safe."

Ethan lowered his voice. "I need to explain to Rachel. She doesn't know what's going on, just that Dad's had a heart attack and there's trouble."

"Then go explain," Sam said. "We leave in an hour."

"SOPHIE, Sophie, honey, time to wake up."

She heard the words, but they seemed so far away. Drowsily, she opened her eyes to see Sam sitting on the edge of the couch, his eyes full of misgivings.

"Are we leaving?"

She was proud of the way she kept the fear from her voice, how steady the words came out.

"Yeah, we need to go."

She pushed herself to a sitting position and took quick stock of the room around her. There were faces she hadn't seen before. A man who looked a lot like Garrett stood against the far wall, his arms sheltering a slender woman with brown hair. Two other men, heavily armed, stood with Steele. The man and woman must be Sam's brother and sister-in-law.

"The key," she said and stopped to clear the cracking from her voice. "Did they get the key?"

Sam reached into his pocket and pulled out a long cylindrical piece of metal.

"Is this it?" he asked as he turned it over in his palm.

It was an odd piece. It didn't at all look like a traditional key. She could understand his skepticism.

She took it from him and ran a finger over the series of etchings on the outside.

"Yes. It's specially engineered. It's quite a piece of technology. On the outside, the etchings are the key part. Each groove fits into a corresponding groove in the keyhole. But it's hollow, as you can see, and on the inside is an encrypted code that is scanned once the key fits the lock.

"It's all computerized, and on the end, where you hold it, is a sensor. If the person's pulse is too elevated or the skin temperature is off the normal body heat by more than a degree, access is denied."

Sam shook his head. "Your father was a paranoid bastard."

"He liked to think he was careful and thought of every eventuality. He didn't trust anyone. But he was also arrogant. He had such a tight security net around him at all times that he thought himself invincible. He didn't think anyone could touch him."

"Motherfucking God complex," Donovan muttered.

Sophie looked up to see that Donovan and Garrett had gathered, as had the man she assumed was their brother Ethan.

She nodded. "In some ways he did consider himself a god. Not a deity. He wasn't a religious man. He had no tolerance for what couldn't be touched or seen. He considered religion a weakness, and he was all about strength or what he perceived as strength."

"How the hell did you ever have the nerve to go up against him?" Garrett asked. "You said you shot him, but how?"

She looked down at her hands. "It's nothing to brag about. I'm not proud of what I did. I did it for selfish reasons. I'm not a noble person."

Sam's hand slid under her chin and tilted it upward until she met his gaze.

"I disagree," he said in a quiet voice that almost shook. "You're risking your life for a woman you don't know. That makes you pretty goddamn noble in my book."

His hand tightened as if just saying the words were unbearable.

"You'll find a way to keep me safe," she said.

Those weren't just words meant to reassure. She believed them. And she wanted him to know that.

Ethan stepped forward and put his hand down to Sophie. "I'm Ethan, Sam's younger brother. I'll be going with you to Rock Springs."

She gingerly slid her hand into his. "I'm Sophie."

He smiled, and it was startling to see someone who so closely resembled Garrett smiling.

"I know who you are. My brother's told me a lot about you."

Steele walked up and touched Sam on the arm. "We're ready to move. Trucks are here, helicopters are waiting, and the jet is fueled."

Her stomach balled into a knot, and she lowered her hands to her lap so no one would see how bad they shook. The key pressed into her palm, and the leather strip that had secured it to her father's neck lay limply across her leg. Deep red splotches stained one side. Her father's blood.

The key had been her insurance policy, but now it was the only thing that stood between Marlene Kelly and certain death. When she gave it up, unless Sam and his men were able to completely bring down her uncle's network, she'd wear a target on her back for the rest of her life. However long it lasted.

Sam reached for her hand and pulled her up to stand beside him. His eyes found hers and he touched her cheek in a tender gesture.

Then he let his hand fall away and tugged her into the protective circle of his men as they walked out of the hospital.

THEY were climbing into the SUVs when a black sedan roared toward them. The clatter of guns was deafening as every single one of Sam's men took cover and aimed at the approaching vehicle. It screeched to a halt a few feet from where Sam stood and Sam shoved Sophie into the backseat.

"Stay down," he barked.

He drew his Glock as the door to the car opened and Resnick popped out, hands in the air. Without waiting for a summons, he strode determinedly toward Sam, his mouth set in a grim line.

"Goddamn it, Adam, I told you to stay the fuck out of our way," Sam said through gritted teeth. He purposely didn't order his men to put down their weapons.

Resnick was smoking like a chimney, and he yanked the cigarette out of his mouth. "I need five minutes of your time, Sam."

"I don't have five minutes. Get out of my way, Adam."

"You're on a goddamn suicide mission, Sam. Goddamn it, listen to me!"

Sam's eyes narrowed and he lowered his pistol. "What the fuck do you know about where we're going?"

Resnick blew out an agitated puff of smoke, then threw the still glowing cigarette to the pavement. It skittered away in a shower of sparks.

"It doesn't take a genius. I have access to more sophisticated satellite imagery than you do. Mouton has moved a fucking army into West Texas. Your men are good, Sam. The best. But are you prepared to take on a goddamn army?"

"What are you proposing?" Sam demanded.

"I have two teams mobilized and en route to Del Rio. They'll coordinate with you."

"Look," Garrett broke in impatiently. "If you're going to talk, do it on the road. We've got to make tracks."

Sam jerked a thumb at Resnick. "Get in."

Resnick hurried around to the passenger seat and jumped in next to Garrett. Sam slid in next to Sophie, who was staring at Resnick like he was a snake.

Sam reached for Sophie and pulled her close as Garrett roared out of the parking lot. "Don't worry," he murmured in her ear.

Resnick turned in his seat to look at Sam. His gaze drifted over to Sophie, and a look of true regret sparked in his eyes.

"I'm sorry for what happened before, Sophie. I never intended to frighten you."

Some of the tension faded, and she relaxed against Sam's side.

"Now, what the hell have you got planned?" Sam asked Adam.

"You'd be walking into a massacre," Resnick said. "A goddamn massacre. It looks like he's pulled in all his men and maybe some mercenaries as well. Who the fuck knows what third world country owes him enough favors that they'd supply him with military power. There's probably a dozen."

"Son of a bitch," Sam swore. "He's got my mother. He wants to trade her for Sophie. That's not going to happen. Our only hope is to go in and take him out."

Resnick nodded and stuck a cigarette into his mouth, though he didn't make a move to light it. He removed it at intervals just like he was smoking it, and his hands shook in agitation. He'd always been a high-strung son of a bitch.

"You know what I think of you and your men, Sam. But you can't do this. You're outnumbered at least four to one. You need to let me even the odds. I have two black ops teams staged and ready to go. They're the best."

"And what do you get out of this?" Sam asked bluntly.

Resnick found his gaze and met it head-on, his eyes glittering with determination. "I want him taken down by any means necessary. Who does it is of no consequence, and if I can aid in that goal, then I'll do what it takes." His gaze swept to Sophie and then back to Sam. "Alex is dead, isn't he?"

Sam gave a short nod.

Resnick's eyes narrowed. "Who killed him?"

Sophie stiffened beside Sam, but he didn't react. "Does it matter?" he asked calmly.

Resnick shook his head and tore the cigarette from his mouth again. "No. No, it doesn't matter at all as long as the bastard is gone."

Sam looked at Garrett, who stared back at him in the rearview mirror. For a moment the two brothers didn't say anything and then Sam finally turned back to Resnick.

"We'll meet your men in Del Rio. They don't go in, they do nothing without my say-so, is that understood? Everything goes according to our plan. My mother and Sophie are to be protected at all costs."

Resnick nodded. "I understand. I got it. I'll make the call."

Sam relaxed and rubbed his hand up and down Sophie's arm. "Thanks, Adam. We appreciate the help."

"Don't thank me. Just nail that bastard to the wall. That's my thanks."

THEY arrived in Del Rio at nightfall. The Kelly jet landed on a bumpy patch of flat soil that had been commandeered by Resnick's teams. They flew in dark, and Sophie's fingers left a permanent imprint on Sam's hands. When they finally rolled to a stop, she sagged like a deflated balloon.

"Rio and Steele are on the ground already. I've notified them of the change in head count. They're awaiting our orders," Garrett said as he ducked through the exit and made quick work of the steps.

He waited at the bottom and reached for Sophie, who preceded Sam from the plane. Garrett set her on her feet and stared at Sam in the dark. Resnick, Donovan and Ethan followed close behind.

"Adam Resnick?"

The voice filtered through the small group like a ghost. They all turned rapidly, drawing their weapons.

"Kyle Phillips, United States Marine Corps, sir. My men are here and awaiting your orders."

"Show yourself, soldier," Resnick said.

There was only a slight shift in the air, and then a dark figure appeared next to Resnick.

Resnick didn't waste time with pleasantries.

"Phillips, this is Sam Kelly and his brothers, Garrett, Donovan and Ethan. You'll be taking orders from them. This is their mission, but it's your job to make damn sure they don't fail."

"Yes, sir."

Phillips turned to Sam and extended his hand. "I've heard a lot about you, sir. It's a pleasure to meet you."

Sam took his hand and gave it a quick shake. "I appreciate you and your men coming, Phillips. What information do you have for me?"

"If you'll come with me, sir, we have vehicles waiting, a quarter mile over that hill. I'll give you the report when we're inside."

Sam took Sophie's hand and Garrett, Donovan and Ethan fell in, surrounding Sophie as they hurried after Phillips. When they reached the line of SUVs, Sam and Sophie got into the vehicle with Phillips and Garrett, while Resnick, Donovan and Ethan got into another.

"We've had the target under surveillance for the last six hours. There was a flurry of movement that ended two hours ago with what we believe was the arrival of his last influx of arms. We have two teams surrounding the house and they're setting explosives now."

"Have they seen my mother?" Sam asked.

"Negative, sir. There hasn't been much movement in the house, and without a man inside, it's tough to see. It was built with defense in mind. No large open windows, few doors, etcetera. Most of the movement has been on the perimeter. They're preparing for war. I have three snipers. We'll position them to do the most damage we can before going in."

"War is what they're going to get," Garrett muttered.

"Excellent," Sam said. "I put my two best sharpshooters for the meeting with Mouton. We could use more around the perimeter."

"We're damn good at what we do, sir. I want you to know that. We won't let you down."

For the first time since this whole bloody business had begun, Sam felt a kernel of relief. He lived and died by his faith in the U.S. military and special ops. There weren't better men anywhere in the world, and he was damn glad to have them with him now.

"I'll need you to brief your men on what's going down," Sam said.

"Yes, sir."

"And I want whatever information you've got on the facility and the number of men and their position. I need to know every inch of this place before we go in. You'll coordinate with Steele and Rio, my team leaders. They'll have the field. My brothers and I are taking Sophie to make the exchange for my mother."

"Yes, sir. We'll take care of it."

"Thank you, Phillips. I appreciate it."

"No thanks necessary, sir. It's my job."

Yeah, a job. He wished that's all it fucking was this time. Just a job.

CHAPTER 28

IT didn't feel right. None of it felt right. Sam eyed his surroundings as the SUV rolled up the winding, dusty road that led to the front gate of Mouton's spread.

Garrett drove and Resnick, who'd insisted on coming along and adding his manpower, rode shotgun. Sophie was squeezed between Sam and Donovan in the middle seat, while Ethan rode in the back.

He glanced sideways at Sophie's pale features and saw grim determination in the set of her mouth. Over her thin shirt she wore a Kevlar vest that Sam himself had secured around her small frame. Hell, he'd wanted to cover her from head to toe with body armor. He wanted no part of her unprotected. What if something went horribly wrong? How could he ever forgive himself if something happened to her or their child?

He was sorely tempted to tell Garrett to turn around so he could take Sophie back. As if sensing his turmoil,

Sophie slid her fingers through his and turned her head to gaze up at him. She squeezed and smiled, and that small reassurance hit him in the gut.

He was a damn fraud. It was his job—his duty—to protect his family, and yet it was Sophie who was determined to protect them all.

He squeezed her hand back, all the words he wanted to say trapped in his throat. He forced his thoughts to the situation at hand.

Steele and Rio had joined Phillips's teams hours before, when night still shrouded the rocky hills. They'd established a tight perimeter around the compound, and P.J. and Cole were in position, their rifles trained on the front entrance.

It was a mission Sam should have felt good about. Phillips's teams had evened the odds. He had absolute faith in his own men. This should be a walk in the park. Only this was personal. This was involving people he loved.

Love. God, he loved her. And it had to hit him now? When he was about to put her in danger? He looked away from her because if he didn't, he was going to lose it.

He had to pull it together. He could not go into this with his head so goddamn messed up. He had to forget love. He had to forget about his mother. He had to forget about Sophie, and oh God, he had to forget about his child.

Just a job. He had to keep objectivity or he was going to make a mistake and he'd lose them all.

Only, his pulse wouldn't slow, and his heart felt like it was going to beat out of his chest. Over fourteen goddamn years of being fearless and stoic in the face of danger, and he was going to fuck it all up now when it mattered the most.

There were three armed guards at the heavy metal gate. The tension level in the SUV went through the roof. Garrett pulled to a stop and cracked the window.

"We're here to see Tomas Mouton," he said coolly.

Sophie went rigid next to Sam.

The guard's gaze swept the SUV, and he gestured for Garrett to open his door.

"Not going to happen," Garrett said. "Tell Mouton we're here. He's expecting us."

The guard's nostrils flared, but he picked up a radio and relayed the information. A moment later the gate began to sweep open, and they were motioned through.

"You stay behind me at all times," Sam said to Sophie, though he'd already gone over the plan a half dozen times. "You don't move, you don't do anything until we tell you, and if I tell you to get down, you drop immediately."

She nodded but never looked away from the house that loomed closer in the windshield.

They stopped directly in front of the main entrance, exactly in the location they'd pinpointed so that Cole and P.J. had clear shots to the front steps.

Everything hinged on a game of chicken and KGI not flinching first. Sam hoped to hell Tomas was the nervous type.

Garrett got out first but stayed behind the open door. Resnick popped out on his side, and then Donovan got out on his side and knocked the seat forward for Ethan.

"Stay in the truck until I tell you," Sam murmured to Sophie as he too opened his door.

Sam stepped into the morning sun, glad that the light was behind them. He'd take any advantage he could.

The seconds ticked into minutes until finally the front

door opened and Tomas Mouton stepped out, flanked by two guards. He looked nervous—a good sign—and when he caught sight of the men surrounding the SUV he halted, and for a moment looked uncertain.

Sam stepped forward until he was shoulder to shoulder with Garrett.

"Where is my mother?" he called out.

The two men were separated by a good twenty yards and a row of four steps leading up to the concrete landing outside the front door.

"Where is my niece?" Mouton returned.

Sam gestured at the truck. "She's inside."

"As is your mother."

Silence yawned, and Sam said nothing, waiting for Mouton to make the next move.

"Bring her out. I want to see her. If you're trying to pull something, Kelly, I'll have your mother executed on the spot."

"As a gesture of good faith, I'll bring Sophie out. That's all. She doesn't make a move toward you until I see my mother. Understand?"

All the air left Sophie's lungs as Sam backed toward the truck and extended a hand inside. She didn't hesitate, didn't want him to witness the terrible fear that streaked through her veins. She grasped his fingers and slid over until she stepped out of the truck.

"Stay behind the door," Sam directed.

When he was satisfied with her position, he moved back ahead of her to face Mouton.

"You see her. Now I want to see my mother. And she better be unharmed, Mouton."

Sophie's uncle's mouth drew into a frown. No, he didn't like threats. She'd seen that look countless times when her father had issued a set-down to his younger brother.

Tomas ignored Sam and looked directly at her. He had a distinct look of unease on his face. And fear. She could almost smell his fear. His forehead was shiny in the sunlight, and when she looked down at his hands, they were balled into fists at his sides.

"The key, Sophie. Show me the key."

Not waiting for direction from Sam, she slowly held her hand up, flashing the metal in the sun so he could plainly see the key and the leather band that had secured it to her father's neck.

The door opened again and the men surrounding her and the SUV all tensed, each reaching for his gun. The guards at Tomas's side reacted by drawing their rifles.

Marlene Kelly came into view looking pale and haggard, but Sophie didn't look at her. No, her focus was on the man nearly covered by Marlene. The man holding one arm tightly around her neck and pressing a gun to her temple with his other hand.

Sweat broke out on her forehead. Her palms went damp, and her stomach clenched in a knot so tight she thought she was going to puke.

It wasn't possible.

She'd killed him.

Sam froze when he saw the man holding his mother like a human shield. Not much of him was visible, but he could see enough to know he'd been had. Not just had, but truly and royally fucked.

Son of a bitch.

He glanced sideways at his brothers, but he refused to look back at Sophie, refused to give her or her bastard father the satisfaction.

God, when he remembered the tears Sophie had conjured as she fed him that sob story about her home life and how she'd shot and killed her father, it made him want to puke. She was good, and he'd been sucked in, hook, line and sinker.

Was the baby even his or had she lied about that too?

"Jesus," Garrett muttered.

It echoed Sam's own thoughts perfectly.

"I believed her too, man," Garrett said quietly so the others wouldn't hear.

Sam went cold. Utterly still, and he turned it all off. Right now nothing mattered but getting his mother to safety.

"Let her go, Mouton," Sam called. "Let her go, and you'll get what you want."

"Welcome home, daughter," Alex called out.

For the first time, Sam turned and put his hand out to Sophie in a stopping motion.

"You don't move a fucking inch until he lets her go."

Sophie stood, stock-still, her face pale and drawn. Her hand clutched the key, that goddamn key—did her father even need it? Was the whole thing an elaborate ruse to get Sam and his men in a vulnerable position?

There was too much Sam couldn't wrap his brain around, but it didn't matter. His mother did.

While he was still faced away from Mouton, he ordered in quick, urgent tones, "P.J., Cole, take the goddamn shot."

"I do not have a shot. Repeat, I do not have a shot," P.J. said.

A split second later, Cole's voice bled through the receiver in Sam's ear.

"Negative on a clear shot."

Sam swore under his breath. He turned back to Mouton, ignoring the pleading in Sophie's eyes.

"It would seem we're at an impasse, Alex."

But were they? Did the bastard even want Sophie? Was he willing to sacrifice her to achieve his means? And what was his purpose? Revenge? None of this made any sense. Why go through such an elaborate charade? Doubt crowded Sam's mind. Had Sophie really betrayed him?

Pushing aside his emotions, he stared Alex Mouton down. Sam needed to get him talking, needed him to make a mistake so P.J. and Cole could take him out.

"No, we aren't," Alex said indifferently. "It really doesn't matter to me one way or another if your mother dies. Can you say the same?"

Marlene made a sound of panic as Mouton dug the point of the pistol harder into the side of her head.

Sam zeroed in on Mouton's hand, how it tightened around the stock. His finger hovered and then closed around the trigger. He was going to kill her. Right here in front of Sam and his brothers. And Sam was helpless to do anything but watch.

Out of the corner of his eye, he caught movement. Garrett whirled around, his hands going to his pants just as Sophie shot past him, one of the grenades from Garrett's belt in her hand.

And so she'd made her move.

She yanked the pin and clutched the grenade in the same hand as the key. Only the leather tie was visible, squashed up next to the grenade.

Her hands trembled and her eyes were wild and fierce with determination. Her gaze connected with Sam's, and he saw so much pain and sorrow that it sucked the air from his lungs.

And he knew. Knew in that moment that he'd made a terrible assumption. She hadn't betrayed him.

SOPHIE couldn't breathe. Couldn't process the nightmare unfolding in front of her eyes.

Her father was going to kill Marlene. She knew it without a doubt. No matter what happened, he would make a statement. Don't cross him. Ever.

She wanted to vomit, but right now she had to be strong. She had to think fast and not betray her gut-wrenching fear. That she could do. She'd hidden her fear and weakness from her father for years. She wouldn't fail now.

Holding the grenade close to her now that she was sure her father had seen it, she leveled a cool stare at him and voiced her demands.

"Put the gun down and let her go."

Marlene's eyes drew up in horror as Sophie walked toward the front steps. Sophie ignored her. She couldn't think about Marlene or offer her any reassurance.

"Let her go or I blow us all up," Sophie said in a voice devoid of the horrific fear that rolled through her body.

"You're bluffing," her father bit out.

"Am I?" She gripped the grenade tighter, her thumb now numb from the pressure she exerted on the handle. "You think I don't know that I die either way? If I go with you, you'll kill me. I have nothing to lose. But you have a choice. You can let Mrs. Kelly go and I'll put the pin back in the grenade and go with you. Or I'll relax my grip and blow me and you and the key to smithereens. Either way *I* die. If you let Mrs. Kelly go, you don't die. Now, what's it going to be?"

Her father shifted but he was careful to keep the terrified Marlene in front of him.

"Honey, don't do this," Marlene said in a scared, shaky voice. "Think of your baby. My grandchild. Don't do it. Go back to Sam. For God's sake, *go back to Sam.*"

"Shut up," Alex Mouton snapped as he angled the tip of the gun harder into her temple.

"Let her go," Sophie demanded.

She pulled the grenade up her body until the hand holding it and the leather strap rested against the straps of her vest. Then she tossed the pin onto the porch where her father and uncle stood.

Tomas swore and immediately dropped down to retrieve the pin. He extended it toward her, his hand shaking.

"You put it back in," he said hoarsely. "Put it back in now."

Her father stared at her for a long moment as if measuring her determination. "All right, Sophie. You're calling the shots. If you want Mrs. Kelly to be freed, you come to me and make the trade. You for her. She doesn't move away from me until you're close enough to dissuade the snipers."

She swallowed and took a hesitant step forward. She wouldn't look back. She couldn't. If she did, she'd only see what she'd never have.

When she was close enough to Marlene, she whispered, "Tell Sam I love him and that I never lied to him."

"How touching," her father sneered.

Lightning fast, he thrust Marlene away from him and yanked Sophie to his chest.

"Run!" Sophie yelled hoarsely.

The world around her erupted in chaos.

Marlene fled toward her sons. The two guards standing on the steps fell, blood running from gaping wounds in their heads. Tomas dove back into the house. Gunfire erupted over the compound. A heavy explosion rocked the ground. Sophie held tighter to the grenade as her father backed through the heavy front door, his arm a stranglehold around her.

Her last glimpse of Sam was as he rushed his mother into the safety of the SUV.

She closed her eyes. Thank God.

CHAPTER 29

"MOM, Mom! Are you okay?" Sam demanded as he leaned over her in the SUV. "Get us the fuck to cover!" he yelled at Garrett.

Resnick and Sam's brothers threw themselves into the SUV and Garrett rocked it over a planter and through a hedge until it dove down a narrow embankment behind a rock outcropping.

"I'm okay, Sam. I'm fine. Just terrified."

Her hands on his face penetrated some of his red haze. He was furious, and he was scared out of his mind.

"We have a hostage situation," he barked into his mic. "Sophie's inside the building. Proceed with extreme caution."

Marlene tried to sit up, but Donovan shoved her back down, his body covering hers. "Stay down, Ma."

She looked up at Sam, torment crowding her tired

eyes. "Sam, you have to get her out of there. She thinks she's going to die."

Sam closed his eyes.

"She told me to tell you she loves you and that she never lied to you," his mom said in a tearful voice.

"Sweet mother of God," Garrett said in a strained voice. "Son of a bitch!"

"What?" Sam demanded as his head swung in his brother's direction.

Garrett held up the key. It was missing the leather tie, the one she'd held in the same hand with the grenade.

"She must have slipped it into my pocket when she nabbed the grenade."

Sam's gut tightened. He remembered well her determination that Tomas never get his hands on the key. How much more determined would she be to keep it from her father?

"Oh dear God," he whispered. "He'll kill her."

Ethan picked himself up off the floorboard of the third-row seat and grabbed at his mom's hand.

"Ethan," she murmured in surprise. "What are you doing here? Where is Rachel?"

"She's safe, Ma," Ethan said gruffly. "Thank God you are too."

Marlene looked anxiously back at Sam. "Are you going after her? You won't just leave her there, will you?"

"Sam, I'll radio for a helicopter. I can have your mom out of here in minutes," Resnick said. "You go. I'll stay here with her."

"I want the rest of you to go with Mom," Sam said. "This is my fight. Your job is to make damn sure Mom gets out of here alive."

"Bullshit," Marlene snapped.

Five pairs of eyes stared at her in surprise.

"Your brothers would never let you go back in alone. Your father raised you all better than that. You get back there and save my grandchild. You save that young woman who just traded her life for mine."

"Don't worry, Ma," Donovan said. "We weren't going to let the dumbass go anywhere without us."

"We're taking heavy fire," Steele said in Sam's ear.

The others turned to Sam, their worried gazes finding his.

"Let's go," Sam said. "I'm not letting this bastard take even *one* of my men's lives, and I'm damn sure not letting that fool-headed female of mine get herself killed."

SOPHIE wrenched herself free of her father's grasp as soon as the doors closed. It felt like the stone being rolled over a tomb. Damn if she'd let fear paralyze her now though.

Her thumb was slick over the lever of the grenade. It would be so damn easy to let go. But she had no intention of dying, no matter what she may have said.

"Put the pin back in, Sophie," her father said.

Tomas stood, hand outstretched with the pin, sweating profusely and shaking. Alex stared at her through the narrow slits of his eyes—cold eyes that betrayed no fear. Was the man made of stone or was he just that convinced that he was indestructible? For that matter, she'd shot him and yet he'd survived. Maybe he *was* invincible.

"I s-shot you."

The corner of his mouth lifted into an almost smile.

"So you did. You impressed me. I wouldn't have thought you had it in you."

Then his eyes changed, growing cold as anger flared in the depths.

"You put me in the hospital for months. I lay there seeing you pointing that gun at me, an arrogant little bitch who thought she'd won. You can't kill me, Sophie. I can't die."

She lifted the grenade again when Alex moved in her direction. Her hand shook, but at the moment she didn't care if she concealed her fear from her father. She was done with it. She was done with him.

"Stay away from me and my baby."

"Give me the key and I'll consider letting you live long enough to give birth to your brat."

A burst of hysterical laughter escaped her. He didn't realize yet that she didn't have the key.

Tomas moved, and in that small lapse of attention as she glanced in his direction, Alex rushed her. He grabbed her wrist and twisted painfully until the grenade dropped from her hand to the floor.

The leather tie drifted downward, and both Tomas and Alex made a grab for the grenade. Alex reached it first, snatched it up and hurled it through the doorway and down the hall.

Sophie hit the floor, her arms covering her belly protectively.

The blast rocked the house, and plaster and wood rained down on her head. Recovering fast, she got to her hands and knees and crawled across the debris-covered floor.

A hand circled her ankle and yanked her back. She

rolled defensively and came face-to-face with the furious eyes of her father.

Dust and bits of the ceiling plaster covered his hair, and he held up the leather tie with his free hand.

"You fucking bitch, where is the key?"

Self-preservation kicked in, and she struck at him with her other foot. Struggling wildly against his hold, she fought to gain purchase with her hands, pushing against the floor in an attempt to gain leverage.

Hope bloomed when she saw him drag his left leg in an effort to keep up with her. His pants leg was ripped from the knee down, and blood dripped onto the floor.

With another desperate kick, she managed to free her ankle, and she turned, scrambling over the floor toward the doorway on the other side. He was on her in two seconds, his body landing clumsily against hers. The sound of his breathing filled her ears as his hand curled into her hair. He yanked viciously, and when her head came up, he slapped her across the face.

Stunned, she hit the floor again, only to have him haul her up and drag her toward the opposing hallway. Tomas was down, pinned under part of the doorway that had fallen in the explosion.

Sophie fought back wildly. She wouldn't die. Not now. And she damn sure wasn't going to die at her father's hands. She aimed a kick at his injured leg.

Cursing, he struck her again, this time with his fist. The cold metal of a gun brushed across her cheek before he lowered it and dug it painfully into her belly.

"Be still and cooperate or I'll shoot you and leave you to bleed out like a gutted pig," he hissed.

"Give it up," she gasped out. "You can't win. Sam and

his men have you surrounded. You can't possibly think you'll make it out alive."

"Watch me."

"Where are you taking me?" she demanded as he dragged her through the house. The sounds of gunfire surrounded them, distant, but growing closer. What if Sam got killed? Or his brothers? What if they couldn't get Marlene to safety?

God, there were so many what-ifs. Sam thought she'd betrayed him. Would he really put her above the safety of the people he cared most about? She wasn't as sure as her father that he'd come for her, even if it was his child he was most interested in saving. In the face of her seeming betrayal, it didn't seem a stretch that he wouldn't even believe the baby was his.

Her father shoved her into the library and toward a wooden panel in the center of the room. The doors slid open, revealing an elevator. He forced her inside, then withdrew a key from his pocket and inserted it into the slot below the button for the floor.

The doors swooshed shut, immersing the interior in darkness. The floor lurched below her and they began their descent.

All the while, he held her arm in his bruising grip. Her face ached and her mouth had swelled and was split in the corner. The metallic taste of blood hovered on her tongue, but she was alive. She wouldn't give up hope yet.

Please, Sam. Find me. Save our child. Save me.

I love you.

The elevator stopped and the doors opened to more darkness. Had they descended to hell?

Her father thrust her forward, and she clumsily

stumbled along the hard floor. He'd slowed now, and he limped heavily, his body bobbing into hers.

She faked a stumble, then let out a cry of anguish. He fell into her, recovered and let out a hiss of pain. But she'd slowed him down.

Her brain short-circuited. She could only slow him down so much in hopes that Sam came for her. She babbled out the first thing that came to mind in a desperate bid to distract him, make him talk, all the clichéd things someone did when she was fighting for her life. What else was there left for her?

"How did you survive? I shot you. You should have died."

Probably not the best thing to do. Remind him of the fact she'd shot him down like he'd shot her mother.

He remained silent, refusing to be drawn into conversation. His only response was to kick at her ankle to spur her movement. She went forward, pretending to fall. Her hand groped for the wall so she didn't go down hard.

"You're trying my patience," he snarled. "Get moving or I'll shoot you and leave you here."

Like a flame to a dry fuse, fury caught fire and burned hot and wild through her veins. "Why don't you then? You're a coward who preys on women and those weaker than you. You shot my mother at the dinner table. What kind of sick fuck does that?"

He actually paused, his fingers still on her arm. She felt a betraying tremble surge through his body. The cold bastard had reacted? To the mention of her mother?

"You think I shot her for some random point?"

He chuckled, but it sounded more like a pissed-off hiss than amusement.

"Your mother was a whore with no loyalty. Just like you. She betrayed me just like you betrayed me."

"What kind of shit have you been smoking? What could she possibly have done to deserve being shot in the head over dinner for God's sake?"

"Shut up," he barked. "Shut the hell up and keep walking."

She opened her mouth to speak again, but he twisted her arm until she cried out in true pain. She fell silent and battled the waves of nausea coursing through her gut.

The tunnel led on forever, but her sense of time had been irrevocably altered by the chain of events leading to now.

She nearly tripped and went down when her foot clipped a divot in the floor. She registered the sound of a hand sliding over the wall and then light flooded her eyes. She blinked, not wanting to be weak and miss an opportunity—any opportunity—to fight, to escape. To live.

Her heart sank when she saw two Hummers parked a few feet away and the long tunnel leading out in front of them.

His hand still wrapped around her arm, he held up his gun with the other hand and pointed it square in her face.

"Get in."

Oh God, she couldn't get in that truck. She couldn't allow him to take her.

A shot roared in her ears. Reflexively she jumped back just as her father hit the truck. His head smacked sickeningly against the passenger window, and for a moment he stood, eyes yawning. Then like a puppet whose strings had been let go of, he sagged and slid down the side of the truck. Blood smeared and streaked a path downward and then pooled beneath him when he finally collapsed to the ground.

She whirled, expecting to see Sam or one of his brothers standing behind her. She prepared to launch herself toward him, her heart pounding in relief. She stopped short, her feet tangling and catching when she saw Tomas standing a short distance away, gun still raised in the direction he'd shot.

Her stomach lurched and she fought the urge to throw up.

She stared numbly at him, not knowing what she was supposed to do.

"He deserved a more painful death," Tomas said in a detached voice. "For what he did to Maria."

Sophie shook her head. "Why do you care what he did to my mother?"

Tomas turned his gaze on her, and she shivered at the coldness she found there. All traces of fear had been wiped from his eyes. No tension, no nervousness. It was as if he'd been freed from the one man he feared above all else.

Wildness blazed and his expression turned triumphant, almost as if he couldn't believe what he'd just done.

"He killed her because she loved me," Tomas said. "He found out. I don't know how he found out. Maybe one of the servants betrayed her. But it's no coincidence that the day after she gave herself to me, he killed her."

Sophie shook her head. The world was crazy. She'd sprung from insanity. Her entire gene pool was one big tainted mess. How could she have ever deceived herself into believing she could lead a normal life when she had lived her earlier life surrounded by crazy?

Completely and utterly overwhelmed, she sank to her knees and finally all the way down, until her butt hit her heels. She buried her face in her hands and rocked back and forth.

"Get up and get in the truck," Tomas ground out.

Her head flew up and she stared at him in disbelief. "You're crazy. You're as crazy as my father. I'm not going anywhere with you. I don't have the key, Tomas. You go. They'll come for you. They'll be here any moment. If you want to survive, you better get out now."

He turned the gun on her, and where before he'd seemed a nervous wreck, now he seemed frighteningly confident and at ease.

"Get up now. Get in the truck."

Slowly she pushed herself upward, her knees knocking together like rocks. The world tilted and swayed, and she nearly fell over again.

She stumbled to the next Hummer, fumbled with the handle and managed to open it. Tomas stalked forward, shoved her inside, then slammed the door behind her. He walked around the front, pointing the gun at her through the windshield all the while. Grim determination was etched on his face. Oddly she was suddenly more afraid of him than she'd been of her father. At least she'd known what to expect before.

Tomas got behind the wheel, transferred the gun to his left hand and cranked the engine.

With a roar, he accelerated down the wide tunnel, the headlights bouncing along the walls. After a few moments, the tunnel lightened as sun poured down the passageway. They burst from the enclosure, and dust rose as he wheeled the truck onto the narrow roadway.

She turned frantically in her seat, searching for direction. Her gaze locked onto the house they'd come from. It grew smaller and smaller as the Hummer streaked through the rocky, arid landscape. Into nothingness. As far as the eye could see, there was nothing but rock and jagged hills.

CHAPTER 30

WHEN an explosion rocked the house, Sam and his brothers flattened themselves on the ground, and Sam's heart nearly stopped.

Sophie. Grenade.

Dear God, what had she done?

"Sam, no!" Garrett barked close to his ear.

He hadn't even realized he'd gotten to his feet and run for the door until Garrett flattened him. He lay on the ground, Garrett sprawled on top of him, his gut about to explode with what-the-fuck.

"Goddamn it, Sam, we're going to do this right, and that doesn't include you getting your ass shot full of holes."

"Get off me," Sam gritted out. "I have to find her."

The sound of a helicopter landing diverted his attention for all of two seconds as he glanced back to see Resnick hustle Marlene Kelly aboard.

Relief for his mother mixed with god-awful fear for Sophie.

Slowly Garrett moved off Sam, and Donovan and Ethan moved up beside them, guns drawn and trained toward the entrance of the house.

"We do this together," Garrett said. "As a unit. Backup. Familiar concept? As in you go nowhere without it."

"Shut the fuck up," Sam growled. "You get off way too much giving me orders."

"Yeah, well, when your head is up your ass, someone has to give them."

Ethan and Donovan crouched on either side of the entrance. Ethan held up one finger, then two, and when he popped the third up, he and Donovan swung around and bolted inside.

Sam and Garrett followed, then moved ahead beyond the foyer.

"We're inside the house," Sam said into his receiver. "Steele, Rio, give me your status."

"Engaged," came Steele's short reply.

"Coming in from the west," Rio said a moment later. "Cleared our area. Backing up Steele to clear the riffraff. No casualties to report."

"Good," Sam murmured. He hoped to hell he'd be able to say the same.

"Over here," Ethan called from the left.

Sam, Garrett and Donovan carefully picked their way across the room to where Ethan stood with his rifle up and pointing down a hall.

"Holy hell," Donovan muttered. "I'd say this is where the grenade went off."

Sam swallowed. His stomach lurched and he swallowed again.

The room was toast. Rubble was everywhere. The walls had collapsed and the doorway was askew leading into the connecting room.

Carefully they picked their way through the destruction. Sam hoisted a large section of Sheetrock, but nothing was underneath it except more debris and the floor. He let it fall and continued a path into the adjoining room.

"There's blood here," Ethan said.

Sam hurried over to where Ethan stood. A beam from the doorway lay to the side, and there was a scraped area on the floor that looked as if someone had been pinned underneath the mess and had shoved their way out. The question was who? Sophie? Her father?

He glanced around the room, but it was silent except for the staccato of gunfire in the distance. There was no sign of Sophie or anyone else. Which meant she'd survived the blast. He could be thankful for that, at least, but she was still in the grip of her father. And that terrified him.

They pushed down the hallway, meticulously combing each of the rooms they encountered. There was nothing. No one. Not even hired help. Either everyone had fled or no one had ever been brought in.

Each time they came up empty, Sam's hope sank a little further. He needed her safe. He needed her back with him.

At the end of the corridor, they reached a dead end. But when they turned into the room, guns up, ready to confront Alex and Tomas Mouton, they found only silence and an empty room.

"What have we missed?" Sam demanded.

His gaze swept the room again, looking for anything that didn't fit. He frowned when he caught sight of a small splatter of blood on the polished marble. Head down, he searched the area around it, looking for more.

There, just a drop.

He followed the sparse sign and came face-to-face with the wood-paneled wood. Deep cherry. Custom crafted. It would have cost a fortune.

"What's up?" Donovan asked.

"The blood trail ends here. There's something behind here. Has to be."

Donovan raised the stock of his rifle and rammed the butt into the wood. It held fast, but the thud sure as hell sounded hollow.

"Amateurs," Garrett muttered.

He shoved by Sam and Donovan, pushed them back away from the wall and then fired a series of rounds into the panel. Wood splintered and fell away. Garrett lowered his gun and then stepped forward and kicked at the fragmented wood.

Ethan joined him, and the two men managed to knock a hole big enough for them to get through. Ethan stuck his head in and then whistled.

"Give me a light," he called back.

Donovan yanked a small flashlight from his belt and thrust it into his brother's hand. Ethan flipped it on and then shined it inside the hole.

"What is it?" Sam asked impatiently.

Ethan withdrew. "Looks like an elevator shaft. No elevator though. If they took it down, it's probably sitting there. Don't see a way to make it come up, so it probably requires a security code or key inside."

"We'll rappel down," Sam said.

Donovan sighed. "I knew you were going to say that."

Ethan gave a slight smile. "Haven't gotten over your fear of heights, flyboy?"

"I like heights just fine. In an airplane. Or helicopter. I don't like dangling from a rope."

"Let's go." Garrett broke in. "Save the chitchat for later."

Sam was already in the process of securing the hook around the steel beam that framed the shaft. After he was securely belted and had tested the hook's hold, he stepped off into darkness and began a rapid descent.

"Goddamn it, Sam, slow your ass down," Ethan growled.

He estimated they were thirty feet down when his boots knocked against a hard surface.

"Throw a beam down here, Ethan," he called.

Just a few feet above him, Ethan turned on the flashlight and directed it down. He landed beside Sam a few seconds later and flashed the light across the surface. They were on top of the elevator.

Donovan and Garrett landed on either side, and while Ethan held the flashlight, Sam bent down to pry open the hatch. As he pulled upward, Ethan shined the light inside the elevator, and Donovan and Garrett pointed their rifles downward.

"Clear," Garrett said.

Not waiting for more, Sam threw the strap of his rifle over his shoulder, then knelt and angled his lower body through the opening. He dropped down and waited with seething impatience for his brothers to join him.

"Goddamn, it's dark," Donovan said after they pried open the elevator doors. He left the others, and Sam could hear him sliding his hands over a surface. "We're in a damn tunnel."

Ethan raised the light, but Sam put his hand out and pushed Ethan's arm down. "Douse the light."

They moved stealthily down the corridor. Sam pressed, almost at a run. When they rounded a bend, he blinked as a distant light source came into view. He held up his hand and motioned silently for his brothers to fan out.

They inched toward the opening, and Sam strained his ears to hear something, anything. As they got closer, the hum of fluorescent light tubes filled the space. Otherwise it was quiet. Too damn quiet.

Sam and Donovan on one side of the tunnel, Garrett and Ethan on the other, the two pairs faced each other, guns up. Sam held up one finger and then two. On three they burst into the opening.

Sam pulled up short at the sight that greeted him. A black Hummer was parked several feet away, and to the side lay Alex Mouton. Or what was left of him.

"Holy fuck," Donovan breathed. "Someone blew half his head off."

Garrett cocked an eyebrow. "Our girl?"

Sam looked around and then in the direction the Hummer was pointed, to see another tunnel. "Tomas must have her. If she shot Alex, where is she now?"

Ethan moved in front of the Hummer and stared down at the concrete. "There was another vehicle here. There are tire marks. Looks like whoever left was in a big hurry."

"Sam, I have a relay from Resnick."

Sam cupped a hand over his earpiece.

"Go ahead, Steele."

"Resnick's in the air. Currently tracking a Hummer

driving balls to the wall off road toward Del Rio. Kicking up a dust trail and evidently not too worried about being seen. He thinks he saw Sophie in the passenger seat. He's going to stay on it."

Sam's pulse kicked up. Nervous energy plowed through his veins and made him jittery. He hadn't felt this kind of adrenaline rush since his first mission.

"Copy that, Steele. We're on it. Are you and Rio okay?"

"P.J. and Cole are kicking some mercenary ass. We're laying low and letting them clean up the stragglers. We're good. Go get your woman."

Sam looked over at Donovan. "Time to show me your skills, tech guy. Get us the hell in that Hummer."

Donovan raised a brow, walked around to the driver's seat, opened the door and stuck his hand in. A second later, the jangle of keys sounded, and Donovan held them up with a smirk.

"Too easy, drill sergeant."

SOPHIE bounced and pitched forward as they hit another rise. Tomas was single-mindedly focused on the path in front of them, and she watched closely while the gun inched lower as his attention became less focused on her.

She didn't say anything. Didn't make a sound even when her head smacked the side of the window. The last thing she wanted was to draw his attention to her. As haphazardly as he was driving, it probably wouldn't take much for that damn gun to go off, and right now it was still aimed at her.

Where were they going? What could he possibly hope to accomplish? He didn't have the key. All his "protection" was back at the house, hopefully getting their asses handed to them by Sam and his men.

Which left her with Tomas. A suddenly scary thought given the fact that he'd just manned up for the first time in his life and stood up to his brother. The last thing she needed was for him to be high on adrenaline and confidence.

She glanced nervously at Tomas when he juggled the gun and tried to reach into his pocket, all the while holding his finger way too damn close to the trigger. She was going to die because this idiot was an inept fool.

He swerved, hit a rock, and his hand fell off the wheel. For a moment they careened dangerously to the right. He swore and yanked the wheel back to the left. Miraculously, the vehicle righted, and they continued on their haphazard trek across the rugged terrain.

Tomas yanked a cell phone out of his pocket and thrust it—and the gun—in her direction.

"You call him," he demanded. "You call him and tell him I want that goddamn key or I'll kill you and his brat."

She laughed. She couldn't help it. An hysterical bubble rose in her throat and escaped through lips that flapped like a fish gasping for air on dry land.

"I don't know how to contact him, Tomas. I've never called him. Shouldn't you know how to call him? You were holding his mother hostage for God's sake."

He swung at her with the stock of the pistol, but she dodged and his hand hit the headrest instead. The Hummer swerved again, and something snapped inside her. Sam wasn't going to get her out of this. Neither was Garrett or the fourteen jillion other men KGI employed.

If she was going to survive this, if she was going to protect her child, she was going to have to do it herself.

When Tomas started to swing at her again, she reached up and grabbed his wrist with both hands and yanked as hard as she could.

Curses filled the air. The Hummer swerved, and he grasped the wheel desperately with his left hand to keep control. He punched his right hand back, trying to hit her in the face, but she dodged and then sank her teeth into his wrist.

She gagged as the taste of blood filled her mouth. He wrenched away and then swung at her with his left hand. As soon as his hand left the wheel, the Hummer hit a huge bump and the world went crazy around her.

Up became down and down became up. She had the vague sensation that she was in deep shit, and then she closed her eyes and prayed.

Her head cracked against something hard. Pain speared through her hand. And then suddenly everything went still.

Though her head throbbed, she cautiously cracked her eyes open. The Hummer had righted. She looked over at Tomas to see him slumped over the steering wheel. Blood splattered the windshield in front of him and she could see it dripping down the side of his head.

Her hand hurt.

Oh God, she was losing it. Was that all she could come up with? She'd just flipped a gazillion times with a man holding a gun, and the only thing that registered was that her fingers ached like a son of a bitch.

She looked down to see her pinkie and ring finger already swelling. The angle of her ring finger looked off, but her brain was so fuzzed all she could do was stare dumbly at her hand.

Out. Get out, Sophie.

She reached across her body with her left hand to open the door. Let it open. Please. She didn't want to have to crawl out the window.

It popped open a few inches and stuck stubbornly.

She bumped at it with her shoulder but only managed to move it a bit. Swearing in frustration, she rotated her body and leaned back toward Tomas, praying the whole time that the bastard was dead. She braced her feet against the door and pushed with all her strength.

The metal shrieked in protest, but she managed to pry it open enough that she could get out. Eagerly she scooted forward until her legs stuck through the opening. When she automatically reached for the door frame to brace herself, she hissed in pain and yanked her injured hand back.

She shook it to try and assuage the horrible ache, and finally opted to rest it firmly against her chest.

"Let's try this again," she murmured.

Realizing the vest was in the way and that she had a better chance of squeezing through the opening without it, she fumbled with one hand on the fastenings until she loosened the vest enough to shrug out of it. Then she sucked in all her breath and eased her way between the door and the truck frame.

As soon as she was clear, she sagged against the beat-up Hummer and blew her breath out in a long exhale.

Somehow she'd come out of this alive. She took it as a sign that someone was looking out for her. The thought bolstered her flagging spirits, and she stared out over the rocky terrain. They'd driven several miles from the house, and the logical thing to do would be to retrace that path.

As she pushed away from the truck, she heard the sound of a vehicle in the distance. She put her uninjured hand to her forehead and scanned the horizon.

A chill went up her spine when she spotted the other Hummer tearing across the rock and sand. She'd seen her father go down. Half the side of his head was gone. He was dead. This wasn't him.

Her heart started thumping fiercely. She took one step forward. Her knees shook, and her mouth went dry. She took one more step when the truck hurled over a rise about fifty yards away. It fishtailed, then came to a grinding halt. The doors flew open, and she heard her name shouted.

Relief poured over her soul like a waterfall.

Sam.

She wanted to run to him, but she was rooted to the spot where she stood like some statue. Sam and Garrett piled out and Donovan and Ethan jumped out behind them. Suddenly their expression changed from concern and relief to horror.

She frowned.

"Sophie!" Sam yelled.

Sam and Garrett broke into a run, and Sam yanked his gun from his belt and aimed at a point beyond her.

Stunned, she turned to see what they were seeing. She recoiled when she saw Tomas stumble from the wreckage. He looked like hell, blood covering most of his face and head. But he took jerky steps toward her, and worse, he had the gun in his hand, and it was pointed directly at her. And she was no longer wearing her vest.

There was a hollow-eyed, vacant expression hovering

over him like gloom. Sophie wasn't sure he had a clue who he was, where he was or what the hell he was doing, but he had that gun pointed at her, and he seemed determined to shoot.

She saw his finger tighten and she hunched in on herself, covering her belly as she tried to drop to safety. The shot exploded across the space just as a blur of movement caught her eye and Garrett exploded past her.

He flew, literally flew, through the air, arms outstretched as he threw himself in front of her body.

The sound of the bullet smacking his flesh was a sound she'd remember for the rest of her life.

"No!" she cried.

She dropped over his body just as a second shot exploded through the air. And a third. She didn't look up.

"Garrett. Garrett!"

She raged at him, beating against his Kevlar vest in an attempt to get him to answer her.

He groaned and rolled to his back, holding up his arms to fend her off.

"God, woman, are you trying to finish me off?"

Tears filled her eyes. Rage suffused her face until her cheeks burned with heat.

"Why did you do that? Are you an idiot?" she yelled. "You don't even like me, Garrett. How could you throw yourself in front of me? What if you die?"

She broke down as sobs tore painfully from her throat. She lowered her head and gathered his large body as close to her as she could, while she wept on his neck.

"Why?" she whispered. "Why would you do something so stupid?"

His hand traced gently through her hair, and then he

gathered the strands in his fingers and pulled carefully until her head came away from his chest and he could look her in the eye.

"Because that's what family does," he said in a soft, pain-filled voice.

CHAPTER 31

SOPHIE stared down into Garrett's eyes—eyes that were glazed with pain and beginning to fade. Warmth spread under her hand, and she looked down to see her palm pressed to his shoulder. Blood seeped through her fingers and over his shirt.

No. No, no, no. The bullet had struck him where he wasn't protected.

She shook her head in denial as tears coursed down her face.

"Sophie, honey, stop looking at me like that," Garrett said gruffly. "You'll have me convinced I'm going to die."

"You're not?" she asked in a quivery voice.

"I hurt like a son of a bitch, but I'm pretty sure nothing vital was hit. That's what the vest is for."

She lifted her hand and swallowed in horror at the sticky blood that covered her palm. Then she looked back at Garrett in panic. Was he lying to her?

"Sophie, move away, let me look at him."

She turned to see Donovan tugging at her arm, his face grim with worry. She allowed him to pick her up, and then she stumbled away as Donovan bent over Garrett.

Immediately she was enfolded in a fierce hug. Sam. She went weak with relief.

"Are you all right? Are you hurt? Talk to me, Sophie. Are you and the baby okay?"

He ran his hands urgently over her body, pushing, pulling, tugging at her clothing as he searched for evidence of injury.

Then he reached out and touched her temple, his fingers coming away covered in blood. She stared stupidly at the blood—her blood. She remembered her hand hurting. Not her head. She hadn't registered that she was bleeding. She stared down at her hand. Garrett's blood. Not hers.

"Son of a bitch," Sam swore. "Ethan, get me something to clean this off so I can see how bad it is."

He all but carried her to the Hummer he'd driven up in. He was exceedingly gentle with her as he set her down on the edge of the seat. Her legs dangled over the edge, and she just sat there. Numb. Suddenly exhausted. Worried out of her mind.

"Garrett shouldn't have done that," she murmured.

She stared over to where Donovan was taking care of Garrett and talking into his receiver in urgent tones.

It bewildered her. Garrett had said it was what family did, but she wasn't family. Certainly not his family. Was she?

Garrett didn't even like her. He had to think she'd betrayed Sam—betrayed them all.

Sam's hands shook as they slid up her arms to grasp

her shoulders. For a moment he held her there, his fingers firm against her skin. Then he lowered his arms once more and gathered her hands in his.

She yelped and yanked her right hand from his grasp and cradled it protectively against her chest. She kept her gaze purposely from his. She glanced over at Garrett again and rocked back and forth, cupping her fingers against her.

They throbbed. Pain streaked up her arm. Her head had started to ache too, and she could feel the warm blood slide slowly over her ear.

Sam watched and worried as Sophie blanked out the world around her. Ethan appeared with a med kit, and Sam grabbed a bottle of saline and some bandages when Ethan opened it

"Go help Van with Garrett. Does he have a chopper coming?"

"Yeah, Resnick is landing now."

Sam nodded and motioned Ethan away. He hadn't even heard the helicopter. He'd been too focused on Sophie.

He carefully wiped at the blood that seeped down her temple and ear. She didn't seem to register what he was doing. Her gaze was fixed on Garrett in the distance.

When he finally got the area cleaned, Sam thumbed the gash and the knot on her head. It needed stitches. He hoped to hell that was all and that she didn't have a serious head injury. She needed transport too.

He tried to pull her wrist away from her chest so he could look at her hand, but she resisted, holding it tense.

"Honey, let me look at your hand. I need to see how badly you've hurt it."

He purposely kept his voice low-pitched and soothing.

Her gaze was still focused on Garrett, and another tear rolled down her cheek.

His heart turned over in his chest. God almighty but he loved her. His skin itched and crawled with the need to hold her and comfort her.

"Soph, let me have your hand, sweetheart."

She looked at him finally, and then she glanced down at her hand, confusion clouding her blue eyes. Slowly she extended it, but held it gingerly in her other hand.

He winced when he saw the two swollen and obviously broken fingers. He gently prodded at her wrist and moved her other fingers. Only the two were injured. It probably hurt like hell, but he couldn't discern any other injuries. He prayed she didn't have anything internal.

He touched a finger to her neck to find her pulse. It was a little erratic, but it beat strongly against his fingertips. Her color wasn't too bad considering. She was pale, yes, but not deathly so. It was her mental state that was bothering him at the moment.

Not even the sound of the helicopter fazed her. She just sat there, her eyes vacant, her face dusty and tear-stained.

"Sam," Ethan called. "You need to get her aboard. Mom and Resnick are going to stay with me and Van. We'll drive out. There's room for both you and Sophie."

Sam gathered her close in his arms and carefully lifted her from the truck. She lay limply against him as he hurried across the ground toward the waiting helicopter.

Donovan leaned down to take Sophie from his arms when Sam arrived.

"How's Garrett?" Sam shouted.

"Stable," Donovan yelled back. "I've stopped the

blood and applied a pressure dressing. He's hurting like a son of a bitch, but he'll make it."

Sam closed his eyes and inhaled deeply in relief. Thank God.

Donovan crouched in the helicopter and situated Sophie on one of the seats while Sam climbed in behind him. Garrett was on a litter on the floor, his legs and one arm immobilized.

He opened his eyes and stared up at Sam.

"Sophie?" he mouthed.

Sam leaned down close to his brother's ear. "She's okay, I think. Thanks to you."

Garrett tried to shrug but then paled in pain.

Sam put his hand on Garrett's chest and stared down fiercely at the big man.

"Thanks, man. I can never repay what you just did for me. You saved . . . you saved my future. You saved *my* life."

Garrett smiled faintly. His mouth worked, but Sam couldn't hear him over the roar of the engine. He leaned closer.

"She means a lot to you, man. I was wrong about her."

Sam returned his brother's pained smile. "So was I."

"All set?" the pilot yelled back.

Donovan hopped out of the back and then gave the pilot a thumbs-up. Sam scrambled up and sat next to Sophie who still stared at Garrett with numb shock.

Sam leaned in close, touched her cheek, then nuzzled through her hair to her ear.

"He's going to be just fine, honey, I promise."

For the first time she seemed aware of Sam, and she

turned her anxious gaze on him. She tried to say something, but he lost it as the helicopter lifted into the air.

She looked back down at Garrett so close to her feet. Garrett smiled. Sam knew it had to be difficult when it was obvious he was hurting, but he lifted his free hand up to Sophie.

She grasped it and Garrett squeezed. He would have dropped his hand back down, but she held tight and leaned over to hold it between her knees.

"I'm okay," he mouthed up at Sophie. "You?"

She only nodded, then grimaced and held up her right hand to show him the swollen, misshapen fingers.

Garrett winced in sympathy, but he kept holding Sophie's other hand as they hovered over the terrain.

Some of Sam's anxiety and the tightness in his chest dissipated as he watched Garrett soften toward Sophie. Garrett looked at Sam, and Sam knew his brother had seen the same fragility in Sophie, almost like she was teetering on the edge of a complete breakdown.

Sam leaned over and wrapped his arms around her. He pulled her in close and slid one hand down to cup her belly. He wanted to feel the reassuring thump of their child, but her stomach was still and rigid.

He wouldn't borrow trouble and wouldn't expend energy worrying needlessly. Their daughter had to be okay. Sophie had to be okay.

He couldn't live without either.

CHAPTER 32

SAM sat in the chair next to Sophie's hospital bed with his foot propped on the edge. And he simply watched her sleep. He watched the little red lines feed across the machine that monitored her for contractions, content that for now, all seemed well with their child.

She'd been poked, prodded and checked over within an inch of her life. Sam had insisted. She'd had a CT scan and multiple X-rays, her head had been stitched up, and her right hand had a partial cast.

The rest of the family was waiting for Garrett to get out of surgery. The bullet hadn't been a clean through-and-through. A fragment of it had lodged in Garrett's shoulder, and they were going in to remove it.

Sam had already called Sean to get a report on their father and to let everyone back home know that Marlene—and Sophie—were safe.

He should have felt on top of the world. The nightmare

was over. Resnick and company were crawling all over Mouton's compounds, but Sam had taken the key from Garrett before he went into surgery.

Whatever was done with it now would be Sophie's decision. Sam wouldn't take that away from her. She'd fought too hard and risked everything to keep it from the wrong hands. He trusted her to do what was right.

"Sam?"

He turned to see his mom standing in the door.

"Hey. Come on in."

"I wanted to see how she was doing but didn't want to disturb either of you."

Sam smiled and motioned her inside. "Sophie's sleeping. She'll probably be out for a while."

He got up, but she all but shoved him back into his seat. "You sit."

He reached for her hand. "How are you, Ma? Really."

She sighed and then smiled. "Better now that I know my boys are okay. Ethan talked to Rachel. She's holding up well. Sean said she's been a rock for Frank and Rusty."

"I talked to Sean too. He said Dad was doing better. Should be ready to go home by the time we get there."

Marlene put her hand on Sam's shoulder and squeezed. "How are *you* doing, son?"

He was silent for a moment, and he looked over at Sophie, watching the gentle rise and fall of her chest.

"I love her, Ma. I want you to love her too."

Marlene smiled. "I already do. How could I not love someone who so fiercely loves my son? She risked her life for me. She's a very courageous woman."

Doubt crowded Sam's mind. "I hope she can forgive—"

"Forgive what?" Marlene interrupted.

Sam sighed. "I didn't trust her at first. I didn't trust her there at the end. I thought she'd lied to me. She has to know that."

"Before you torture yourself needlessly over something that may not be, wait and ask her. I think things will be a lot better than you think."

He smiled and reached up to cover her hand where it lay on his shoulder. "You always have a way of simplifying things and making me feel better. Sometimes I feel six years old again, confident in the knowledge that Mom can fix everything."

She leaned down and kissed his cheek. "I hope you never lose that, baby. I don't know a mother alive who won't always try to make things better for her children, no matter how old they are."

"There are going to be changes, Ma. You need to realize that. This . . . what all that's happened . . . has changed everything. I need to know that you and Dad are safe. That the family is safe."

Her smile was achingly sad as she stared down at him. "I know, Sam. And I want you to know something. I want you to know how proud your father and I are of you. Even with everything that has happened, I wouldn't change who you are and what you do for anything. Sometimes sacrifices have to be made in order to make the world a better place. Your father has always believed that, and he's passed that ideal on to each and every one of his sons. Yes, your father will grumble and make noises over change, but he'll accept it with the same grace that he's always accepted knowing that each of his sons risks his life every day because he wants to make the world safer."

"I love you. Do you know that?"

She enfolded him in her arms and squeezed. "I know, but it's nice to hear."

"I didn't even ask about Garrett. Is he out of surgery? Is that why you're here now?"

She nodded. "They took him to recovery a while ago. They said I could go back when he starts to come around, but they don't expect that for another half hour or so. I wanted to come check on you and Sophie."

"Thanks. I'm good."

"I won't even ask if you're bringing her home," Marlene said with a smile.

"Over my dead body will she go anywhere else," he said gruffly.

Marlene glanced at the monitor with a wistful look. "I admit, I never expected you to give me my first grandchild, but in a way it's fitting. You're the oldest."

Sam leaned forward. "Did I tell you? Of course I didn't. How could I? She's having a girl. I saw her for the first time at the hospital where Dad is."

Marlene's face lit up. "A girl! Oh, won't that be so much fun. She'll have you wrapped around her finger for sure."

Sam's chest expanded, and he felt such a surge of anticipation that it made his skin tingle. He imagined a blond-haired, blue-eyed little girl. The spitting image of her mama.

"They both will," he said huskily.

His mother chuckled. "Yes, I suspect you're right."

She patted his cheek and cast one last look in Sophie's direction. "I'm going to go back to Garrett. I expect he'll be grumpier than a hungry rattlesnake when he comes around. I'll need to make sure he doesn't scare off the nurses with all his growling."

Sam laughed and rose to hug her. For a long moment he just hung on to her. She felt very precious in his arms. He had a lot to be grateful for. He owed her life to Sophie.

"I can arrange to have you go home ahead of us so you can get back to Dad. He needs you."

She hugged him fiercely. "Right now my sons need me more. I'm not going home without Garrett. Your father would have a kitten if I even thought of leaving. He'd want me to be here."

She pulled away, gripped his arms and stared hard at him. "I know you're worried about Sophie, but you need rest, Sam. Even a couple hours in the chair would be better than nothing. You said yourself she'd be out for a while."

The corner of his mouth lifted. "Okay, Ma. I'll rest. Promise."

After a final pat to his cheek, she turned and walked out of the room.

SOPHIE opened her eyes, and the first thing she saw was Sam slouched in a chair beside her bed, his head tilted sideways in what looked like an extremely uncomfortable position.

She was on her side, her casted hand resting on her hip. Her other hand was tucked underneath her pillow. Not wanting to move, she lay there still, watching as Sam slept.

He hadn't left her. During the helicopter ride, the landing, the hustle and bustle as the emergency room had run countless tests and the obstetrician had examined her and assured her the baby was doing well.

He'd been with her through it all, his steady, reassuring presence more comforting than anything she could imagine. No words had been exchanged. They hadn't had a single moment alone to talk, and now that they were by themselves, she couldn't bring herself to wake him.

He looked exhausted.

Carefully she brought her casted hand down over her belly. To her delight, the baby bumped and kicked and did a little somersault inside the womb. She glanced down, her chest tightening at the wonder of knowing her daughter was alive and well.

When she looked back up, she was surprised to see Sam watching her, his gaze intense as it drifted to her hand.

"Hi," she whispered.

He lowered his feet from the bed and sat forward. He rubbed his hand over the stubble on his jaw and then through his hair in a weary motion.

"Hey yourself. How are you feeling?"

He scooted the chair closer and cupped his hand over her forehead. He stroked over her hair in a soothing motion, then leaned down to kiss her brow.

A light fluttery feeling rose in her chest and escaped in a breathy sigh.

"Okay. Nice actually. A little numb maybe. I feel almost disembodied. I suppose that sounds weird. I feel like I'm up high somewhere. Removed from reality."

She dropped her gaze, embarrassed by the babbling.

"Makes perfect sense," he said softly. "You've been

through a lot. You're entitled to feel a little out of it. I'm glad you're not hurting. Is our little one moving around? I saw your hand bump a bit when you put it over your stomach."

She smiled and then reached tentatively for his hand. She bumped awkwardly against his fingers with her cast, but she clutched on and guided him to her belly.

His face lightened, and suddenly the gray, tired look lifted as he stared in wonder at his hand.

"That's so amazing. I wonder what she thinks of the world around her. If I were her, I'd want to stay inside her mama where it's safe forever."

"How is Garrett?" Sophie asked hesitantly.

"He's good. Out of surgery. My mom was down a while ago. They removed a bullet fragment from his shoulder. He's probably bitching with the best of them right now."

"Thank God. I was so worried. I couldn't have lived with myself if he'd died."

Sam moved his hand from her belly and touched her cheek. His thumb brushed across her lips, and he stared at her with so much emotion in his eyes that her belly clenched.

"And I couldn't have lived with myself if *you* had died, Sophie."

Her chest hurt. She couldn't breathe.

He pulled away and then stuck his hand in his pocket. He reached for her fingers with his other hand, opened them and then brought the hand from his pocket and laid something on her palm. She looked down to see the key she'd dropped into Garrett's pocket.

She sucked in her breath and stared at the shiny piece

of metal lying across her hand. Then she looked back at Sam, searching for an explanation.

He closed her fingers over it and stared intently back at her.

"You decide, Sophie."

Warmth traveled up her body and wrapped around her heart.

She opened her mouth to respond, but a knock sounded at the door. To her surprise, Adam Resnick stuck his head in, but he didn't make any move to enter. Sam looked at her and waited.

"Come in," she called softly.

He had an unlit cigarette tucked between his lips and his hands shoved into his pockets as he cleared the entryway.

"Sophie," he said around the cigarette, and then as if remembering it was there, he hastily reached up and snatched it from his mouth.

"How are you feeling?"

"Okay. Maybe." She laughed a little. "I'm not sure yet."

Resnick nodded. "I won't keep you long. I just wanted to check in on you." He hesitated for a moment, glanced over at Sam and then focused back on her. "And I wanted to thank you."

Her eyes widened in surprise. "Thank me? I didn't do anything."

"You did more than you think. Your father's network is crumbling as we speak. We've rounded up dozens of his followers. He and your uncle are dead. It's only a matter of time before we take apart his system."

She glanced down at her hand, felt the imprint of the key. And she knew what she needed to do. Sam had given her the choice. The freedom to place her trust in whom she wanted. She trusted him. And now she'd trust Resnick to do the right thing. As Sam had trusted her.

Slowly she raised her hand and extended it in Resnick's direction. She let her fingers fall open to reveal they key.

Resnick stared at her, his brow furrowed.

"Take it," she said huskily. "You'll find the vault underneath my father's home in Mexico. In it is everything that made Alex Mouton who and what he was. His wealth. His contacts. And if he was dealing in nuclear weapons, it's all there."

She carefully related the facts she'd given Sam when she'd first told him of the key. Resnick halted her midway through and pulled out his BlackBerry. He typed furiously as she dictated.

When she was finished, Resnick stared at her with admiration and gratitude reflected in the dark pools of his eyes.

He reached into his shirt pocket and pulled out what looked like a business card. But when he handed it to her, she saw that it only had a single phone number written in ink across its surface.

"If there's anything I can ever do, you have only to call."

She stared at the card between her fingers. A great weight lifted from her shoulders. It was over. It was truly over. Her father was dead. Her uncle was dead. Anyone who could possibly harm her or her child was gone.

She was safe.

"I'll leave you to rest," Resnick said in a quiet voice.

She looked up as he turned to Sam and extended his hand. Sam stood and shook it firmly.

"Thank you," Sam said. "I owe you now."

Resnick shook his head. "No. Never that. I'll be in touch."

Sam nodded and Resnick walked out the door. When he was gone, Sam leaned over and pressed his lips to her temple.

"I'm so proud of you," he murmured.

She turned so that their eyes met and their mouths were just a breath apart.

"Thank you," she whispered.

He trailed the back of his hand down her cheek, and she was struck by the intensity of his gaze. He was so focused on her that on another man, she'd have sworn his expression meant he was looking with all the love in his heart.

"I sat here watching while you slept, and I went over what I wanted to say to you. And then I realized how much I needed to say to you. I thought about how much we need to talk about. And it went on and on."

He turned his hand over and palmed the side of her face. His thumb trailed over her lips, then traced the shape of her mouth.

"But then I realized that all the talking in the world doesn't change one single fact. It doesn't clarify it, make it better or worse. It doesn't change what is."

She stared at him, her heart beating so hard that she could feel her blood pulsing, hear the roaring in her ears.

"I love you, Sophie. I can't tell you at what moment I fell in love with you. Maybe it was that first time I looked across the bar in Mexico and there you were. Maybe it was the first time we made love. Or maybe it was watching you fight for our child. And then for my mother. It doesn't matter. I love you. That's it. That's all. I hope to hell it's enough."

Her heart squeezed. She'd always tried to imagine what it would be like to hear those words. To know that she was loved. Nothing had come close. There was so much joy. It hurt. It shouldn't hurt, but she felt too small for her skin, like she'd burst right out of it.

"I love you too."

She'd always imagined those three words being so difficult to say. It was so easy, so freeing. It was the most wonderful feeling in the world.

Sam smiled, and his voice sounded scratchy and a little hoarse. "I know you do, honey. God, I do know. You've proved it time and time again. But thank you for saying it. I needed to hear you say it."

His elbows were on the edge of the bed now, and their faces were close—so close she could hear each of his breaths. She could feel his nervousness and his uncertainty, and she marveled that she could do that to him. That she could make this man of action be hesitant, even for a moment.

He tugged her hand from its resting spot over her waist and let it rest over his palm. He put his other hand over the top and rubbed his thumb idly across the back of her hand.

"Answer me something, Sophie. What do you want? What do you want most in the world?"

There was vulnerability in that question. Was he afraid she'd want something beyond him? Out of his reach?

"I want us to be a family," she said softly. "I just want us to be a family. You loving me and our daughter. Me loving you. I'll always love you, Sam. I'll never betray you."

Some of the tension fled his expression. His eyes burned. Deep, intense blue.

"You'll have a family, honey. You'll not only have me and our daughter, but you'll have brothers. A sister. You'll love Rachel. And there's Rusty."

At her grimace, Sam smiled. "Don't worry. She's a pain in the ass to everyone. You'll have a mom and a dad. They're the best and they'll love you every bit as much as I do."

He leaned in and kissed her, his lips melting over hers in the sweetest of touches.

"And you'll have me. Always."

Her stomach dipped, and she imagined this was what riding on a roller coaster was like. Or flying. Facing into the sun, riding so high that you couldn't see the ground.

She wanted to laugh. Wanted to close her eyes and savor this moment forever.

She was free. Finally free.

Free to love. Free to live her life the way she wanted. Free to choose.

"I choose you," she whispered.

He smiled and kissed her again. Between them, their daughter rolled once, then quieted as though she didn't want to disturb the precious moment between her parents.

"And I choose you, Soph. Always you."

"I don't know how to live a normal life," she admitted. "I don't know what it's like not to be afraid. I've never not been afraid."

"I can't offer normal," he said. "But I can promise you that you never have to be afraid again. You'll always have me to protect you and our child. Not just me, but my entire family."

"I'm afraid." Then she laughed. "See? I don't know how not to be afraid. What if I screw up?"

He touched her nose, his eyes serious, and soft with love.

"I'll help you. We'll take it one day at a time. Trust me, Soph. Trust me to love you and make you happy."

She rested her cast on his shoulder and leaned into him until their foreheads touched.

"One day at a time. I think I can safely make that promise."

CHAPTER 33

SOPHIE never got tired of the view from Sam's dock. She sat at the edge, dangling her feet in the water as the sun slipped lower in the sky. Her protruding belly made it difficult for her to sit too far forward, so she leaned back, bracing her palms on the sun-warmed wood, and turned her face upward.

Three weeks she'd been here with Sam. Three weeks since they'd come back from West Texas. It had taken a while for everything to sink in. She'd had plenty of time to think during those weeks. The quiet times were good for her soul, but they also gave her time to doubt.

She rubbed at a spot on her belly where she was convinced a tiny foot poked and then shifted to alleviate its discomfort. Her feet kicked up and she sent droplets skittering across the surface of the water.

"Hey, Soph."

She glanced up, shielding her eyes with one hand, to

see Sam standing behind her, hands shoved into his jeans pockets.

"Mind if I sit?"

She smiled and patted the worn wood beside her. He squatted and then maneuvered his legs over the edge of the dock. It was then she noticed he was barefooted and his jeans were rolled up over his ankles.

He didn't say anything, but then he'd been extremely patient with her long periods of reflective silence. He seemed to understand that she was struggling to come to terms with everything that had happened.

They sat side by side, their feet making ripples in the water below. She put her palms down and curled her fingers over the edge of the dock. She tried to make her voice sound casual, like she was embarking on meaningless conversation.

"Do you ever worry about being a good parent?"

As if picking up on the worry she'd tried so hard to conceal, he turned and cocked his head, his eyes narrowing.

"All the time."

He reached for her hand and laced their fingers together.

"I worry too," she admitted. "So much is made of nature versus nurture, but in my case, both aren't good options. Where does that leave me? How can I be certain I won't become a monster like my father? I know it sounds silly, but then I remember that I shot my father in cold blood."

He pulled her into the shelter of his arm and brushed a kiss across the side of her head.

"Have you ever considered that you'll be ten times the mother of anyone else *because* of your upbringing?"

She shook her head. "I worry so much. Some days I'm

convinced I'll make sure our daughter never doubts for a minute how much I love her. Other days I worry that I'll screw up her life forever."

Sam chuckled. "Welcome to parenthood, honey. I don't think there's a parent alive who doesn't have those same fears, no matter what their upbringing was like."

She laid her head on his shoulder and absorbed his warmth and strength. "Think so?"

"I know so. You should talk to Ma. She swears over and over that she screwed up so many times that it's a wonder any of us boys turned out normal. Dad argues we didn't and that it's all her fault."

Sophie laughed and enjoyed the loosening in her chest. She relaxed and stared over the water, soaking up the beauty of the perfect day. The sun was beginning to set, and streaks of pink and gold painted the horizon.

"You know what I regret?"

Sam's arm tightened around her waist. "What's that?"

"That we never got to do all the normal things a couple does. You know. Go out on dates. See stupid movies. Go dancing. I used to dream about dancing in a crowded room at New Year's. Sort of like a fairy tale." She smiled as the childhood fantasy came alive in her mind. "Me and Prince Charming waltzing as confetti rains down around us, and all the noise and cheering at midnight."

She was startled from her daydream when Sam pulled away and got to his feet. She stared up at him in surprise, wondering if she'd made him angry with her silly rambling.

But he simply stood over her and extended his hand down.

Still confused, she reached up and let him help her to her feet. Then he pulled her into his arms and pressed his cheek to hers.

His body moved slow and sensual against hers. In a loose circle, he turned them, swaying in rhythm to the wind.

She sighed and closed her eyes. God, how she loved this man.

"Marry me, Sophie," he whispered close to her ear.

She stiffened and pulled away, shock making her mouth fall open.

He smiled gently and kissed her open mouth. "It shouldn't shock you that I want to marry you."

"I-I . . ." She trailed off lamely and blinked furiously as tears threatened.

"Marry me," he said again. "Say you'll grow old with me, that you'll have a dozen children with me. That you'll love me every bit as much as I love you."

"Are you sure?" she whispered.

He rested his forehead against hers and wrapped both arms around her, until she was molded tight to his body. The baby kicked as if in protest, and they both glanced down at where their daughter lay.

"I've never been more sure of anything in my life. I love you, Soph."

"I love you too, Sam. So much. And yes. I'll marry you."

He smiled and she felt a tremble work through his body. She marveled at the fact that he seemed so happy with her response. His entire face lit up.

"Dance with me."

She melted into his embrace as he turned them around. They danced as the last of the sun's rays slipped over the horizon. They danced to the tune of the gentle waves lapping at the shore. They danced until the stars twinkled overhead and the moon splashed onto the surface of the water like liquid silver.

TURN THE PAGE FOR A SPECIAL PREVIEW OF
MAYA BANKS'S NEXT KGI NOVEL

HIDDEN AWAY

NOW AVAILABLE
FROM BERKLEY SENSATION!

GARRETT lugged his two bags through the door of the cottage and grimly surveyed the surroundings. When he'd imagined a beach-front house with great views and just steps from the water, he'd envisioned something a little more modern. Flat-screen TV, front porch with a hammock, fully stocked kitchen and maybe a hot tub that overlooked the beach.

What he'd gotten was a ramshackle cottage that looked like it didn't survive the last hurricane season, with a dilapidated front porch and sagging steps. The inside smelled like his grandmother's house—musty and old. The furniture was threadbare and at least thirty years old. The kitchen had been designed in the sixties and had appliances to match. Worse, there wasn't a TV at all, and his hopes for a hot tub went down the toilet.

With a shrug he dropped his bags and began opening

windows to air the rooms out. He'd certainly had worse accommodations during his years in the Marines.

He peeked out his bedroom window down the beach to where Sarah's cottage stood in the distance. It wasn't optimal. He'd prefer closer proximity to the woman he was supposed to shadow, but the houses were sparse along this stretch of the shore.

The first order of business was a trip into town for food, and he planned to take the path down the beach that went directly in front of her house. He didn't want to be too obvious right off the bat and force a meeting, but if she happened to be out and around when he passed, it was as good an opportunity as any to meet his new neighbor.

As he went out the front door and stood on the tilted porch to look out over the ocean, he realized this wasn't going to be as bad as he imagined. As much as he protested the need for any recovery time, a few weeks on a beach to exercise, eat good food and not trip over all the people who currently inhabited his house sounded pretty damn good. If it put him back to one hundred percent so he could go back to work, he'd take the downtime.

He felt a little ridiculous in the beach khaki shorts, the muscle shirt and the flip-flops, but with the hint of scruff on his jaw and the fact that he hadn't cut his hair on his usual schedule, he passed for a man only concerned with kicking back and relaxing.

The sun beat down on him and warmed his shoulders as he set off on the worn path down the beach toward Sarah's cottage. He flexed his arm and was happy to note that his shoulder was limber and not stiff despite the long time he'd spent traveling and cooped up in a way-too-small seat with no legroom. Puddle jumpers weren't built for men his size, and they were damn claustrophobic to boot.

Sand got between his toes and between the bottoms of his feet and the flip-flops. Worthless shoes. He stopped periodically to shake the sand from his shoes and then continued on down the beach.

He was careful not to show any undue curiosity as he neared Sarah's cottage, though he memorized every detail of the place from his periphery. Like his, it had seen its better days, although hers had underwent fresh paint recently. Still, it would take nothing to get inside. A good kick to the door—or hell, even the walls—and it would probably knock right down.

He continued past, wondering if she was as unconcerned as she appeared by using her real name and having zero security measures in place—or if she was extremely naïve. It wasn't like people got lessons in school on how to be a fugitive. Not that she was classified as a fugitive, but she may as well be. There were certainly enough people interested in her whereabouts.

The closer he got to town, the higher the dunes on his left stacked up. There were a few shoddily fashioned walkways up over the dune to turnouts on the road. Public access to the beach, but he hadn't come across a single beachgoer on his walk into town.

The sand ran smack into a rock outcropping and cut into the stone steps leading up to the coffee shack. He climbed the stairs but circled around the front to cross the cobblestone street to where the market was located. Outside the front were stands of fresh fruits and vegetables. He bypassed those for now and went inside to find the essentials. Red meat.

He soon learned that to the locals, meat meant fish or other seafood. He grumbled through the selection of ground meat and winced at only finding two steaks. He bought up all the pork chops and put a healthy dent in the chicken breasts. He wasn't a fish person. Oh, he'd put a hook in one, but eating them didn't appeal. Not enough substance.

Which reminded him, he really needed to check out the local bait shop, pick up a surf-casting rod so he could spend some time fishing. It would give him a good excuse to be on the beach, where he could watch Sarah's cottage and get an idea of her routine.

At least the locals appreciated beer. There was a ton of variety, and well, when it came to beer, he wasn't picky. He picked up several six-packs, tossed them in the cart and headed down the aisles to see what else he needed to feed himself for a while.

Eggs, stuff for his protein shakes. Then he frowned. What were the odds of his cottage having a blender? He was lucky to have a few pots and pans to cook out of. Cheese, bread, mayo, mustard and ketchup. Definitely ketchup. What meal was complete without it?

He smiled at the memory of his mother grumbling about his need to pour ketchup on everything.

When he finally rolled the cart to the front of the store, he was treated to several curious stares. It was then he realized that most everyone else had a basket with maybe one day's worth of food. It took a while to check out since there was only one clerk, and the line piled up behind him as everyone waited for all his groceries to be tallied.

A young guy who looked to be in his teens approached Garrett as he finished paying.

"You want I deliver the groceries to where you stay? I can get my friends to help. We work cheap."

Garrett eyed the eager kid. "How cheap?"

"Twenty euros. Apiece."

"I wasn't born yesterday," Garrett said dryly. "I'll give you twenty American and you split it with your friends."

The kid beamed at him. "Deal."

Garrett pulled out his wallet. "I'm the last cottage down the beach from the coffee shack."

"Yes, I know it. I'll bring them down and leave them on your porch. Don't be long. You wouldn't want your meat to spoil."

No, he didn't want his food to spoil. Who knew how long it took the grocery to restock their non-fish meat items.

Since the kid was taking the groceries, Garrett ambled down to one of the shops that boasted fishing supplies. He walked in to see the shopkeeper sitting behind the register with his feet propped up on the counter. He had a floppy hat pulled low over his eyes, and it looked like he was taking a nap. Garrett was nearly by him when the guy tipped up the brim, gave him a cursory once-over and then nodded.

"Feel free to look around. If you need any help, just holler."

Garrett was surprised to hear an American drawl. Not just American, but clearly Southern. "Got a recommendation for something to do a little surf fishing with?"

The shop owner slid his feet off the counter and they landed with a clunk on the floor. He pushed back the hat and sized up Garrett more fully. Then he grunted. "Military, though probably not for a few years. Injury to your shoulder. Recent. Looking for some R and R and don't much like other people. Am I right?"

Garrett raised an eyebrow, immediately suspicious.

"Relax. I read people. Nothing much else to do around here when what little tourist season we have is over." He stuck out his hand to Garrett. "Rob Garner. Retired army. Opened up shop here five years ago. Doesn't take much to live here and the scenery's good. I got in at a good time. In a few years the rest of the world will catch on to what we have here and the property values will soar. Then I can sell and live high on the hog."

Garrett returned his handshake. "Garrett Kelly. Marine Corp. And yeah, here for some R and R and no, I don't like people much."

Rob laughed and clapped his hands together. "I don't have much use for them myself. Now, if you want to do some surf fishing, I'd suggest a casting rod that you can get out there a ways with. Then you can slip it into the holder, kick back with a beer and wait for the fish to bite. All the casting and reeling those bass fishermen do is for idiots. Fishing's supposed to be relaxing."

Garrett cracked a smile. "Fuckin' a."

"Come on, I'll get you what you need. For bait you can use shad or shrimp. Cut bait is good too."

Garrett watched as Rod pulled down a twelve foot rod, handed it to Garrett and then went down another aisle to get hooks, surf weights and liters. A few moments later, he piled everything onto the counter. "You're all set. I'll ring you up and you can be fishing this afternoon if you want."

"Thanks. I might do that. Got the beer already. Maybe I'll grill some steak and dinner on the beach."

Rob nodded. "Yep, that sounds like a pretty good damn day to me. Enjoy it. If there's anything else you need, don't hesitate to come back in."

Garrett broke down the rod to make it more manageable to carry then collected the bag with all the other supplies. With a nod, he headed back outside.

Hopefully the kid had delivered the groceries while Garrett was in the bait shop. Breakfast had consisted of a dry bagel on the plane, and his stomach was doing some serious protesting. A steak and a little fishing sounded next to heaven.

He glanced over to the market to see a woman step out, bag clutched close to her chest. She glanced furtively left and right and then strode toward the coffee shack. His pulse picked up. If he wasn't mistaken, he'd just gotten his first real life glimpse of Sarah Daniels.

On impulse, he crossed the street toward the coffee shack. He'd intended to take the main road back, but carrying the fishing pole and supplies, he had a ready excuse to take the beach path.

When he rounded the corner of the shack, he saw her head bob down the stone steps leading to the beach. He waited a moment to give her a bigger head start and then took off after her.

At first she didn't realize he was following her. Which further cemented his opinion that she was hopelessly naïve. When she did look over her shoulder, her eyes flared in alarm. Then she made a concerted effort to shield her reaction. She even offered a semblance of a smile as she took in the fishing gear he carried before turning around and increasing her pace.

Twice more she turned just enough that she could

see him, and each time she speeded up. By the time she reached her cottage, he could tell she was alarmed by the fact that he still trailed her. She hurried her steps, and in her haste to open the door, she dropped one of the bags she carried.

She yanked the door open and then turned so she could see him while she picked up her things. Her gaze never left him as she shoved the items back into her bag. Garrett found himself strangely transfixed and unable to look away. The pictures hadn't done her justice, nor had they captured the haunted, frightened eyes rimmed with shadows. She looked infinitely fragile, scared out of her mind, but he also saw something else. Maybe it was the way she tried not to look scared or maybe it was the subtle stiffening of her shoulders and the rebellious twist to her lips. She was a fighter, not the timid mouse he'd imagined.

Awareness prickled over his skin and tightened the hairs at his nape. He rubbed the back of his neck in an attempt to dispel the momentary discomfort. His reaction irritated and intrigued him all at the same time.

He offered a friendly wave and continued on his way, though he found it hard to drag his gaze away from her. He didn't want her to feel threatened by him, because he planned to see a lot more of her.

"Maya Banks writes the kind of books I love to read!"
—Lora Leigh, #1 *New York Times* bestselling author

FROM *NEW YORK TIMES* BESTSELLING AUTHOR
MAYA BANKS

SHADES OF GRAY

A KGI NOVEL

P.J. and Cole were sharpshooting rivals on the same KGI team and enjoyed a spirited, uncomplicated camaraderie. Until the night they gave in to their desires and suddenly took their relationship one step further. In the aftermath of their one-night stand, they're called out on a mission that goes terribly wrong, and P.J. walks away from KGI, resolved not to drag her teammates into the murky shadows she's poised to delve into.

Six months later, Cole hasn't given up his search for P.J., and he's determined to bring her back home where she belongs. Bent on vengeance, P.J. has plunged into a serpentine game of payback that will make her question everything she's ever believed in. But Cole—and the rest of their team—refuse to let her go it alone. Even if it means sacrificing their loyalty to KGI, and their lives…

**INCLUDES A NEVER-BEFORE-IN-PRINT KGI NOVELLA
IN THE MASS MARKET EDITION ONLY!**

mayabanks.com
facebook.com/AuthorMayaBanks
facebook.com/LoveAlwaysBooks
penguin.com

M1255T0213

Meet Gabe, Jace, and Ash: three of the wealthiest, most powerful men in the country. They're accustomed to getting anything they want.

Anything at all.

FROM *NEW YORK TIMES* BESTSELLING AUTHOR
MAYA BANKS

THE BREATHLESS TRILOGY

RUSH
FEVER
BURN

PRAISE FOR THE NOVELS OF MAYA BANKS:

"Hot enough to make even the coolest reader sweat!"
—*Fresh Fiction*

"Superb...[an] exciting erotic romance."
—*Midwest Book Review*

"You'll be on the edge of your seat with this one."
—*Night Owl Reviews*

mayabanks.com
facebook.com/AuthorMayaBanks
facebook.com/LoveAlwaysBooks
penguin.com

M1266AS0213

LOVE
ROMANCE
NOVELS?

For news on all your favorite romance authors,
sneak peeks into the newest releases, book
giveaways, and much more—

"Like" Love Always on Facebook!

 LoveAlwaysBooks

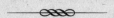